Books by Mark Cheverton

The Gameknight999 Series
Invasion of the Overworld
Battle for the Nether
Confronting the Dragon

The Mystery of Herobrine Series: A Gameknight999 Adventure
Trouble in Zombie-town
The Jungle Temple Oracle
Last Stand on the Ocean Shore

Herobrine Reborn Series: A Gameknight999 Adventure
Saving Crafter
The Destruction of the Overworld
Gameknight999 vs. Herobrine

Herobrine's Revenge Series: A Gameknight999 Adventure
The Phantom Virus
Overworld in Flames
System Overload

The Birth of Herobrine: A Gameknight999 Adventure
The Great Zombie Invasion
Attack of the Shadow-Crafters
Herobrine's War

The Mystery of Entity303: A Gameknight999 Adventure
Terrors of the Forest
Monsters in the Mist
Mission to the Moon

The Gameknight999 Box Set
The Gameknight999 vs. Herobrine Box Set
The Gameknight999 Adventures Through Time Box Set

The Rise of the Warlords: A Far Lands Adventure
Zombies Attack!
Bones of Doom
Into the Spiders' Lair (Coming Soon!)

Wither War: A Far Lands Adventure
The Wither King (Coming Soon!)
The Withers Awaken (Coming Soon!)
The Wither Invasion (Coming Soon!)

BONES OF DOOM

THE RISE OF THE WARLORDS BOOK TWO

AN UNOFFICIAL INTERACTIVE MINECRAFTER'S ADVENTURE

MARK CHEVERTON

SKY PONY PRESS
NEW YORK

Copyright © 2017 by Mark Cheverton

Minecraft® is a registered trademark of Notch Development AB

The Minecraft game is copyright © Mojang AB

Sky Pony Press books may be purchased in bulk at special discounts for sales promotion, corporate gifts, fund-raising, or educational purposes. Special editions can also be created to specifications. For details, contact the Special Sales Department, Sky Pony Press, 307 West 36th Street, 11th Floor, New York, NY 10018 or info@skyhorsepublishing.com.

Sky Pony® is a registered trademark of Skyhorse Publishing, Inc.®, a Delaware corporation.

Visit our website at www.skyponypress.com.

10 9 8 7 6 5 4 3 2 1

Library of Congress Cataloging-in-Publication Data is available on file.

Cover design by Brian Peterson
Cover artwork by Vilandas Sukutis (www.veloscraft.com)
Technical consultant: Gameknight999

Print Paperback ISBN: 978-1-51072-738-0
Print Hardcover ISBN: 978-1-51072-832-5
Ebook ISBN: 978-1-51072-742-7

Printed in Canada

ACKNOWLEDGEMENTS

I'd like to thank my family for their continued support through this incredible writing adventure. Without their help, these stories would likely not have materialized on the page. I would also like to thank the great people at Skyhorse Publishing for continuing to publish my books. They have been fantastic to work with, and their faith in my writing keeps me motivated. I look forward to having many more Minecraft-inspired novels published by them.

NOTE FROM THE AUTHOR

A big THANK YOU goes out to all of my readers who sent me emails through my website, www.markcheverton.com, telling me how much you enjoyed traveling through the Far Lands with Watcher and his friends in the first book of this new Minecraft-inspired series. Your kind and supportive words have motivated me to work towards making this book even better than the last. I hope I'm successful.

I can't wait to see the fan fiction many of you write about the characters in my stories. There are a lot of Gameknight999 stories on my website, under the *Blog* section, but I hope you'll carve a space in your imaginations for Watcher and his friends. It's always a lot of fun reading what all of you create; keep up the great work.

With a new survival world starting on the Gameknight999 Minecraft Network, I'm hoping to build some of the ancient structures from this story for you to explore. If you go to www.gameknight999.com, you can find information about the server. The server's IP address is **mc.gameknight999.com**.

Be sure to come to the server and say hello to me, Monkeypants_271, and my son, Gameknight999. Though I don't have as much time as I'd like to play on the server, I'm there now and then to help people build or maybe have the occasional Paintball battle. Soon, we'll have SkyWars and maybe some other games where you can test your skills against those of myself and my son.

I hope I see you on the server, and I hope you all send me emails letting me know what you think of this new series. I love hearing your ideas for new stories, though I'll probably give you the answer I give many people: "I love your idea! You should go write it!" I have faith in you to do your stories justice, so sit down and put your fingers to the keyboard, and release the stories that hide in the recesses of your imaginations.

Fearlessly believe in yourself without doubt or caution. The first step to success is believing you can do a thing . . . all the rest is just details. See yourself achieving your goal in your mind, then find the path to make that dream a reality. We abandon our goals only because we no longer believe they are possible. Belief is everything!

CHAPTER 1

The skeleton warlord, Rakir, shoved the terrified zombie down the shadowy passage, expecting the foolish creature to trigger some kind of lethal trap; soon, the skeleton would get what he wanted.

The idiotic zombie walked along one wall of the corridor, moving about a dozen blocks ahead of the company of skeletons. When the monster lost the motivation to continue walking through the dark and terrifying passage, the warlord had a few arrows shot in its direction, forcing the decaying creature to continue.

Shuffling its clawed feet slowly across the stone floor, the zombie glanced anxiously about, looking for tripwires or other traps hidden in the darkness . . . but it was too late. The zombie stepped right on an unseen pressure plate. Instantly, a series of pistons extended, pushing the cold stone walls together, crushing the monster. Flashing red, the zombie took damage, his HP (health points) quickly dropping lower and lower until the decaying creature disappeared, destroyed by the mechanism. The walls receded back into their original position, looking like every other part of the corridor, waiting for their next victim.

"You see, zombies *are* useful after all." The skeleton warlord laughed a dry, hacking laugh that sounded more like he was choking than chuckling. "Get a skeleton up there with a pick axe." He turned to his companion. "General Rusak, find some volunteers. That was our last zombie and we have many more passages to search."

Rakir adjusted his enchanted iron armor, then glanced up at his general. Rusak was larger than any other skeleton he'd ever seen. His bones were thicker and longer, allowing him to loom over the other monsters. He wore a full set of iron armor, something few skeletons could do because of the weight. Rakir didn't have that problem; his enchanted armor felt as if it were made of leather, only many times stronger.

"I'm sure I can find some skeletons who want a promotion." The general laughed a hollow laugh, his jaw clicking together with each chuckle. He pointed at a nearby monster. "You, come here . . . now!"

The skeleton's posture slumped as he shuffled forward, an expression of hopelessness on the monster's pale face; refusing a direct order was a crime that carried with it a lethal punishment.

"Hurry up, you fool." Rakir grabbed the skeleton by his bony arm and pulled him forward. Another monster with a pick axe finished destroying the pressure plate, then stepped aside for the new "volunteer."

"Here, take this torch and search the passage ahead. We're almost to our destination," Rakir said.

The skeleton moved carefully into the passage, the flickering light from the torch splashing on the walls and floors. The illumination revealed a ceiling that was impossibly high; it was at least twenty blocks high, if not more.

"There's a trip wire here," the skeleton "volunteer" said.

Rusak motioned for another soldier to destroy the trip wire, allowing the squad of skeletons to move further into the ancient passage.

"Warlord, how do you know if there are any ancient relics in this place?" the skeleton general asked.

Rakir glanced at his general. "The new Wither King, Krael, told me."

"Why should we trust that creature?" Rusak said. "Withers always have a plan of their own that benefits them at the expense of everyone else."

"You are right to be cautious." Rakir ran his bony fingers along the cold stone wall, his fingers making a scraping sound. "Krael showed me a book written by one of the monster warlocks. It had the location of many relics hidden all throughout the Far Lands."

The sound of something slithering along the ground echoed through the passage. The skeleton warlord held up a bony fist, stopping his warriors in their tracks. They all pulled out bows and scanned the passage for threats.

Rakir stepped quietly to a hole in the tunnel wall and peered through the gap, the other skeletons backing away, afraid. They all knew strange things could happen in the Far Lands. They were far from the center of the Overworld. In fact, they were hundreds of millions of blocks from its center. At the edge of Minecraft, where the fabric of existence was stretched tight, strange and unpredictable things were known to happen.

It was here in the Far Lands, hundreds of years ago, where the Great War between the NPC wizards and the monster warlocks took place. Great beasts and magical weapons were conjured into being as the two sides played a deadly game of tug-of-war, using the inhabitants of the Far Lands as the rope. The end result of this colossal struggle was not clear, much of it clouded by the fog of time. But one thing remained certain . . . tensions between monsters and villagers were still high.

Suddenly, a silverfish scurried out of the hole, the tiny little creature squeaking as it scraped its armored tail along the stone floor. The skeletons relaxed, as did Rakir, and put away their weapons for now.

Rakir turned back to his general and continued. "This ancient structure was one of those locations on the wither's map. It was built by the zombie warlock, Zo-Kol the Destroyer. That monster sought to keep this prize from the skeletons in those ancient days, during the Great War. If the skeleton warlock had been given this great weapon, maybe the outcome of that war, hundreds of years ago, would have been different and monsters would rule the Far Lands."

"I still don't trust that wither king."

"Nor do I, General, but I will gladly use any of the ancient weapons the great warlocks created and left behind for us."

Rakir stopped and stared up at his general. The hulking skeleton gazed back, his one eye black as midnight, the other a dull red. A long scratch extended down Rusak's face and passed across the crimson eye, the remnant from some NPC blade. The scar gave the skeleton an even more terrifying appearance.

"With these magical weapons, I will lead the skeletons to take over all of the Far Lands. Once all is under our control, we will spread through the rest of the Overworld. I'm sure there's no one that can stand against us."

"Yes, sir," Rusak replied. "You are probably—"

"There are some side passages up here," the skeleton scout shouted ahead of them. "We've disarmed the traps; it's safe to approach."

Rakir and Rusak ran through the long corridor, the dozen skeletons in their company following fast on their heels. The skeleton general's armor clanked as he ran, the metallic plates slamming together with each step, but the warlord's armor was completely quiet; the enchantments put on the iron plates by the ancient wizards of the past not only kept the metallic coating light, but also silent. Behind the two commanders, the rest of the skeletons struggled to stay close, their bodies encumbered with non-magical, light-weight chain mail.

The monsters jingled like a set of angry windchimes, the sound filling the passage. The skeleton warlord listened to the clinking noise and smiled, then focused on the monsters up ahead.

"Show me what you found," Rakir demanded when he reached the monsters' sides.

"There is a passage heading to the left and right." The skeleton "volunteer" pointed with his bow. "But this main passage continues up ahead. I was able to see some redstone lanterns in the distance along the main passage, but the side passages are lit with torches. Which way do we go?"

"Ignore the side passages," the skeleton warlord commanded.

"But Rakir, there may be relics in there." Rusak glanced down one of the smaller corridors, then brought his gaze back to his commander. "Perhaps we send a couple skeletons down each one?"

"No. Krael told me to follow the redstone lanterns." Rakir moved closer to his general and spoke in a soft but firm voice. "The wizards and warlocks of old only used redstone lanterns in the magical areas. The redstone somehow enhanced their powers."

"Do you think this wither king can be trusted?" the general asked.

Rakir nodded.

"Very well." The general turned and faced the other skeletons. "Continue forward. Everyone carry a torch and watch for traps." Rusak turned to the lead scout and pointed down the passage with a bony finger. "After you."

The monster swallowed uncomfortably, then continued through the passage.

After thirty or so blocks, the scout triggered a trap that shoved him into a deep pit filled with cacti. His HP didn't last very long. Another "volunteer" was chosen and the party continued forward. After three more traps, and three more "volunteers," they reached the end of the passage.

Before them stood a cylindrical chamber. The floor and walls were obsidian, with thick columns of redstone lanterns stretching up to the ceiling high overhead. A thick layer of dust and grime covered the stone-brick floor, the dirt adding to the stale and ancient feeling of the chamber. Across the floor, the gray dust was featureless, almost smooth, the absence of footprints suggesting no one had visited this chamber for hundreds of years. At the center of the room was an altar made of quartz. Atop the altar was a crafting bench, cracked with age and covered with dust. Floating just above was a bow made of pale bone. The white, ornately-carved surface of the bow seemed to glow with a lavender luster, and small sparks of purple hovered around the taut string.

"What is it?" Rusak asked in awe, his jaw clicking ever so slightly.

"Behold, the Fossil Bow of Destruction," the warlord said. "Krael promised it would be here; he did not lie . . . this time." He smiled. "The wither king gave me many such locations as this, each an old structure with hidden weapons of magic just waiting to be taken by us. We have patrols out searching for them as we speak. Soon we will have many ancient and enchanted weapons, making the skeleton army the strongest fighting force since the Great War between the wizards and the warlords."

Rakir moved to the crafting bench. His footsteps caused tiny little clouds of dust to billow into the air. Cautiously, he reached out and grasped the weapon. Pain instantly engulfed him, making the warlock want to scream. But he would never show that kind of weakness in front of another skeleton. When he realized he wasn't going to die, and the pain began to fade away, the skeleton warlord smiled.

"Only a true descendant of a wizard or warlock may use this bow." Rakir backed away from the ancient crafting bench and held the weapon out to Rusak. "Anyone else would be destroyed." He looked up at his general, challenging him with his cold gaze. "Do you want to try?"

Before Rusak could answer, one of the skeletons shouted from the chamber's entrance. "Zombies coming. There are probably two dozen, if not . . . more." The skeleton's voice cracked with fear. "They're armored and heavily armed. We can't fight that many. Do we surrender?"

"Never!" snapped Rakir. "Let's see what this fabulous weapon will do."

The skeleton warlord moved to the entrance and stared down the long passage. He could see the shuffling monsters approaching.

"They're too far for our bows." General Rusak moved to the warlord's side. "We should lure them closer, into a trap, and hope their numbers can be cut down by our arrows."

"Watch and learn," Rakir said with a wry smile.

The warlord held the Fossil Bow before him, his bony fingers squeezing it tight. Rusak handed him an arrow, but it was brushed aside. Rakir grabbed the string and pulled it back. Instantly, a shimmering arrow appeared on the weapon. He aimed high in the air, judging the distance to the targets, which was still great. He focused his attention on one of the zombies, fixing the monster's position in his mind. A burst of pain spread through his body, causing the skeleton warlord to flash red, taking damage as his HP was drawn from his body to power the magical weapon. Then he released the string. The magical arrow leapt off the bowstring and streaked into the air, its enchanted shaft making a faint whistling sound as it flew.

"You're too far away," Rusak said.

"Watch."

"All the zombies need to do is step aside and the arrow will miss," the general said.

"Just watch," the warlord said, scowling at his general and silencing him with his gaze.

The skeletons watched the glowing projectile travel in a graceful arc, climbing higher and higher, then slowly descending. The zombies saw the incoming missile and all moved to the walls in hopes of getting out of the projectile's path. But the arrow turned slightly, tracking its target on the left wall. The zombies, seeing this, all moved to the right wall. The arrow changed course again, staying fixed to its next victim. The zombies moaned in fear, uncertain what to do.

The arrow struck the lead zombie, pushing the monster back, onto the ground. The decaying creature just had time for a terrified moan, then disappeared, the single shot from the enchanted weapon powerful enough to destroy all the monster's HP.

"You see? This magical weapon is incredible." Rakir gave his general a satisfied smile.

"I want to try," one of the skeletons said.

He snatched the bow from the warlord's hand. Rusak made a move toward the offending monster, but Rakir raised a hand, stopping his general.

"Watch and learn," Rakir said.

The skeleton pulled the bow string back. Instantly, the monster was overwhelmed with pain. He flashed red as the bow sucked on his HP. Flailing his arm about, the monster tried to drop the bow, but he could not make his hand release its grip. Flashing red again and again, the skeleton fell to his knees, trying to push the bow away with his other hand, but it was hopeless. The creature shouted in pain and fear as the enchanted bow slowly consumed him. Finally, the monster fell to the ground and disappeared, his HP consumed by the Fossil Bow of Destruction.

"I told you, only an ancestor of the wizards or warlocks can wield this weapon." Rakir bend down and picked up the weapon. "I am a descendant of the great skeleton warlock, Ragnar the Tormentor."

Rusak nodded in awe. "Perhaps *his* magical powers pulse through your veins."

"Perhaps," Rakir said. "But now, it's time we destroy the rest of those pathetic zombies."

He stared at the decaying green monsters in the distance, then pulled back the string and fired again and again. He launched a dozen quick shots, the last being released before the first even found its target. The glowing arrows streaked through the air like magical missiles, tracking the creatures with uncanny precision. They fell upon the zombies, each shaft taking a monstrous life. In seconds, all the zombies were gone.

"That weapon is incredible," General Rusak said with a grin. "It will give us an unbelievable advantage against the zombies and spiders."

The skeleton warlord nodded. "Tensions have been high since the disappearance of the zombie warlord. The spiders try to expand their territory while the zombie kingdom struggles in chaos. The Fossil Bow of Destruction will give us the advantage, allowing us to control the other monsters. Once we have enough relics from the wizards and warlocks, we'll then move against the villagers."

General Rusak smiled.

"Today begins the reign of the skeletons." Rakir glanced at the other monsters around him. Quickly they began to cheer his name, lest they become the next victim themselves. "Soon all will grovel before us, both monster and villager alike. With this bow, we will destroy any that stand in our way."

"Nothing will stop us, warlord," General Rusak said.

"Perhaps you are right." The skeleton warlord put the enchanted bow into his inventory, then lowered his voice so only the general heard. "The new wither king, Krael, gave me a warning."

"What did he say?"

"He told that that the descendants of the great wizards can use this bow as well." Rakir removed it from his inventory again. The purple light from the enchanted weapon threw a lavender glow on the cold stone walls.

"Every one of those descendants will want to take this bow from us. Before we can begin our campaign to take over the Far Lands, we must first destroy anyone who might challenge us."

"You mean the offspring of the wizards?" Rusak asked.

The skeleton warlord nodded. "Krael told me the descendants are similar to the wizards, in that they all have red hair and are expert archers."

"Red hair?" Rusak asked, confused.

"Yes, the wizards had red hair, as did all their children." Rakir waited for these words to sink into his general's thick skull. "Spread the word; all skeleton scouting parties are to search for any red-headed villagers that show even the smallest bit of skill with a bow. They must all be destroyed, and their villages burned to the ground. None can be left alive, for the descendants of the great wizards of old are the only threat standing in our way of dominating the Far Lands."

"It will be done as soon as we get back to the Hall of Pillars," the general said.

"Good. Let's get moving . . . there's a world out there I must dominate and villages that need destroying." The skeleton warlord laughed a hacking laugh which echoed off the walls of the long passage, making the very fabric of Minecraft cringe.

CHAPTER 2

Watcher peered over the edge of the massive hole, looking at the ancient watchtower that lay half-buried in the deep hole, the tower jutting up out of the cavity almost as if it were climbing its way into the sky. Along one edge of the massive pit, he could see a small group of skeletons leaping from block to block, slowly descending towards the bottom and the entrance to the watchtower.

They'd been following the company of skeletons through the forest since the NPC scouts had spotted them. Watcher wanted to know what they were doing so close to their village . . . and now they knew. They were looking for the old watchtower.

"Er-Lan does not like skeletons," the zombie next to the young NPC whispered. "They came to Er-Lan's zombie-town many times, raiding for supplies."

"When was that?" Blaster asked. The boy moved next to Watcher. He was taller than both Watcher and Er-Lan, his curly black hair sticking out in all directions. "I assume it was before the zombie warlord started attacking our villages?"

Er-Lan nodded. "It was when this zombie was still part of the zombie nation." He glanced at the two boys, then cast a quick look at Planter, her blond hair shining in the bright sunlight. "Now, Er-Lan is part of this family."

"You got that right," Planter said with a smile.

Watcher placed a hand on the zombie's shoulder. "I don't like skeletons either. In fact—" he leaned in close and whispered "—I'm terrified of them. From far away, I'm okay, but when they're up close, they scare me, almost to death." His voice shook a little. "I hate 'em."

"Why does Watcher have so much hate for the skeletons?" Er-Lan asked.

The monster adjusted his chain mail, making a brief clinking sound that echoed down into the hole. Instantly, everyone froze and ducked behind a tree. One of the skeletons glanced back up toward the noise, but acted like it saw nothing.

"When I was very young, a skeleton attacked my mother and me." Watcher's voice took on a wistful tone. "We ran, but found ourselves cornered with a cliff at our backs. If it weren't for one of the soldiers from the village, that monster would have . . . well, you know."

The zombie nodded.

"That was when I decided I wanted to be a villager soldier, just like our rescuer."

"And now you *are* a soldier," Er-Lan said.

Watcher nodded and smiled. "But I'm just an archer. I don't use a sword or have heavy iron armor or—"

"A smart person uses the tools that are best suited to their hands." Er-Lan held out his hand and spread his green decaying fingers wide, the dark claw at the end of each one sparkling under the morning sun.

Just then, Planter moved next to Watcher and peered through the branches at the monsters as they moved deeper into the hole in which the ancient structure sat. Her hair smelled like sweet melons . . . he'd never noticed that before, but it was fantastic.

"Why do you think the skeletons are going into the Wizard's Tower?" Planter asked.

Watcher glanced at her. Sunlight streamed through the leafy canopy, and coated her blond hair, making the flowing locks seem to glow with a magical radiance. It seemed more vibrant than usual . . . in fact, everything seemed more vibrant than usual around Planter. She seemed different somehow to Watcher, but he couldn't figure out exactly what it was.

Watcher glanced down at her clothing. Her green smock merged with the leaves of the trees, allowing her to blend in with the foliage, but the bright yellow stripe down the middle of her garment made her stand out. Gently, Watcher pushed her behind the trunk of an oak tree, so she would be well hidden.

She smiled at him, and Watcher felt as if he were melting. For some reason, a content and satisfied peacefulness settled over him when he was near Planter. It was as if, with all his faults and inadequacies, he was accepted by her, no matter what. He could just be himself, no pretending to be brave, no trying to look strong, no . . . nothing. All Watcher had to do was be Watcher, and that felt . . . fantastic.

"They must be looking for something," Blaster replied. The young boy put on his favorite leather armor, which was dyed black. "Let's follow them and see what they're up to." He turned to Watcher. "Your sister, Winger, should have made it back to the village by now. We'll have help soon."

Watcher nodded, then moved to the edge of the massive hole that had been excavated around the ancient tower. With an arm across his chain mail armor to keep it from making too much noise, he jumped onto the rocky surface, following the redstone torches that marked the safe trail down. The three companions moved along the roughhewn walls much faster than the skeletons, having the benefit of the flickering torches that showed the easier path.

"Everyone hide, they're looking around." Watcher ducked behind a block of stone, his three friends doing the same.

With his sensitive vision, the young boy peeked around the edge of the block. The largest of the skeletons down below them glanced up and around at his surroundings, the monster's chain mail reflecting the few rays of sunlight that managed to penetrate the depths. With arrow notched and bowstring pulled back, the monster scanned the area, looking for an innocent victim to destroy.

"Do you think . . . they saw us?" Planter asked, her voice cracking with fear.

"If they had, they'd be firing at us." Blaster adjusted his black leather cap, then glanced quickly around the moss-covered block. "They're moving again." He stood. "Come on, let's keep following."

Blaster continued down the rocky path, jumping from block to block, the others following closely. They finally reached the entrance to the structure. A hole had been carved into the ceiling of the ornately-decorated building, the multicolored roof stretching out into the darkened cavern that lay hidden under landscape above.

"Why do you think this building sank into the ground?" Watcher asked. "It's almost as if it fell into some kind of sinkhole, then was buried."

"Who knows why the ancient wizards did anything during the Great War? It was hundreds of years ago." Blaster headed down the brick stairs that led to the ground floor of the structure. "I'm more interested in what the skeletons are looking for now. My dad and I searched this place a while back. I'm sure there are still passages in there that we missed; many were blocked off by cave-ins, fallen sand, and gravel blocking the way."

"You hear that?" Watcher stopped on the stairs and cupped his hand around his ear. "It sounds like digging."

"Let's hurry and see what they're doing." Planter put on an iron chest plate, donned chain mail leggings and helm, then pulled out an enchanted bow. The magical power in the weapon bathed her in a lavender glow, shining light onto the walls and floor. She notched an arrow, then followed Blaster down the steps.

The three friends reached the last of the stairs. Before them stood a massive, cylindrical tower that stretched high into the air. Sunlight streamed through the stained-glass windows, casting colorful beams of light to the floor. The last time they'd been here, Blaster had shown them his cache of weapons. That had been months ago, after the zombie warlord had invaded their village and taken most of the inhabitants captive. Watcher and his friends had traveled far to free the NPCs and stop the zombie-warlord from destroying any more villages. It has been a terrifying adventure that took them to the Capitol where they'd faced off and destroyed the wither king, Kaza. Watcher had hoped his adventures were at an end, and he wouldn't need to come here again. But with the new enchanted weapons they'd discovered in the Capitol, at least they were more prepared for battle.

Watcher moved around the tower and followed the sound of the digging. Hiding behind the edge of a wide doorway, he spotted the skeletons at the end of a long corridor, each of them digging through a pile of gravel blocking the passage. As soon as the pale monsters created a large enough opening that refused to cave in on them, they moved deeper into the structure.

"Come on, let's follow them." Reaching into his inventory, Watcher pulled out an enchanted sword. The thin blade gave off an iridescent purple glow, adding to the light from Planter's bow. Its shining, mirror-like surface reflected his own worried expression, as if the blade were seeing into his very soul. The blade was called Needle; it was the weapon that had been used to destroy the king of the withers deep within the ancient chambers of the Capitol. The blade had first belonged to Planter, but in that terrible battle with the wither, Needle had somehow bonded to Watcher. It would now only respond to Watcher for some reason.

They ran down the long, brick-lined tunnel, the high ceiling overhead lost to the darkness. In the distance, the skeletons moved carefully through the passage, a torch held high overhead. Occasionally, a trap of some kind would trigger, destroying the lead skeletons, but once each was identified, the monsters stopped and disarmed the tripwires or pressure plates, then continued, their numbers slowly diminishing, even though there were still many of the bony creatures in their party.

Suddenly, the skeletons took a side passage, abandoning the main corridor. Watcher ran forward, his leather boots making a quiet scuffling sound that echoed off the walls, the chain mail wrapped around his chest jingling softly. *I hope they can't hear us,* the young boy thought. *There are at least dozen skeletons in their party. If they attack us, we'd be in trouble.*

Watcher reached the side passage and peeked around the corner. The narrow corridor was lit with redstone lanterns, the glowing cubes embedded in the floor and in the impossibly high ceiling. At the end of the hallway, he spotted the skeletons approaching an entrance to a large room bathed in darkness.

"Blaster, you ever been down here?" Watcher asked.

The dark-haired boy shook his head, causing tangles of black curls to slip out from beneath his leather cap. "My dad . . ." He stopped for a moment to remember his father. He'd been destroyed in the zombie attack that fell upon their village, led by the late zombie warlord. "My dad said there would be more traps deeper into the structure. We figured it wasn't worth the risk."

"Apparently the skeletons didn't mind sacrificing a few of their own to get in here," Planter added, shaking her head.

Another trap went off, causing the walls of the narrow passage to suddenly fall away, revealing a set of dispensers on either side. Arrows streaked out from the gray blocks, impaling the skeleton who had triggered the mechanism. The pale monster quickly fell to the ground, its HP almost immediately consumed. Once the monster was off the pressure plate, the arrows stopped and the walls moved back into place. With an iron pick-axe, one of the skeletons destroyed the stone pressure plate, then the group moved quickly into the large room. The light from their torches moved far into the shadows and away from the entrance.

"Come on, we need to see what they're doing," Blaster said. "We can't let any relics from the wizards or war-locks fall into the monsters' hands."

"Skeletons will use all relics for evil," Er-Lan whis-pered, a hateful tone in his voice. "They cannot be trusted."

Blaster nodded his agreement and slapped the zom-bie on the back, then gave him a smile.

Watcher sprinted down the passage, his keen eyes watching the ground with caution; they didn't want to trigger any traps themselves. The footsteps of his three friends echoed off the walls, giving the young boy a feel-ing of security.

At the end of the passage, Watcher peered around the corner, looking for the monsters. To his surprise, he found himself staring into the stacks of a huge library. It was bigger than any library he'd seen in a village or stronghold. The bookshelves were stacked six-high, the spines of the books covered with dust.

"Er-Lan did not expect to find books." The zombie gazed at the countless tomes in amazement.

"Wait here," Watcher said.

Quickly, he dashed to the nearest stack and grabbed a book. Spinning on his toes, he darted back to the entrance. As soon as he exited the chamber, a purple glow enveloped the book in his hands, then it turned to dust and fell through his fingers, sprinkling the ground before him.

"I guess we aren't taking any books with us." Blaster kicked at the pile of dust on the ground. "Let's get in there and see what they're doing."

Both Watcher and Planter nodded, then the friends moved quietly into the massive library.

High overhead, wooden beams ran the length of the chamber to hold up the stone ceiling. Along the center of the room, three huge chandeliers hung down, the structures made of dark wood and stained glass, their torches all extinguished. But where the chandeliers met the ceiling, a circle of glowing redstone lanterns cast faint illumination on the chamber.

"I see their torch at the far end." Blaster reached into his inventory and pulled out a pair of long, curved knives, his preferred weapons. "Follow me."

They moved through the library, hugging the shadows. Blaster's black-leather armor made him nearly invisible in the darkness. But then Watcher noticed that an iridescent glow painted the walls of the passage; their enchanted weapons were making them easy to see. He put away Needle and had Planter do the same with her enchanted bow and their magical armor, and they moved forward using mundane weapons and chain mail instead.

The four friends walked quietly between the shelves of books, the dust from the floor slowly floating up into the air with each step. It made it difficult to breathe without coughing or sneezing, but they all knew silence was their best weapon. Er-Lan's clawed feet made a scraping sound as they dragged across the stone floor; it reminded Watcher of the sound made by silverfish.

At the end of a row of bookcases, a single skeleton stood over a table, holding a huge book. He set it down and leafed through the stained and brittle pages. As they approached, Watcher drew a normal bow from his inventory and notched an arrow. Carefully he drew the arrow back, getting ready to attack if necessary. The bow creaked slightly. The skeleton turned and stared straight at them.

"Villagers . . . in the library!" the monster croaked out in warning.

Instantly, the sound of rattling bones filled the chamber. Torches burst into life, throwing a flickering yellow glow onto the surroundings.

Watcher and his friends retreated back between the tall bookcases, hoping to vanish into the darkness. The monster at the table now moved to end of the aisle, a huge, wicked-looking battle axe in his bony hands. Watcher dropped his bow and drew Needle while Planter pulled out her own enchanted bow.

More skeletons gathered behind the axe-wielding monster. At the same time, a half-dozen monsters sealed off the other end of the aisle . . . they were trapped.

Cold beads of sweat trickled down Watcher's forehead as he glanced to either end of the bookcases, trying to come up with some clever idea that would help them to survive . . . but he couldn't think of anything. His brain was overwhelmed with fear.

The skeleton commander took a step closer, the terrifying monster turning Watcher's blood to ice.

"What are you doing here, villagers?" the axe-wielding monster asked.

Watcher tried to speak, but he'd lost his words. He couldn't even think.

"We could ask you the same," Blaster replied. "This building was built by the NPC wizards before the Great War. Skeletons have no place here."

Er-Lan moved next to Watcher and put a clawed hand on his shoulder. "Be strong . . . Er-Lan is with you," the zombie whispered.

Somehow, his friend's words calmed his fear. Just then, a noise came from the entrance to the library; it sounded like pieces of metal clanking together. He smiled.

"The skeletons will no longer play the victim to zombies or villagers." The monster took a step closer, his axe sparkling in the torchlight. "I have come to take the knowledge from this place and bring it to my warlord, Rakir. We will use what is written in these ancient tomes to find every ancient relic made by the great monster warlocks. When we have gathered enough of them, the skeleton nation will then sweep across the Far Lands, destroying all that oppose us. It will be the beginning of the Age of the Skeletons."

The clanking grew louder. Some of the skeletons glanced over their shoulders. Watcher knew he had to keep their attention on them.

"Sounds very . . . ambitious." Watcher's voice cracked with fear, making the skeleton leader grin. "But you forget, villagers like me will stop you." The young NPC tried to stand up tall and hold out his sword, but his hand was shaking so much that he almost dropped Needle. "The weapons from the Great War are better off left buried. More weapons will only cause more violence."

"You are a fool," the skeleton said with a sneer. "We will take what we want and there is no one who can stop us. What's unfortunate is that none of you will live long enough to see that happen." The skeleton turned his pale head and glanced at his fellow monsters, then smiled eerily. "Skeletons . . . attack!"

CHAPTER 3

Suddenly, a battle cry boomed off the chamber walls, causing dust to fall from the ancient books. The skeletons glanced about, uncertain what was happening. Planter and Blaster were equally confused, but Watcher just smiled.

"Villagers . . . ATTACK!" a voice bellowed from the darkness.

A huge NPC, clad in glowing iron armor, crashed into the skeleton formation, his diamond sword swinging left and right, tearing HP from bony bodies. More villagers emerged from the darkness, this time from the other end of the aisle.

The skeletons, startled by this attack, stepped back, moving closer to Watcher and his friends as they tried to get away from the crazed villagers. The NPCs now had the skeletons surrounded instead of the other way around.

Blaster laughed, then charged at the skeletons, swinging his curved blades through the air with deadly precision. Planter knelt and fired her enchanted bow, hitting monster after monster with her pointed shafts.

Watcher drew Needle but was terrified. These skeletons, being almost within arm's reach, extinguished any courage he had like a tidal wave on a single, flickering flame. He pushed his back to the dirty bookshelf and tried to be invisible, hoping the monsters would just go away.

One of the monsters turned when Planter's arrow pierced its back. The skeleton brought his bow up as Planter was reloading. He was getting ready to shoot her.

"No you don't!" Watcher moved faster than he thought possible. He leapt in front of Planter just as the skeleton fired. The arrow streaked through the air, heading for Planter's chest . . . but it never made it. Needle moved as if someone else controlled the blade. The enchanted weapon flicked the pointed shaft out of the air, causing it to tumble to the ground.

The monster quickly pulled out another arrow and took aim.

"I said NO!" Rage bubbled up from within Watcher as the monster tried to shoot at his dearest friend again.

Watcher knocked the arrow aside, then charged into the fray. Needle tore through the monster's HP like a bolt of metallic lightning. After the monster fell, Watcher turned to the next enemy. Fear started to creep back into his mind; the skeletons terrified him beyond reason, but the thought of these bony creatures hurting Planter . . . *his* Planter . . . he wouldn't allow it.

A monster wielding a heavy iron sword charged at Watcher. Stepping back, the boy waited as fear bubbled to the surface. The monster chopped at him. Spinning quickly, Watcher ducked, then slashed at the creature's legs, causing it to flash red, taking damage. Ducking under another attack, Needle slashed at the skeleton's exposed ribs, doing more damage. For every attack the skeleton made, Watcher returned with two of his own. In seconds, the monster was gone, his HP finally consumed.

Glancing around, Watcher found the other skeletons had been destroyed as well.

"That was fun." Blaster patted Watcher on the back, then removed his leather cap. Dark curls sprang forth, all tangled and disheveled, as if they hadn't seen a brush since the Great War.

"I thought there would be more of them." Cutter sheathed his huge, diamond sword, then scanned the room with his steely gray eyes, looking for stragglers. He was the biggest villager in the room, maybe even the biggest anywhere. His skill with his diamond sword was legendary, only eclipsed by his courage. Nothing seemed to frighten Cutter; it was something Watcher admired.

Satisfied they were safe, the big NPC moved to Watcher's side. He wore enchanted iron armor with ornate decorations on the front and back, clearly the work of some ancient blacksmith with magical powers.

"When your sister, Winger, told us a company of skeletons were in the Wizard's Tower, I thought there would be at least a couple dozen monsters." Cutter ran his finger across the spine of a book. A clean streak was left behind, showing golden letters in the standard galactic alphabet used by the ancients.

"I thought there would be more too," an NPC girl said.

She stepped into the flickering light of a torch, her long brown hair spilling down the back of her chain mail. A pair of bright, blue eyes scanned the faces of the NPCs, then stopped at Watcher's and smiled. She ran to him.

"You're okay, brother?" she asked with a smile.

"I'm glad you brought all the NPCs, Winger." Watcher hugged his sister. "We were a little bit surrounded."

Winger smiled. "When I told the others it was the Wizard's Tower that was being invaded, of course two certain villagers *had* to accompany us, even though they wouldn't be much use in a battle."

"Let me guess, our father and Mapper?" Watcher asked.

She nodded.

Two men stepped forward. Watcher's father, Cleric, was wearing his always-clean white smock with a gray stripe running down the middle. The hem of the garment was, not unusually, dirty from the thick layer of dust covering the floor. In the flickering light of the torch, his full head of grayish-white hair glowed in the flickering light like strands of silver.

"Sometimes, it takes more than blades and arrows to win a war," Cleric said in a confident, almost indignant voice.

The brother and sister giggled.

The other villager, Mapper, was bent with age. His head was bald, a ring of gray hair on the sides of his head trying to hang on to its youth despite the scalp slowly advancing over the years, driving the gray hair into retreat. His deep brown eyes, filled with subtle flecks of gold, widened when he noticed the many thousands of books on the shelves. He smiled. "This is remarkable."

"What is this place?" Cutter's deep voice boomed through the air. "A library?"

Watcher nodded to him.

"Why would the ancient wizards build something like this?" the big NPC asked as he removed his shimmering, enchanted helmet and ran his stubby, square fingers through his short cropped, sandy-brown hair.

"They made this to protect their knowledge and history," Mapper said in a scratchy voice.

"This is probably the greatest find we could ever hope for," Mapper continued, his wrinkled face filled with wonder. The old man's bald head was covered with tiny, square beads of sweat, the moisture reflecting the light from the many flickering torches being placed throughout the library. "Do you know what this place is?"

"Well . . . yeah, it's a library." Watcher led them to the others.

"Watcher, it's not just any library, this is *the* library." Mapper stopped to stare at the books on the shelf.

"What are you talking about?" Watcher's question went unanswered; Mapper was lost to the wonders of the ancient tomes standing before him.

"Son, this library was put together by one of the great wizards," his father, Cleric said. "Her name was Alexandria, and stories say she was the keeper of knowledge for the wizards before the Great War. This is the Library of Alexandria." Cleric paused to let that sink in, but no one reacted. "Didn't any of you learn *anything* in school?"

Many of the villagers just shrugged.

The old man sighed and shook his head. "Anything the wizards learned was entombed in this library. Even knowledge stolen from the monster warlocks was stored here. This is the greatest storehouse of knowledge in all of the Far Lands."

"Will there be information about magical weapons in here?" Cutter asked.

Cleric nodded.

"That's why the skeletons were here." Watcher pulled out a torch and placed it on the ground, the flickering light making it easier to see. "They were looking for weapons."

"Or maybe just information about weapons," Watcher's sister added. Winger pulled long strands of brown hair from across her face and tucked them behind an ear. "We'll need to guard this place closely. The information here could be dangerous."

"You're probably right, daughter." Cleric patted her on the back, then moved toward the front of the room. His white smock now seemed dingy; likely, it had gotten dirty on their trek through the dust-covered library. "I wish we could see better in here. Some of these books are probably very interesting."

"Watch this," Mapper said with a smile.

The old NPC moved to the front of the chamber, his boots scuffing the ground, creating tiny clouds of dust.

Watcher followed his friend, just wanting to make sure he was safe in these strange surroundings.

Mapper stepped to a button that was on the stone wall. It was almost invisible against the gray stone, but the villager seemed to know it was there.

"I read about this, once, in a stronghold library." Mapper smiled, then pushed the button.

A ball of fire appeared next to the button, then moved up the wall. When it reached the ceiling, the flame floated through the air until it hit the first chandelier. Instantly, all the torches came to life, spreading a warm yellow glow throughout the chamber. The ball of fire then moved to the next chandelier and the next, igniting every torch. Panes of stained glass built into the light fixtures cast a multitude of colors throughout the library, throwing warm oranges and reds on the walls, with yellows and blues covering the floor. It was a spectacular sight.

The villagers all gazed around them at the incredible scene. Some wiped off books and read their spines while others searched the rest of the library for relics.

"Don't try to take any of the books out of here," Watcher said.

"Of course not," his father replied. "They'll turn to dust just like in a stronghold library. The magical enchantments that surround this chamber keep the books from falling apart over the centuries."

"Oh, my." An expression of awe covered Mapper's square face as he pulled out a thick book and slowly opened to the pages.

"What is it?" Cleric quickly moved to his side.

"This book has a list of ancient relics with their last known locations." Mapper flipped the pages. "Let's see what it says about the Library of Alexandria." He stopped at the page describing the library, then mumbled as he read through the page. "It doesn't make any sense."

"What did it say?" Planter asked, her long blond hair looking like spun gold in the orange light that shone down upon her. It made Watcher smile. Out of the corner of his eye he saw Cutter staring at her as well, a smile on his big face. It caused his own smile to fade for some reason, Watcher's feelings were replaced with something else he didn't like or understand. It was like an anger levied toward the big NPC, but for no reason other than because Cutter was looking at her.

"Well, it says 'Follow the redstone' and that's all." Mapper looked at the other villagers. "I don't see any redstone in this library."

"Everyone, spread out and look for redstone," Cutter commanded.

The villagers moved throughout the library, wiping away dust from the floor with their boots. As they searched, Watcher gazed up at the ceiling, lost in thought. He stared at the three chandeliers, each hanging from a single wooden fence post. Mounted in the ceiling, a circle of redstone lanterns glowed faintly around the first chandelier, but the second had a smaller circle of lanterns, and the third an even smaller circle.

"Ha ha." Watcher laughed as he stared straight up.

"What is it?" Winger asked. She moved to her brother's side.

"Look . . . it's up there." Watcher pointed at the ceiling.

"I don't see anything," his sister replied, confused.

"Look at the number of lanterns in the circle around the main support for each chandelier," Watcher explained. "The first circle has a radius of four blocks, the second has a radius of three, then the last has two."

"Where's one?" Planter asked, now on his other side.

"Exactly," Watcher nodded.

Moving to the center of the chamber, Watcher counted the number of blocks between each chandelier . . . it was eighteen. Moving to the last chandelier, he stood directly beneath it, then counted eighteen blocks away from that point.

"I think we need to dig here." Watcher pulled out a pick axe and tore into the mossy brick cube.

Chips of stone flew in all directions, some of the tiny shards cutting the backs of his hands, but Watcher didn't slow. Two more strong swings, and the cube shattered.

"Well, look what we have here," Cleric said, peering over Watcher's shoulder.

In the excavated hole sat an ender chest. The dark cube glowed with a strange green light, lines of pale green on its side. But this chest was different than the ender chest Watcher and Blaster had found months ago in the Wizard's Tower; this chest had a gold circle drawn across the top, a bright-red ruby placed at the center.

"This is no ordinary chest," Mapper said. "I think it's a linked chest."

"What does that mean?" Cutter asked as he approached, the rest of the villagers now gathering around them.

"It means there is similar chest linked to this one," Mapper explained. "Open one and you gain access to everything in the other. It's sorta like a teleportation system. Items in one box are instantly made available in the companion chest, no matter the distance between them."

The old villager knelt and carefully opened the linked ender chest. Inside, they found five pairs of enchanted diamond boots, the crystalline items almost looking as if they were made from ice. They felt cold to the touch and almost froze his fingers as Mapper pulled multiple pairs of boots out and set them on the ground. He then pulled out a golden battle-axe. It shimmered with magical power, the enchantments pulsing within the weapon as if the axe had a heartbeat. Mapper also lifted a handful of red-tipped arrows from the chest, each dripping the smallest amount of liquid from the tip, and placed them on the ground.

Planter reached down and picked up the axe, her

eyes wide with wonder. As soon as she touched it, the handle pulsed with light, then grew dim.

"I think it just bonded to you," Cleric said. "Best you keep it."

She nodded. "What do you think these arrows do?"

"They're healing arrows," Watcher said. "We used them to destroy the Wither King."

"I remember," Planter replied, smiling.

Mapper gasped, then withdrew a duplicate chest to the linked ender chest. "Here is the companion to this chest. It will give us access to both."

"So whatever is in one, you'll be able to retrieve from the other?" Blaster asked.

Mapper nodded.

"Then we fill it with books." Blaster moved to a shelf and pulled off those with the most ornate writing on their spines. He dumped the books into the chest. "If we keep the books in the chest, then they'll still be in the library and won't fall apart."

Blaster smiled . . . the others looked confused.

"That means we can have access to any book we put in here. We can get to all this knowledge while we're looking for the ancient relics." Watcher bent over and picked up a pair of the diamond boots. He stared down at them, inspecting every inch. They were cold to the touch and colored a glacial blue, like diamond, but the frozen surface caused Watcher to wonder if they were actually hewn from solid blocks of ice. Putting the ten pair of boots into his inventory, the boy noticed a fine layer of frost on his fingers, and their tips felt slightly numb . . . interesting.

"What do you mean, son? Looking for ancient relics?" Cleric asked.

"The skeletons knew what they were looking for here," Watcher put the rest of the boots into his inventory. "They're clearly looking for the magical weapons from the past. We can't let them get their hands on them. If they gather enough of them, they could become more powerful than the zombies, or spiders, or endermen, or—"

"Or us," Blaster added.

"Exactly." Watcher nodded. "We must stop the skeletons from getting these weapons. And the only way to do that is to hide the most important books that tell where the relics are hidden, and then find them ourselves."

"Agreed," Cutter said. "Fill the chest with what look like the most important books, then hide it again." He turned to Mapper. "Search for the next closest relic. We'll head there first, as long as we don't run into any—"

"SKELETONS!" the lookout shouted.

They rushed to the entrance of the library and peered down the long corridor. Bony white monsters skulked in the shadows, trying to get close. There were only four or five of them, not enough to be of any concern in battle, but battle wasn't what Watcher was worried about.

The monsters spotted the villagers in the light from the library. A few of the creatures fired their arrows, but they were too far away; the arrows embedded themselves harmlessly in the brick floor. As more villagers filled the entrance, the skeletons began to look scared, and soon turned and fled.

"We have to stop them," Watcher said. "If they get word back to the skeleton warlord about this library, then they'll be back . . . in force."

"Half of you stay here and make sure that chest gets filled and hidden," Cutter said. "The rest of you, follow me."

Cutter charged down the passage with Watcher and the others following close behind. The skeletons were far ahead; it seemed impossible to catch them, but they had to try. If they failed, then those monsters would tell the skeleton warlord, and he'd descend upon this library with his whole army. If that monster had control of the information in this library, who knew what kind of damage he could do to the Far Lands?

CHAPTER 4

The skeleton captain stood on the edge of the massive hole that had once covered the ancient tower. Peering down into the depths, he marveled at the meticulous skill needed to construct such a colorful and ornate structure. He had to admit, those NPC wizards could build some fantastic structures.

"Our scouting party is coming out," one of the skeletons said. "They look like they're running from something."

"Or someone," the captain mused.

The fleeing monsters climbed the steps that led through the roof of the structure, then ran along the edge of the hole, leaping from block to block as they worked their way out of the hole.

"Captain Ratlan, it looks like the main group of skeletons are missing," a pale lieutenant reported. "What do you think happened?"

"Maybe we ask them when the scouts get up here." Captain Ratlan stood and addressed the rest of his troops. "Everyone get ready to leave. As soon as the scouts report, we're heading to the next location on the map given to us by our warlord, Rakir."

"But how did the warlord know about these

locations?" The lieutenant seemed nervous about asking these questions.

Captain Ratlan put a hand on the monster's bony shoulder, easing his fears. He encouraged the skeletons under his command to speak honestly, without penalty or repercussions; they never knew he took his revenge out on them later, when they weren't expecting it.

Ratlan eyed the skeleton suspiciously. "After the last wither king, Kaza, was mysteriously destroyed, a new wither king emerged. His name is Krael, and he gave the locations of many ancient sites to the skeleton warlord. With the weapons we will uncover at these sites, we will soon dominate the Far Lands."

"There's something wrong!" One of the skeleton soldiers were pointing at the Wizard's Tower.

Emerging from the structure was a small group of villagers. At the front was a large NPC wearing enchanted armor; he was giving orders to the others, clearly in command. But the smaller one interested captain Ratlan the most. He was a short and skinny villager, with no muscles to speak of . . . but he had reddish-brown hair and carried an enchanted bow.

The small villager stopped and drew back an arrow, aiming at the fleeing skeletons.

"He'll never be able to hit any of them," his lieutenant said. "They're moving much too fast."

"Watch," Ratlan cautioned as he moved behind a tall oak tree.

The villager released the arrow, then drew and released two more in quick succession. The shafts flew through the air, aimed not at the monster's position, but where he *was going* to be. The arrows hit the lead skeleton, destroying his HP and making him disappear. Before the other monsters could react, the archer fired more shafts at the fleeing creatures, slowly, methodically eradicating them.

"Skeletons, open fire!" Ratlan yelled.

The skeletons on the edge of the hole fired their own

arrows down at the villagers. The large NPC pulled out a shield and held it in front of the small archer, allowing the skinny boy to continue firing. After six more shots, the last of the scouting party was destroyed. The villagers cheered, then retreated back into the Wizard's Tower, except for the skinny boy. He put away his bow and pulled out an enchanted sword. Skeletons fired at the young NPC, but the villager was able to deflect all the arrows with his magic blade, remaining completely untouched.

"Stop firing," Ratlan commanded, then stepped out into the open to stare down at the tiny archer. "We must tell the skeleton warlord. This red-headed archer must be a descendant of the ancient wizards; only someone from that bloodline could shoot so well."

The villager stared up at the skeleton, then turned and went back into the structure. Stepping away from the gigantic hole, the captain turned and faced his skeletons. "Hurry . . . we run."

"Are we going to the next place on the map?" the lieutenant asked.

"No, this information is far too important." Captain Ratlan turned his gaze on his company of skeletons, a worried expression on his bony face. "We must get this information to Rakir right away; there is a wizard in the Far Lands. That boy may not know it yet, but when he realizes his lineage, that little archer is going to be a big problem." He moved back to the edge of the hole and peered back at the sunken tower; the archer was still gone. "Come on, brothers and sisters . . . we run for the Hall of Pillars. Anyone that cannot keep up will be left behind. There is nothing more important than this information. Rakir will want to destroy that archer, but first we need more skeletons . . . lots more skeletons. Then, we'll crush that boy and make him sorry he was ever born."

Ratlan pointed at a small group of monsters. "I want you skeletons to go back into the structure and destroy that boy-wizard. They won't be expecting you; surprise will be your ally."

"But what about all those villagers and the wizard?" one of the monsters asked.

"Are you questioning my order?" The captain reached into his inventory and pulled out an iron sword. He glared at the skeletons, as if daring them to refuse.

The monster shook his head, then led the others back down into that hole.

"You will meet us in the Hall of Pillars after your victory," Captain Ratlan said. "The warlord will be proud and there will be promotion for each of you upon your return."

The monsters sighed as they continued down into the sink hole while the others watched.

Turning, the skeleton captain ran through the forest, heading for their ancient home, the Hall of Pillars, and their commander, the skeleton warlord, Rakir.

CHAPTER 5

"**Y**ou got them all, Watcher, nice shooting." Blaster patted him on the back.

Watcher walked back up the steps and stood on the roof of the Wizard's Tower, staring up at the oak tree, where he'd seen that skeleton. The monster was gone now.

"Yeah, nice work with your bow." Cutter's voice boomed through the building.

The big NPC climbed the steps and stood next to Watcher. "I always knew you were the right person to be commanding our archers. You proved it today."

"I didn't get them all," Watcher said in a low voice.

Blaster and Planter now stepped off the staircase and stood on the roof with the others.

"What?" Cutter asked.

"I said, I didn't get all the skeletons." Watcher pointed to the oak trees with his enchanted bow. "There was one standing right up there, watching as I shot at the skeletons trying to escape. I think it was their commander, because he ordered the others to attack."

"That may be true, Watcher," Planter said, "but none of those skeletons saw the library. They know nothing about it."

"Maybe you're right." The young boy put away his bow. "It's just . . . the ones up there in the forest ran away as if they knew something important. I feel like they're gonna tell the skeleton warlord about the Wizard's Tower."

"They already know about its presence," Blaster said. "After all, they were already here, so it's no secret."

"Relax." Planter put a hand on Watcher's shoulder.

Her touch felt like gentle waves of electricity, filling his soul with joy. Watcher turned to look at her, but she'd already headed back down the steps, Cutter and Blaster following.

"Come on, let's check on the others." The big NPC's voice echoed off the stairway. "We need to collect all the relics, then get out of here."

"Yeah, we need to reset the traps leading to the library, to dissuade any more monster visitors," Blaster said. "Maybe I'll add a few of my own as well."

"No TNT," Planter shouted, her voice getting softer as she descended further down the steps. "We don't want you blowing this place up just to keep some skeletons out."

Blaster gave her a pouty face, then laughed and started down the stairs. Cutter reached out and stopped both Blaster and Watcher, allowing Planter to go first.

When they reached the bottom, Watcher stopped to check their surroundings as the rest of them continued through the long passage, heading toward the library. Cutter moved next to Planter and said something to her, making her giggle . . . her laughter was like music to Watcher's ears. He watched the two walk away until they disappeared into the darkness, then he realized he was alone. Usually, Watcher would have been nervous . . . no, scared to be alone in a place like this, but he knew they'd destroyed all the monsters and everything was safe. He stood there in the darkness, thinking about this library and the skeleton staring down at him. There was a strange look of recognition on the monster's face, as if the creature knew Watcher . . . or perhaps knew something about him . . . but that made no sense.

Why didn't the rest of the skeletons come down and attack? Watcher wondered. *They had no idea how many soldiers we had . . . they should have attacked.*

A strange itch formed in the back of Watcher's mind. It was an itch that couldn't be scratched. He'd learned it always happened when things just didn't add up.

Pushing the thoughts aside, he walked down the hallway, pulling out his enchanted bow, just to be safe. The enchanted weapon sparkled with magical power, casting an iridescent purple glow around him.

A strange sound echoed off the cold stone walls. Watcher stopped next to a dark side passage and listened. The multiple reflections off the walls made the noise difficult to identify.

I think that sounded like . . . no, it couldn't be . . .

Suddenly, a pair of skeletons stepped out of the shadows at the end of the passage, one of them firing an arrow at him. Watcher froze, the presence of the monster filling him with dread. He watched the arrow as it arched through the air; it would fall short. Drawing one of the Healing arrows, he fired, then drew and fired to the left and right of the first arrow.

Watcher's first healing arrow struck one of the monsters in the shoulder. The skeleton flashed red, taking damage as the potion slowly poisoned the undead creature. The other two arrows missed the creature, but it didn't matter. The healing potion was slowly finishing him off. The monster gasped in surprise and fear as his HP went to zero and he disappeared.

Charging toward the remaining attacker, Watcher changed the range, making it difficult for the skeleton to figure out the correct angle for his next shot. He fired multiple arrows into the air, spreading his shots across the width of the passage. They fell upon the monster just as it loosed another arrow toward Watcher. The villager's arrows hit the monster, causing it to flash red while the skeleton's arrow flew well over his head.

Fear electrified every nerve, making Watcher feel as if he was burning from within. He glanced over his shoulder. Planter and Blaster were running toward him. They were on the other side of the monster and would soon be within range of the skeleton's bow. He crouched and notched three normal arrows to his string, saving the last arrow of Healing for later, then fired them at the creature. The projectiles spread as they flew. It was impossible to hit a distant target with all three arrows this way, but the shafts covered the width of the passage. The skeleton saw the arrows and backed up, hoping to change the range and cause his adversary to miss.

Watcher just smiled.

The arrows, aimed higher than before, flew past the original position of the skeleton and fell down upon the creature. The leftmost shaft struck the monster in the chest, taking the last of his HP. He disappeared, a terrified expression on his pale face.

"Yes!"

Just then, more clattering filled the air. This time, it was right behind him. Spinning around, Watcher found a skeleton had emerged from the side passage with bow in hand.

He froze, unable to move. The monster pulled back the arrow and took aim, its bow creaking with strain. At this range, the monster couldn't miss.

A flash of green shot out of the passage and smashed into the skeleton. The two figures rolled on the ground, struggling for control of the weapon. The dim lighting made it difficult to see what was happening, or even to discern the identity of his savior.

"HELP!" Watcher cried out as he drew an arrow and pointed at the struggling combatants, but held his shot. There was no way to tell who was who.

Planter moved to his side, her bow held at the ready, but she too couldn't find a target to shoot.

Boots pounded on the ground as Cutter and the others raced to his side.

The skeleton's bow skidded across the stone floor, out of reach. Watcher quickly clamped a foot on the weapon, then pulled out a torch and held it high over his head. At his feet, he found Er-Lan, his zombie friend, wrestling with the skeleton.

With the claw on each finger extended, the young zombie wrapped one arm around the skeleton, and with the other, held the claws to the monster's throat.

"Stop struggling, or the skeleton will not survive," Er-Lan said.

The skeleton turned his head and looked at his assailant, then glanced nervously up at the young boy.

"Stop fighting and answer our questions, and you will not be harmed." Slowly, Watcher lowered his bow.

The skeleton stopped struggling, then peered past Watcher and the assembly of villagers approaching, many with swords drawn. The monster's dark eyes grew wide with fright.

"Don't worry, they won't hurt you, as long as you cooperate." Watcher held up his hands to signify they had the situation under control.

Two villagers grabbed the arms of the skeleton and raised him to his feet, pinning the monster to the wall. Planter quickly went to Er-Lan's side and helped him up, wrapping her arms around him and hugging the zombie tight.

"You saved us again," she said.

"Er-Lan was just making sure my friends were safe." The zombie blushed slightly, his green skin turning a warm shade of brown for just a moment.

"Thank you, Er-Lan." Watcher put a hand on the creature's arm. "If you hadn't been there, this skeleton might have killed me."

"Er-Lan would never let that happen," the monster said.

"This is great and all . . . but let's focus on the

skeleton." Blaster stepped up to the monster and drew one of his curved knives. "We want to know what you were doing here. If you answer truthfully, we'll spare your life. But if you lie . . . well, it won't be pretty."

The skeleton swallowed nervously, his eyes glued to the keen edge of the knife. Blaster moved the tip of the blade to the creature's chest, pressing it against one of his ribs. The monster flinched, feeling the razor-sharp point.

Blaster moved closer, so they were nose to nose. "Talk now . . . or die." He drew his other knife and held the blade to the creature's neck.

"Okay . . . okay . . . I will talk," the skeleton stammered. "We were sent here to look for ancient relics. The skeleton warlord is collecting all he can find."

"Why?" Blaster scowled, moving his knife a little closer.

"Please, put the knives away, and I will tell you what you want to know."

"Blaster . . . take a step back," Watcher said.

The NPC nodded and moved back, but kept his knives out and ready.

"How did you know to come here to look for relics?" Cleric asked, his aged voice sounding calm and wise.

"The warlord was given the locations by a wither . . . the wither king," the skeleton said.

"The wither king?" Watcher was confused. "I thought we destroyed that monster."

"There is a new wither king. I don't remember his name, but he wears the Crown of Skulls. I saw it." The skeleton took his gaze from Blaster and focused it on Watcher. His eyes went to the young boy's reddish hair and an expression of surprise came across his face.

"What is it?" Mapper pushed through the crowd and stood next to Watcher. "What did you just notice about our young friend here?"

The old man put an arm around Watcher's shoulders. At the same time, Blaster took a step forward again. A look of fear came across the skeleton's bony face.

"The hair . . . it was just the hair . . . it's red." The skeleton seemed terrified, but not because of Blaster or his knives; rather, it was because of Watcher.

"What about his hair?" Blaster asked.

"The ancient wizards, they all had red hair and were great shots with a bow." The skeleton pointed a finger at Watcher. "He is a descendant. He is a wizard. The monsters of the Far Lands all know to fear the wizards, for they will bring back the Great War to the Far Lands and try to destroy all monsters."

"I'm not a wizard," Watcher said, confused. "I'm just me."

"He was able to use the Mantle of Command to destroy the last wither king," Mapper said. "It was the enchanted armor from the zombie warlord. The relic was made to be used only by monsters, yet Watcher was able to use it."

"And my sword, Needle." Planter turned and looked at Watcher with an expression of astonishment on her beautiful face. "Once he touched it, no one else could use it. It was like the sword recognized him, somehow."

"Interesting . . ." Mapper stepped back and cradled his chin in his wrinkled palm, lost in thought.

"The wizards must be stopped," the skeleton whispered, his voice barely audible.

The monster suddenly grabbed Blaster's wrist. At the same time, he struck Blaster with his knee, right in the boy's stomach. Blaster fell back, releasing his grip on the knife. Moving faster than anyone thought possible, the skeleton raised the knife and brought it down toward Watcher in a killing blow.

Er-Lan leaped forward. The zombie blocked the attack with an arm, then tore into the monster with his razor-sharp claws. Surprised, the skeleton turned his dark eyes toward the zombie, but Er-Lan didn't stop. He continued to slash at the monster, taking his HP to zero in just seconds. The skeleton disappeared, a look of confusion and fear on his bony face.

Blaster's knife clattered to the floor.

"Er-Lan, you did it again!" Planter said and put her arms around the zombie again.

This time, the decaying creature did not blush, he just stared down at the three glowing balls of XP and the pile of skeleton bones that lay on the ground.

"The skeleton is gone." The zombie's voice was filled with sadness. "He was there and now he's gone. Er-Lan destroyed him."

"That's right!" Cutter slapped the zombie on the back. "You acted fast and now that skeleton is no more. Great work!"

The zombie looked up at Cutter with tears in his eyes, then turned and shuffled off into the darkness to be alone.

"What's with him?" Blaster asked.

"I think that was his first time in battle," Cleric said. "Destroying another living thing takes a toll on one's soul. I'm not sure Er-Lan was ready for that."

"Well, at least that skeleton is gone." Blaster picked up his knife and put it back in his inventory. "What about the things the skeleton told us?"

"He thought I was one of the wizards because of my hair and skill with a bow." Watcher paced back and forth, lost in thought. "The skeleton near the oak trees looked at me the same way. He saw me shoot and destroy those escaping skeletons; I bet he thinks I'm a wizard as well."

"Our prisoner was willing to trade his life to destroy Watcher," Mapper said. "How do you think the skeleton warlord will react to this news?"

Watcher looked up at the old man. "He'll send his entire army here to try and destroy me. Our village will be leveled to the ground and everything in the library will be his."

"Don't worry about the library," Winger said. "We

took some of the stone-bricks and sealed off the passage. You can't even tell there's anything there. It looks
like a dead end."

"That's great, but that doesn't help everyone in the
village." Planter pulled out the small, golden axe they'd
found in the linked ender chest. She passed it from hand
to hand as the magical weapon pulsed with energy.

"You're right. Those skeletons are gonna destroy
everything around here." Watcher turned to Cutter. "We
need to evacuate the village before the skeleton warlord
gets here with his army. If we can't convince the rest of
the village to leave, it'll be a massacre."

"Don't worry." Cutter moved to Watcher's side and
gazed down at the boy. "I'll ask everyone nicely, and
then I'll ask not-so-nicely. They'll evacuate if they know
what's good for them."

"Then it's a plan," Cleric said. "We'll explain this to
the village; it will make it easier on them. Besides, when
a new journey in life is started, it's always best to start
it with friends."

"You're full of all kinds of warm and fuzzy thoughts
. . . aren't you?" Blaster said.

"That's my thing." Cleric smiled.

Blaster rolled his eyes, then headed out of the
Wizard's Tower with the others close behind. Last to
leave was Watcher. He peered into the darkness and
found Er-Lan, then guided the zombie toward the
stairs.

"I know what you did for me was hard, Er-Lan, but
you saved my life again."

"But this time, it cost the life of another. That does
not sit well with Er-Lan."

Watcher sighed. "I understand, and I'm sorry you
were put in this position. It's my hope you'll never have
to do that again."

"Er-Lan hopes Watcher speaks the truth." The zombie turned and shuffled through the passage and toward
the exit.

As his friend shuffled away, Watcher had the strangest feeling that everything was about to change, and not for the better. Chills slithered down his spine as a strange sensation filled his entire being. Somehow, Watcher could sense that something dangerous was hunting them. And if that unseen adversary caught them, he was sure many of his friends would perish. The young boy shook with fear, glancing at the shadowy passage around him. Then, as quickly as the sensation appeared, it was gone, and he was alone in the Wizard's Tower, terrified.

Quickly, he ran for the exit, all the while glancing over his shoulder, looking for that invisible predator.

CHAPTER 6

Captain Ratlan and the surviving members of his company ran across the countryside without stopping. Everything was a blur as they sprinted through forests, then swamps, and through deserts. It took days and their HP dropped dangerously low. When necessary, Ratlan stopped to hunt for food, shooting cows and pigs so he and his companions could feast on their bones, for that's what skeletons ate: bones. When one of their party fell, the doomed skeleton's HP exhausted, the rest of the party consumed their comrade, sharing stories about the deceased's bravery; it was the skeleton way. Every one of them knew this was the way of the world; a skeleton's death frequently fed his own family.

Finally, Captain Ratlan slowed as an extreme hills biome came into sight.

"Skeletons, we're almost there." Ratlan slapped one of his comrades on the back.

"I see the Triplets." One of the monsters pointed to a group of steep mountains. There were three tall peaks spaced close together, each topped with a frosting of snow. "I can almost hear the wonderful echoes of the Hall of Pillars." The monster closed his eyes for a moment and smiled.

"Come on, let's get to the Leap of Faith." Captain Ratlan smiled at his fellow skeletons. "I miss our home."

He ran through the stream that marked the boundary of the extreme hills biome. Following a trail that was well known to all skeletons, they headed for the trio of mountains. The path took them past smaller hills, with multiple trails joining the main path, then led them to the side of a hill, a dark passage carved through the very center of the mound. They could go around, but would lose valuable time. With their bows in their hands and arrows notched, they moved into the darkness.

"Watch for spiders and zombies," Ratlan warned in a low voice. "Since the destruction of the zombie warlord, the other monsters have been more aggressive. We must be careful."

The other skeletons nodded, then notched arrows to bowstrings. They moved through the dark passage, following the ancient path through the mountain that would eventually take them home. Fortunately, there were no other monsters in the tunnel. They moved out of the darkness and back into the late afternoon light.

Weaving around the occasional oak and spruce tree, Ratlan was grateful to be out of the tunnel and into the open, where their bows could be more effective; confined spaces were something all skeletons hated. As he ran, the skeleton smelled something burning and smiled. Ash began to fill the air, dimming the rays of the sun as the glowing square slowly approached the horizon.

We're getting closer, the captain thought with a smile.

They came to a deep crevasse, the bottom of which was filled with lava. Smoke and ash floated into the air, creating a subtle gray haze. As they ran, their steps created tiny little clouds of ash that circled around their feet, obscuring the occasional tuft of grass or shrub.

The roar of falling water filled the air. Ratlan smiled and glanced up; a waterfall cascaded down the side of one of the mountains in the Triplets, the cold liquid crashing into the crevasse and mixing with the lava. Steam billowed up from the collision of hot and cold at the bottom of the ravine, causing the ash to become sticky, like a gray ooze that coated everything nearby.

Right near the waterfall, the crevasse narrowed to a gap only two blocks wide. The skeletons ran straight for that point and leapt across the chasm with practiced ease. They followed the trail along a curving path, moving around smaller hills until they reached a point between the tree tallest peaks . . . the Triplets. The trail ended at a wide pit, cloaked in darkness.

Captain Ratlan stared down into the hole. No features were visible in the darkness, just an inky blackness waiting to swallow those foolish enough to enter the abyss. It was as if the opening extended all the way through Minecraft and into the dark void.

"I always wonder why the sunlight is never able to penetrate the Leap of Faith," one of the skeletons asked, pointing into the darkness.

"It's said the ancient skeleton warlock, Ragnar, cast a spell on it, keeping out the sunlight," Ratlan explained. "Now, only those that know the path can make it through the Leap of Faith without falling to their deaths. During the Great War, the NPCs were heading for the Hall of Pillars. Ragnar the Tormentor cast his spell on this entrance, protecting the skeleton people from the atrocities of the NPCs. This magical opening still protects our people from attack."

The captain moved to the edge and jumped on the lone block of stone. "You all remember the path . . . right?"

The skeletons nodded.

"Then let's go home."

Ratlan turned to the right and leapt into the darkness. His feet landed on a stone block, the magical darkness now embracing both stone and skeleton. Continuing through the ancient parkour course, the captain jumped from block to block, following the invisible trail that was taught to every skeleton born in the Hall of Pillars. In minutes, he'd reached the bottom. Standing before him was a large, cylindrical tunnel lit with redstone lanterns running along the ceiling, their glow barely strong enough to illuminate the wide passage.

Captain Ratlan waited for the rest of his troops, then ran through the passage. It bored straight through the flesh of the Far Lands, making a gentle curve as it descended deeper and deeper underground.

Shadowy recesses in the walls caught the monster's eye. Ratlan knew bony surprises awaited anyone foolish enough to enter the tunnel uninvited. He smiled and waved to his brothers and sisters he knew were hiding in the shadows, ready for any invasion.

Finally, the passage ended, opening into the historic Hall of Pillars, built hundreds of years ago, before the Great War. The skeletons gazed in wonder at the amazing view. Tall columns of quartz, each with embedded redstone lanterns, stretched up to the ceiling, which was impossibly high and lost in the darkness high overhead. The white pillars stood out in stark contrast to the stone-brick floor, each equally spaced from their neighbors, creating a grid-like array of columns stretching across the chamber.

"Come on, we must give the skeleton warlord our news." Ratlan sprinted into the chamber, his footsteps echoing off the ancient floor. The echoes from their bony feet filled the Hall, letting the monsters on the other end know someone was approaching. As they neared, ghostly shapes emerged from the haze of Minecraft; hundreds of skeletons, each with arrows drawn back, waited for the intruders. When they saw it was their comrades, the defenders lowered their weapons.

"I must speak to the warlord, immediately," the captain yelled.

"Bring him to me," a scratchy voice said from the far end of the Hall.

Ratlan pushed through the skeletons until he finally reached the far end of the huge room. A large throne, built from fossilized bone and redstone blocks, sat against the wall. Redstone lanterns embedded in the floor cast a warm yellow glow around the structure, pushing back the darkness. Sitting on the throne was the skeleton warlord, Rakir. In his hands he held the most fantastic bow Ratlan had ever seen. The weapon glowed with magical enchantments, but more interesting was its construction: the bow wasn't made of wood like every other bow wielded by the skeleton army; instead, it was crafted from enchanted, fossilized bone.

Captain Ratlan instantly went to one knee and bowed before his commander. "Warlord, I believe a descendant of the wizards has been spotted."

"What?!" Rakir instantly stood and stepped forward. "Stand up, you fool, and tell me what you saw."

"We went to the location given to us by the king of the withers, and—"

"I gave you that location," the warlord snapped. "Only Rakir commands the skeletons. That idiotic wither, Krael, told me of the tower's location, and I decided it was worthy of our inspection."

"Yes, sire." Ratlan lowered his head, trying to avoid his commander's wrath.

"Well . . . what did you find there?"

"We found nothing. The scouts were all destroyed."

"So, there could be weapons there in that ancient tower; we still don't know." Rakir glanced at his general, Rusak, then back to the captain.

"There was something more important than weapons, my warlord," Captain Ratlan said.

"More important than weapons?" Rusak boomed.

Ratlan cowered, knowing of the general's lethal temper. "As my scouts were leaving, they were fired upon by a young NPC archer. He hit the scouts from an impossible distance using an enchanted bow. His skill was incredible."

"That means nothing," Rakir said, his voice harsh and grating. He stood and paced back and forth, his impatience growing. "Just because he was a good shot, it doesn't mean he's–"

"He had red hair as well," Captain Ratlan said.

"What?" Rakir stopped pacing and moved to stand directly in front of the skeleton.

"He had red hair and wielded his bow better than anyone I'd ever seen."

The skeleton warlord's eyes grew wide with surprise, and then he scowled.

"Well . . . except for Rakir, of course." The skeleton captain reached up and wiped his sweating brow.

"So, you think this was a descendant of the ancient NPC wizards?" the warlord asked.

"That's the only explanation. He hit my skeletons from thirty blocks away while they were jumping from block to block. Only a wizard could do that."

"Interesting . . . interesting indeed." Rakir turned and motioned for another skeleton to step forward.

General Rusak stepped out of the shadows and moved to his warlord's side, his iron armor clanking as he walked.

"General Rusak, did you hear what the captain said?" The warlord gazed up at the huge skeleton.

"Yes," the general replied. "I heard and am concerned. We cannot let the wizards regain their power. They probably know the locations of all the ancient relics. When they get those weapons, they're certain to attack the skeleton nation. We must protect ourselves." The huge skeleton moved closer and lowered his voice to but a whisper. "The Great War is not over."

"Exactly." Rakir nodded his bony head, then pulled his enchanted bow from his inventory. "With the Fossil Bow of Destruction, built by the great skeleton warlock, Ragnar, himself, we will capture more relics and grow stronger and stronger. The zombies already fear the skeleton army; with their warlord destroyed, they are leaderless and in chaos. But now, we have a new target. That wizard must be destroyed before he gathers all his power."

The skeleton general smiled an eerie, toothy smile.

"The map given to me by the king of the withers will tell us where to search for the ancient weapons." Rakir began pacing again. "We know the boy-wizard and his cohorts were at the buried Wizard's Tower. The map will show us the nearest artifact; that will surely be where the villagers will be heading." He turned and faced his commander. "General Rusak, you will lead a battalion of skeletons. Take what you need and find that wizard. Your priority is to find that boy and destroy him. He must not be allowed to find his powers. Capture the relics that are in his path if you can, but his destruction is paramount." The warlord leaned toward his general and stared into Rusak's one good eye. "Failure will not be tolerated . . . do you understand?"

The skeleton commander nodded, his eyes, even the ruddy and sightless one, filled with fear.

"Now go, and return when you have good news for me."

"As you command." Rusak bowed, then walked to the Hall's exit, gathering soldiers and supplies as he went.

Sixty pale monsters followed their general, their armor clanking and jingling as the monsters marched.

"Success!" the skeleton warlord shouted to the general's back. "Success or death!"

Rusak held a fist up into the air as a salute, the other monsters doing the same, then disappeared into the shadows, heading toward their new adversary and prey, the boy-wizard.

CHAPTER 7

I t took little effort to convince their friends and neighbors to abandon their village. None were excited about facing an invasion by the skeleton warlord and no one wanted to stay behind. They all knew if any were captured, they'd be tortured into telling where Watcher and the others went . . . no one looked forward to that. It was best if they all stayed together, which made Watcher happy. "There's safety in numbers," his father, Cleric, had told him when he was younger.

Gathering the supplies and items they needed, they left their community with Cutter in command and Watcher in charge of the newly formed archer corps. The responsibility for commanding the archers weighed heavily on Watcher; he wasn't sure he was up for the job, but Cutter seemed to have faith in him . . . that faith was something he didn't understand, nor have for himself. Standing tall, Watcher pretended to be totally confident and know what to do, but that was far from the truth . . . he was afraid of this responsibility, afraid he'd fail.

Mapper and Cleric promised everyone they would return to their village soon, but few believed the old men. They'd learned when an army of monsters is descending upon your home, things change and life is never the way it was again.

The community moved through the forest as quietly as possible, the more experienced travelers helping out the old and infirm. In all, there were maybe seventy of them, every villager armed except for the very young and the very old. Those villagers were given the task of holding the healing potions and food, allowing the rest of the NPCs to carry more of the heavier weapons and armor. Watcher had learned long ago: the Far Lands was a dangerous place and they had to be ready for anything. His father was fond of saying, "It's always better to *be* prepared than *wish* you were prepared." He made sure they had everything they might need.

As their village was slowly obscured by the forest, Watcher gazed back at his home with a heavy heart. The last time he'd abandoned his village it had been in flames, having just been attacked by the zombie warlord. Now, they were leaving home again, this time because of the skeleton warlord.

These warlords are becoming a problem, he thought. *Why can't they just get along and leave us alone?*

"Hey . . . you okay?"

Watcher turned and found Planter at his side, the setting sun nestling itself behind the horizon, just over her shoulder. Deep orange and red light filled the sky and cast a warm radiance on his friend, making her long, blond hair glow with a soft luster as if it were made of the finest gold. She smiled at him . . . the sight was breathtaking. Her green eyes seemed to glow like magical emeralds. *I could get lost in those green eyes for an eternity,* he thought. *Wait, what am I thinking?!*

The fear lurking deep in his mind seemed to fade when he thought about Planter. Watcher knew he didn't need to pretend to be confident or strong or brave when he was around her, he could just be himself. Planter filled in what he lacked, their personalities seeming to merge as if in a delicate dance, one reinforcing the other;

they were each more complete when together than when apart. She accepted him as he was, and always had . . . he was just beginning to notice that in her, and it made his heart soar just a bit.

"Ahh . . . what?" He'd been daydreaming again; that frequently happened when he was around Planter.

"I said, 'Are you okay?' You look a little sad."

"Well, I was just thinking about the last time we fled from our village. You know, when we were chasing the zombie army."

Planter nodded. "Yeah, I was thinking about that too. It seems like a hundred years ago, but was just a couple of months."

"I hoped the fighting was over, and then we—"

A stick cracked off to the left. Watcher turned and peered into the darkening forest, looking for threats. Slowly, with his hands up, Er-Lan emerged from the darkness and headed for Watcher and Planter.

"Er-Lan . . . over here." Planter waved to their zombie friend.

The green creature lowered his arms and slowly pushed his way through a group of villagers to get to his two companions, the zombie's chain mail armor swinging back and forth. He'd been given a full set of iron armor after helping free villagers captured by the zombie warlord, but the thick metallic coating had been too heavy for the young zombie. Instead, he chose the lighter chain mail.

"The armor looks good on you, Er-Lan," Planter said.

The zombie smiled.

"Yeah, you look like a real warrior now," Blaster said as he ran past, putting on his black-dyed leather armor.

The boy gave Watcher and Planter a smile, then darted ahead of the column, scouting their surroundings. He quickly disappeared into the shadows, his black-leather armor making the boy nearly invisible in the darkness.

"Er-Lan does not want to look like a warrior." The

zombie tugged uncomfortably at the sheets of chain that hung over his shoulders. "Looking like a peaceful zombie would be better."

"I know." Watcher adjusted the monster's armor, twisting the shoulders so it hung better on his diminutive frame. "We all just want you to be safe, and this chain mail will help protect you."

The young zombie growled his annoyance, then nodded.

"Everyone hurry up," a voice said from behind. "We need to move quick and quiet."

Cutter shoved through the crowd of villagers, urging them along with a gentle but firm hand on a back or shoulder. He directed a handful of warriors to position themselves on either side of the group, just to be safe. When the big NPC reached Planter's side, he slowed and glanced up at the darkening sky. The stars were beginning to shine through the blue veil of daylight, sparkling like a million gems.

"We need to get everyone moving faster." The big NPC glanced at Watcher, then back to Planter and smiled. "Who knows when the skeleton warlord will get here with his troops? I want as much space between us and his army as possible."

"I agree." Watcher nodded. "But we need a plan. Where are we going? The next village is down the stone path—you know, the one we followed when the zombie warlord captured all our friends."

"I know that's the closest one." Cutter sounded annoyed. "But with all the young kids and elderly with us, it'll take us a couple of days to get there. Our best bet is to go where the skeleton warlord doesn't expect. That's why we aren't heading for any communities on the main road. I sent runners to those villages, warning them of the skeleton army. Hopefully, they'll evacuate just to be safe, and hide in the forest."

"You know, instead of hiding in the forest, I have a better idea." Watcher glanced at Planter and stood a little taller as he walked. "They could head for the ancient church instead. If they patch the holes in the walls with some cobblestone, they'd be safe."

"That's a great idea, Watcher," Planter said.

The young boy beamed with pride, then glanced up at Cutter, one side of his unibrow raised in question. The big warrior looked at the two of them, then gave a sigh.

Cutter pointed to one of the scouts. "You heard Watcher's idea?"

The villager nodded.

"Then go tell the plan to the other villages," Cutter ordered.

The NPC nodded and took off running, weaving his way around trees until he disappeared into the forest.

"So, Cutter, where are *we* heading?" Planter asked.

"There's a large village in the savannah, a day's march from here." Cutter pointed with his diamond sword to the south, their current direction. "I've heard rumors that the NPCs are a bit strange there, but that community is off the main road that stretches between the villages. I doubt the monsters even know about it. We'll rest up there for a couple of days, then send some scouts out and see what the skeletons are doing. When the skeleton warlord has moved on, we'll go back home."

"That sounds like a great plan." Planter turned and looked at Watcher, expecting him to say the same thing.

That doesn't sound like much of a plan at all, Watcher thought. *That skeleton said they had to destroy me, because they think I'm a descendant of the great wizards from the ancient days. Waiting in a village for a couple of days doesn't do anything . . . they'll be back, I know it.*

"One should always control the battle rather than be controlled by it," a voice said from behind.

Watcher glanced over his shoulder and found his father and Mapper behind them.

"What's that supposed to mean?" Cutter asked.

Cleric just shrugged, then smiled at his son.

"It means we need to control the situation instead of just watching it. We need to be more aggressive." Watcher said. "Sitting around in a village seems like it would help the skeletons."

"Okay, professor, what's your plan?" Cutter stared down at the boy with his steel-gray eyes.

"Well . . . ahh . . . maybe we go find as many relics as possible." Watcher's voice was weak, barely a whisper. "The more we find, the fewer the skeletons can use against other villagers."

Cutter laughed. "What do you mean, just go searching all of the Far Lands?"

"Ummm . . . we could . . . ummm . . ." Watcher stammered.

"That's exactly right," an old voice croaked from behind. Mapper moved between Watcher and Planter. "One of those books in the Library of Alexandria had the location of many artifacts listed in it."

"That's great, but the Wizard's Tower is probably filled with skeletons right now." Cutter shook his head in exasperation.

Mapper placed a hand on Cutter's muscular arm. "I put that book in the linked ender chest. I can find the location of the closest relic right now."

The old man stopped beside a birch tree. Pulling out a torch, he placed it onto the side of the tree, then pulled the glowing ender chest from his inventory. He placed it on the ground, the flipped open the lid. Cleric moved to the old man's side and gazed into the chest, Watcher looking between them. The chest was filled with many books, each dusty and worn. Mapper reached for one with gold writing along its spine. He opened the aged tome, careful to keep it inside the chest. While the book remained in the ender chest, it was still in the Library of Alexandria, and wouldn't turn to dust.

Mapper flipped through the pages, mumbling as he read.

"Let's see if we can find us a relic," the old man said.

Suddenly, a shadowy figured emerged from behind the birch tree. Watcher jumped back, then saw the large smile stretching from ear to ear . . . it was Blaster in his dark armor.

"Blaster, you need to warn us when you do that," the young boy chided.

"What's the point of being sneaky if you warn people you're there?" Blaster smiled, then turned and faced Cutter. "I scouted the forest and heard clicking in the treetops . . . there must be spiders nearby."

"Everyone spread out and look for the spiders," Cutter said, his voice booming through the woods.

"No . . . we must stay together!" Watcher snapped.

"Don't listen to him." Cutter glared at the young boy. "You can't find an enemy when you don't go looking for 'em."

A quiet tension spread across the villagers as the big NPC glared down at the young boy. Watcher took a step back and lowered his gaze to the ground, but then a gentle hand pushed him forward. Glancing over his shoulder, he found his sister, Winger, standing behind him.

"Tell us your plan," she whispered.

"Well . . . ahhh . . ."

"Say it loud," his sister snapped.

"Right." Watcher looked up at Cutter. "We stay together. Get scouts up on top of the trees. Spiders like to sun themselves; somehow, they gain energy from the sun . . . that's where they'll be." He turned and pointed at a couple of scouts. "Everyone else, set up a perimeter around Mapper. We need to give him time to read his book and find the closest relic."

"This is ridiculous," Cutter said with a scowl. "They're just a bunch of spiders. We can just spread out and attack them, one at a time, until they're all destroyed."

"Not everyone is as good with a sword as you, Cutter." Watcher pointed at some of the younger kids from the village. They looked scared. "We need to work together and not abandon each other so we can keep everyone safe."

The big warrior gave him a frustrated stare, then nodded.

Watcher smiled. "Scouts, follow me."

Using blocks of dirt, the young boy built steps that led to the leafy blocks overhead. With an axe in hand, he climbed the steps, cutting through the leaves as he moved to the top of the tree. Crouching, Watcher scanned to the north while the other scouts moved next to him and checked the other directions.

"I see something to the west," one of the scouts said. "But I can't tell what it is."

Watcher looked to the west. With the sun completely settled behind the horizon and the moon not yet risen, the forest canopy appeared almost black. The sparkling stars overhead gave barely any light by which to see, but Watcher's eyesight was legendary amongst his fellow villagers. Peering into the darkness, the young boy could see something moving in the distance, but wasn't sure if it was a spider or not. He glanced up at the stars, the shining pinpoints of light like sparkling gems sewn into the evening tapestry. Looking back to the west, it seemed as if there was a collection of ruby-red stars on top of the oaks. And then a group of the crimson stars blinked and bobbed up and down; they were moving across the treetops.

"That's them," Watcher said.

"You sure?" a deep voice asked from below. "It looks pretty dark out there."

He glanced down and saw Cutter staring up at him.

Watcher nodded. "Yep, I can see their glowing red eyes. That's the spiders."

"So we go out there and attack." Cutter's statement sounded like a command, but also a question.

"No, I have a better idea." Watcher moved down the stairs and pointed at Blaster. "I need you to do something, and it's gonna make you really happy. You think you can prepare a little surprise on the treetops for our spidey-friends without being seen?"

Blaster replaced his black, leather tunic and pulled on his black cap; he nearly disappeared in the darkness, only his smile revealing his presence, like the Cheshire Cat. "What do you have in mind?"

Watcher quickly explained.

Blaster nodded, then tossed a set of dark, leather armor to Er-Lan. "Come on, I need your help. With your claws, you'll be a natural climber."

Er-Lan glanced at Blaster nervously, then to his friend. Watcher gave the zombie a smile and nodded. "You're gonna help save a lot of these villagers around you if you help."

The zombie nodded, then removed his chain mail and donned the shadowy armor. The two disappeared into the darkness, a block of TNT in Blaster's hand.

In the distance, an axe could be heard cutting through blocks of leaves, then everything was silent. Watcher moved back to the treetops and crouched behind a block of oak leaves, staring off to the west. The red pinpoints of light were still there moving about. It seemed they were a little closer, which worried him . . . what if they saw Blaster and Er-Lan, and attacked?

Just then, a dark object moved across the tree-tops, blocking out the glowing eyes of the spiders. Then another shape, not as quick as the first, moved from one tree to another. Watcher couldn't see what they were doing, but he was confident Blaster knew what he was doing.

Moving down the steps to the forest floor, Watcher glanced at Mapper. "Do you know the location of any relics yet?"

"I'm still reading," Mapper replied. "Many of these pages are faded and damaged. I've found a few, something called the Trident of Pain and the Lightning Helix and the Static Snare, but those things are far away from here."

"Make sure you mark where they are on a map . . . maybe we'll want to go get them some time in the future."

Mapper nodded, then glanced up at Watcher. "I need more time."

"We'll give you as much time as we can." Watcher pointed at a group of villagers. "We need defenses built around Mapper. Build a wall out of dirt that goes up to the treetops. We'll want holes in the walls for archers. Build quietly, we don't want to tip off the spiders to our location . . . at least not yet."

The NPCs sprang into action. Winger and Cleric went with them, one of them directing the construction defensive wall on the north side of their party while the other took the opposite. They made the barricade two blocks thick, expecting this to be a fierce battle. Once the spiders knew they were there, they'd likely throw everything they had at them.

Watcher moved back to the tree tops and scanned for the spiders. They were still milling about, some of them a little closer. Suddenly, a pair of dark shadows appeared before him, both smiling.

"We're ready," Blaster said as he took off his black leather cap, Er-Lan doing the same.

"Okay, this is your show." Watcher moved back and got out of the way.

Across the treetops, a line of dirt could now be seen, extending off into the darkness. Atop the brown cubes, redstone dust was spread, with a redstone repeater occasionally breaking up the crimson line. At their feet, a lever was mounted into a block of stone right at the end of the trail of red dust.

Blaster removed the rest of his leather armor and replaced it with a full set of iron. He then pulled out a torch and held it high over his head.

"They'll see you." Watcher reached up for the torch.

Blaster smiled and gently pushed him back.

Drawing a sword from his inventory, Blaster banged it on his chest plate, creating as much noise as he could.

"Spiders are filthy, cowardly creatures!" His voice echoed across the forest. "The spider warlord is the biggest coward of them all. I don't see her out here. She must be skulking in some cave, hiding with creepers!"

Instantly, angry clicks filled the air. The red eyes all turned toward Blaster, then grew larger as they approached.

"They're coming, flip the switch." Watcher's voice sounded anxious.

"Hold . . ." Blaster's voice was strong and clear.

"Archers, get to the wall and be ready." Winger's voice floated up to them from the forest floor.

"They won't be necessary," Blaster said.

"They're getting closer," someone said.

"Hold . . ." Blaster's voice was like iron.

Cutter pushed his way to the tree tops and stared at the oncoming storm of spiders. He drew his diamond sword and started to advance. Blaster grabbed the back of his enchanted iron armor and pulled him back.

"Hold . . ." the boy said again.

Cutter growled his frustration but held his position.

The moon had risen, and now the spiders were bathed in the silvery lunar glow. There were maybe twenty-five of them and they seemed frothing with rage as they charged toward the group.

"Did I mention the spider queen is a coward?" Blaster shouted.

The spiders screeched and ran faster, charging straight toward Blaster.

"Almost there," he whispered. "Almost there . . . and . . . NOW!"

Reaching down, Blaster flipped the lever at his feet. Instantly, the line of redstone dust turned bright red, burning a crimson glow across the treetops. The glow dimmed as it moved farther from the lever, but when it reached the repeater, the redstone became brighter. The radiant dust stretched off across the treetops until . . .

BOOM . . . BOOM, BOOM . . . BOOM, BOOM, BOOM . . .

TNT blocks detonated behind the spiders, pushing them forward. Those that survived were then hit from the left and right by more explosives, delayed by just a couple of seconds. As they struggled to stand, the main battery of explosives detonated, tearing a huge hole in the forest and swallowing the spiders in the bright, fiery maw of Blaster's trap.

"Archers, get ready to attack," Winger's voice said on the forest floor.

Blaster turned and glanced at Watcher, a huge smile on the boy's face. "I don't think that's gonna be necessary." He slapped Er-Lan on the back and laughed. "That was fun."

Er-Lan just growled something unintelligible.

Watcher stared out at the forest. None of the spiders survived the explosion, or if they had, they had been wounded and thrown to the forest floor. Likely, they'd be running away as fast as they could.

"I found it!" Mapper exclaimed.

Watcher moved down to the forest floor and peered over Mapper's shoulder.

"There's an ancient temple in the desert, not far from here." The old man marked the position on a map, then closed the book and shut the linked ender chest. Putting the chest back into his inventory, he stood on wobbly legs and smiled. "We keep going south, and when we hit the savannah, we head south-west, toward the desert. We'll be there tomorrow."

"Great, let's get moving," Cutter said.

The army continued to the south, eyes watching the dark forest with renewed concern. Spiders were usually solidary creatures and did not like working together. But with such a large group of spiders in the treetops, it could only mean the spider warlord was becoming more active.

I wonder what the spider warlord is up to, Watcher thought. *The last thing we need right now is* another *warlord to deal with.*

He shook almost imperceptibly as thoughts of a spider army floated through his mind. Something about the whole scene nagged at him, but with so many other dangers around them, it quickly was swallowed up by other fears and concerns.

With a sigh, he followed the rest of the army, weaving around trees as his keen eyes scanned the forest for more monsters.

CHAPTER 8

The temperature in the savannah was much higher compared to the forest biome, but it was nothing compared to the desert. Watcher had never been in a desert before and wasn't prepared for the sweltering fist of heat that slammed into him when he stepped onto its sandy ground.

Beads of sweat instantly trickled down from his forehead, most of them being trapped by his wide, reddish-brown unibrow, though some of the moisture managed to make it past the fuzzy barrier and leak into the corners of his eyes. Reaching to his face, Watcher wiped away the stinging sweat and glanced around at the parched terrain.

The villagers passed through the warm savannah through the evening and into the early morning. Now, with the sun having just risen, they moved into the desert, the full and crushing heat of the sun blaring down upon them.

"I heard there are villages in the desert in some parts of the Overworld." Mapper drank from a bottle of water. "It's a mystery why anyone would choose to live in these conditions."

"Sometimes it is not choice, but necessity," the

young zombie said. "If one is born in the desert, then the desert becomes home."

"Perhaps you're right, Er-Lan." Mapper nodded, then grew silent as he contemplated the statement.

"How much farther must we go?" Watcher asked.

The old NPC pulled out the map and held it up, comparing it to their surroundings. "Well, I can see that mountain range over there corresponds to this one on the map." Mapper pointed to the steep, sandstone mountains, then dragged a finger across the map. "There should be a river ahead, then after we climb the next sand dune, we should be able to see the desert temple."

"Then let's move faster," Cutter said. "We've had enough of a break. It's time to run again."

Many of the villagers moaned, but they all knew the big NPC was right.

Cutter charged across the hot sands, having removed his iron armor while they were walking. The metallic coating had almost been too hot to touch already; it would have been unbearable in the full heat of noon. The rest of the villagers kept pace with the warrior, running while drinking water or potions of rejuvenation. Many were encouraged to eat, keeping their hunger at a minimum so their HP would stay high. They moved across the sand dunes and around dried scrub brush. Green cacti were the only things with any semblance of life in the arid domain, the prickly plants like silent sentinels, watching the intruders as they passed.

"I can hear water up ahead." Watcher's hearing was the best in the village, like his eyesight. The young boy ran faster, now sprinting.

They crested a large dune, then raced down the other side, some of them stumbling and rolling down to the river at the foot of the hill.

Watcher splashed into the stream and just fell backward, the cool water reviving his overheated body. It was the greatest thing he'd ever felt. The heat was pulled from him, refreshing not just his body, but also his mind. Holding a hand over his face, he blocked out the harsh rays that were now pummeling them with the relentless power of the sun, the noonday heat nearly unbearable.

Cutter pointed to a couple of villagers. "Go take over for the scouts. They need to get into the water and cool off."

They nodded and ran off to the points of the compass to find and relieve the distant sentries.

Watcher climbed out of the river and sat on the bank, letting his legs dangle in the cool water. Suddenly, he was covered with water as someone dropped into the river right next to him. A joyous laugh greeted his ears as he turned and found Planter in the water smiling up at him. He offered a hand to help her out. She grabbed hold and climbed out of the river and sat next to him. But instead of just releasing the grip, he held on for a moment, staring down at their hands. Her hand felt electric, as if their nerves were all singing in harmony.

"Ah . . . Watcher . . . you gonna let go?" She laughed.

"Oh, yeah." He released his grip, but let his fingers drag against hers.

What am I doing? He was confused. That was something he saw his mother and father do many times when he'd been younger. Doing that to Planter seemed weird, but also felt right, making his chest feel lighter, as if he could fly.

Planter glanced at him, equally confused. She was about to say something to him when Mapper plopped down on the other side of Watcher.

"What do you think the skeletons will do when they find the village and Wizard's Tower deserted?" he asked the two of them.

"I bet they'll try to follow us," Planter said.

"Maybe, but I think it's more likely they'll continue hunting for magical artifacts." Watcher looked away from Planter, embarrassed. He stood and brushed the sand from his leggings. "That skeleton we captured said something about knowing where many of the artifacts were located. They'll probably head for the closest artifact on their map."

"That'll be this desert temple," Mapper said, his voice becoming very serious.

Watcher nodded. He glanced around for Cutter, but couldn't find him. "Then we better get there before the skeletons do." Watcher leapt into the air and placed a block of sand under his feet, then did it again so he was two blocks high. "I know you're all tired, but this is a race, and if we come in second place, things will likely get very bad. We need to find as many magical weapons as we can so the skeletons won't get them. If the monsters get them, they'll be used on villagers like you and me. . . . We need to get moving."

Without waiting to see the reaction of the other villagers, Watcher jumped to the ground and climbed the sand dune that hugged the far side of the river. As he jumped from block to block, slowly ascending the gradual slope, the sound of soggy feet thumping on sand filled the air from behind.

Watcher smiled.

"Aren't you the motivated villager?" Blaster said to his right.

"If the skeletons are out looking for relics, then we need to do the same to maintain the balance of power," Watcher said as he wiped his brow, then glanced at his friend.

Blaster wore no armor nor cap. His dark hair was a tangle of black, interlocking curls that stuck out in all directions, and his red-and-white smock was wrinkled and dirty, as usual.

"If either side gains more power than the other, that's when the war will start." As he thought about the idea of war, Watcher could feel tension building not only in his body, but also in his mind, everything stretching tighter and tighter. Cleric moved up to his other side and leaned in close, listening.

Watcher lowered his voice so only Blaster and his father could hear. "We must keep the relics out of the hands of the warriors. If they realize we have more power than the monsters, they'll likely want to attack and destroy them all, right dad?"

Cleric nodded, a proud expression on his wrinkled face.

"We must not let the future of the Far Lands become embroiled in a war that will destroy everything." Watcher glanced over his shoulder at the other villagers following him up the sand dune. "We have much to protect, and war is not the best solution. We can't let that happen."

"The future is already written," a growling voice said.

Er-Lan moved next to Cleric, the zombie's leaps up the sandy blocks synchronized with his own.

"What do you mean?" Watcher asked.

The zombie sighed. "The future has already been determined, and the creatures of the Far Lands have already been given their parts to play." Er-Lan gazed at Watcher. "All one can do is accept what will happen and . . ." A single tear tumbled from his eye. "And mourn those who will be lost to fate."

"Er-Lan, are you okay?" Watcher tried to reach out and place a hand on his shoulder, but Er-Lan moved away, then cast his gaze to the ground.

"It is not important," Er-Lan said.

"Clearly it is important, to you." Watcher was concerned for his friend.

"Er-Lan says too much," the zombie grumbled in a low voice. "And Er-Lan sees too much."

"What?" both Watcher and Blaster asked, the friends confused.

The monster didn't answer, instead, he slowed, then stopped, likely to put distance between himself and the villagers.

Watcher glanced at Blaster and his father. "Either of you understand that?"

They both shook their heads.

Cleric looked back at the zombie, then spoke in a low voice. "Not really, but he seems like he's hurting over something. Maybe that's just the zombie way."

"No, this is something different . . . something important." Watcher wiped his brow again. "I think I need to—"

"There it is!" Blaster exclaimed.

They'd reached the top of the dune. Before them, a desert temple sat on a pristine patch of sand, not a single footprint visible anywhere. Watcher ran down the slope and sprinted for the ancient structure. It looked like a huge pyramid made of sand and sandstone, with tall, square turret-like structures on either side. The looming towers were embedded with orange blocks of wool. The decorative pattern was in the simple lay-out of a cross, with a set of blocks across the top. To most, it was just some geometrical arrangement, but to Watcher's keen eye, the design was like the shape of a person with an orange helmet being lowered onto his head, the helmet matching the person's skin or armor. It felt like a message or a clue cast onto the endless river of time hundreds of years ago by the ancients, and now its wait had finally ended as Watcher burned the image into his memory, though he had no idea what it meant.

Blaster punched him in the arm. "You comin'?"

"Oh, yeah." Watcher looked back at the villagers still climbing the hill. "The temple is on the other side of the sand dune . . . we're there." The villagers cheered. "Come on, everyone."

Watcher and Blaster ran down the hill while Cleric waited to help Mapper, the rest of the army following. They approached the entrance and went in, carefully looking for traps or tripwires. The sandy structure was noticeably cooler inside, the ancient building able to withstand centuries of exposure to the desert heat.

To either side of the doorway, passages stretched off into the two side towers, steps visible going up into the parallel structures. Moving farther into the sandy building, Watcher could feel the immense age of the place. A thick layer of dust covered the floor, likely undisturbed since the end of the Great War. Sunlight streamed through a hole in the very top of the pyramid, the rays scattering off the many particles of dust, making the air sparkle as if enchanted.

He moved further into the structure, finding four thick columns that stretched up from the floor to the pale ceiling. Colorful blocks were embedded into the floor, creating a geometric pattern of oranges and yellows, a single blue cube at the center. Off to the side, a set of stairs were carved into the sandy ground, leading down into the darkness.

"This way." Watcher pulled out another torch and placed it by the stairway, then held another in his hand as he descended.

A purple glow covered the narrow steps as he went down. Behind him, Planter followed with her golden axe in her hands, the magical enchantment pulsing within the weapon splashing an iridescent glow on the walls. The rest of the NPC army followed Watcher, cautiously entering the descending passage.

The stairs were ancient, their surface scuffed and worn by the thousands of feet that used these steps hundreds of years ago. Cracks spread across many of the stairs, showing their age.

They descended deep underground, the staircase turning to the left, then right until it ended at the opening to a long hallway. Redstone lanterns glowed overhead, offering faint illumination, pushing back the shadows. All along one wall, metal doors stood closed, each separating the passage from large rooms. Watcher opened a couple of the iron doors only to find empty rooms. All had furnaces lining one wall, some with fires still smoldering within, while others were dark and cold.

The corridor stretched off into the distance for at least thirty blocks, with doors located only on the right side of the tunnel. The left side seemed to leak bits of ash and the occasional drop of lava; Watcher was sure there was a huge lava lake on the other side of those stone blocks.

They followed the passage to the end, where it turned to the right, then opened into a large, deserted chamber, the walls, floor, and ceiling made of impenetrable bedrock. Redstone lanterns embedded in the corners of the room cast some light into the room, but the dark gray of the bedrock made it feel as if Watcher were standing inside an endless shadow.

On the far wall, an iron door stood closed, a button mounted next to it. A wooden sign hung over the top of the door. Watcher moved closer and held his torch up high.

"Can anyone read it?" he asked.

Cutter stood beneath the sign and reached up, brushing off the centuries of dust that covered the writing. Coughing as he breathed in the dust, the big NPC stepped back.

"What's it say?" Planter asked.

Watcher moved closer and held his torch up high. "It says 'THE END OF RAINBOWS.' That's a strange thing to put over a door."

"What's that supposed to mean?" Winger asked. "Is it a warning . . . all rainbows are gonna go away?"

"It's not a warning . . . it's a hint," Cleric said. "The sign is giving us some piece of information we need."

They both glanced at Mapper, hoping for some insight from the old villager.

Clearing his throat, Mapper spoke in a low voice. "Maybe we should just open the door and see what's inside."

Watcher nodded, then stepped forward and pressed the button. Instantly, the iron door creaked open, revealing a dark chamber. When he took another step, his foot pressed down on a pressure plate hidden in the shadows. A click sounded from beneath the floor. Torches flared into life around the walls of the chamber, throwing a warm yellow glow across the ancient room.

With a gasp of surprise, Watcher stepped back, allowing the others to see. "No one enter . . . just look."

The other villagers took turns glancing into the room, then stepped back and debated the best strategy.

The room was covered with colored blocks in every hue imaginable. Metal pressure plates sat on each square, covering the entire chamber. The walls of the room were made of dispensers, the pattern on the metallic cubes looking like a surprised face, the opening in the dispenser being the face's mouth. Another iron door was embedded into the far wall; clearly that was their destination.

"What do you think comes out of those dispensers?" Planter asked.

"Who knows," Cleric said. "Maybe arrows, or fireballs, or . . ."

"Or poison," Er-Lan added. "Zombie teachers say the wizards used dispensers to shoot poison at monster warlocks. The dispensers could shoot many lethal items."

Cleric nodded. "Er-Lan is right. We don't know what they do, but you can be sure it's something dangerous. This room is a huge obstacle meant to keep the contents of the next room safe."

"It's a maze," Cleric said. "We must step on the correct blocks to cross and get to the next door. If the wrong block is stepped on, that will likely trigger the dispensers."

"But we have no idea what pattern is needed." Watcher glanced into chamber. "That room is seven by seven in size. That's forty-nine blocks in total. There are likely millions of combinations."

Mapper stepped to the entrance, then stepped back and stared at the sign over the door. The old villager began swaying to the left and right as he became lost in thought, humming softly. And then suddenly, he froze and became perfectly silent. He turned and faced Cleric, a smile painted across his square face. "I know the pattern."

"How?" Watcher asked.

"The sign tells us . . . it's the parts that make up a rainbow."

"What are you talking about?" Planter asked.

Mapper sighed. "I remember teaching this to you when you were younger, all of you." A stern look came across his wrinkled face. "Don't you remember . . . the rainbow?"

"So what?" Blaster asked. "We've all seen a rainbow."

"Exactly, and what are the colors in the rainbow?"

"Of course . . . the rainbow!" Watcher moved to the doorway, then glanced over his shoulder. "What's the first color?"

Mapper sighed again and shook his head. "Didn't you learn anything in school?"

Watcher just shrugged.

"ROY G BIV," Cleric stated slowly, as if it were obvious.

Mapper nodded and smiled.

"Right." Watcher nodded, then took a step forward, his foot on the red square.

"What are you doing?!" Cleric exclaimed.

Watcher glanced away from his father. "Someone must test out the theory."

All of the dispensers remained silent.

He stepped to the orange square, then found a yellow one. Still nothing from the dispensers. He continued through the pattern, green, then blue, then indigo, then violet. But he was one block short from the door.

"I didn't make it." Watcher carefully glanced over his shoulder. "I need one more color."

The others glanced at Mapper as he stared up at the sign again. "The end of the rainbow . . . what could that mean?"

"My mom used to tell me about a chest of gold at the end of the rainbow," Blaster said. "I bet it's a gold block." He stuck his head into the chamber. "Is there a gold block?"

Watcher nodded, then extended his foot toward the shining block.

"Wait!" Planter shouted, concerned.

The young boy froze, then retreated back to the violet block.

"The sign doesn't say the *end of the* rainbow," Planter said. "It says the *end of rainbows*. It's like the death of a rainbow. What happens when a rainbow dies?"

"It disappears," Watcher shouted, "leaving only blue sky."

"No, that can't be right," Cleric said. "Let's think this through."

"We don't have time," Watcher said. "If I'm wrong, you can try the gold block."

"Nooooo!" Cleric shouted

But Watcher ignored his father. Moving his foot slowly, he pressed it on the sky-blue block. A click sounded from beneath the block. Watcher shut his eyes and waited for the barrage of arrows or fireballs. But then, another click filled the room, followed by a metallic screech. Opening his eyes, he found the door before him had swung open, revealing a long, dark passage.

"It worked!" Watcher stepped into the passage as the cheers of the other villagers echoed off the chamber walls. But as soon as he took another step, the iron door slammed shut behind him, plunging him into complete darkness.

A strange noise seemed to envelop him from all sides, even over his head. He heard the moans of zombies, the clicking of spiders, the rattling of skeleton bones, and the dry chuckles of endermen. The voices of monsters wrapped around him like a poisonous fog, moving closer and closer. But there were also sounds he'd never heard mixed in with the other terrifying voices. A strange, high-pitched squawking punctuated the voices of the angry mob.

In the darkness, Watcher's famous imagination created armies of monsters closing clustered about him, their claws, teeth and fists getting closer and closer. He couldn't tell if he was inventing the sounds he'd heard or if there really was an army of monsters surrounding him. His heart pounded in his chest and he took short, gasping breaths. Sweat trickled down his face, some of the salty cubes flowing into his eyes, stinging. Every nerve in his body felt as if it was aflame as waves of fear crashed down upon him. His mind was overwhelmed, making rational thought impossible. All he could do was stand there, close his eyes, and hope the end would come swiftly.

CHAPTER 9

"Faster, we must move faster," General Rusak growled. "Run, skeletons . . . RUN! We have a wizard to destroy."

The monsters cheered as they charged through the terrain. The skeleton horde was heading east, hoping to find the stony trail south of the village, then follow it to the soon-to-be-destroyed community. The general dug his heels into the skeleton horse on which he rode and looked around at his other commanders, who were also mounted.

Suddenly, one of the scouts galloped back to the bony army, waving his hands over his head. Rusak reined in his mount and waited for the scout.

"What is it?" the general asked.

"Tracks . . . lots of them," the skeleton reported, out of breath. "It looks as if the NPCs have left the village and are heading to the south-west."

"Toward the desert?" Rusak didn't expect an answer.

He pulled out the map given to the skeletons by the wither king, Krael. There was a marking in the desert to the south-west; it was a location of some ancient relic.

"They must be after the magical weapon in the desert." Rusak pondered his options, then motioned for the army to stop. "Commanders, come here with your skeleton horses."

The other leaders galloped to him.

"Our enemy is searching for the enchanted weapons left behind after the Great War." He glared at all his subordinates, making sure they all understood the gravity of the situation. "Only a wizard would know where to look. The skeleton warlord was right. The boy-wizard is a grave threat and must be destroyed. We must catch him and destroy him, then take every ancient weapon we can find." He dismounted and handed his reigns to one of the skeleton warriors standing nearby, then glared at the dozen commanders that stared down at him. "Each of you dismount."

The commanders did as instructed.

"Give your mount to another skeleton." General Rusak watched as his soldiers mounted the bony animals. "Warriors, I want you to ride to the NPC village and burn it to the ground." He glared at the monsters. "Leave nothing standing, do you understand?"

"But General, the NPCs are already gone," Captain Ratlan said. "What good will that do."

"It will serve as a punishment and a warning to those who help the wizards. The retribution by monsters for helping the enemy will be swift and brutal." General Rusak smiled an eerie, toothy smile, then turned back to the now-mounted soldiers. "After you have destroyed the village, then search the Wizard's Tower. There may still be weapons for us to use against the NPC criminals, and we must have more weapons. When you have finished, return to the south west and join us in the desert." He glared at his soldiers, making sure his orders were understood. "The only reason the NPCs would be looking for the creations of the ancient wizards is because they are preparing for war. We must be ready as well."

The skeleton nodded.

"Now go." Rusak drew an enchanted broadsword

and pointed it toward the north. "Destroy that village and erase it from the face of the Far Lands."

The small squad of skeletons cheered, then kicked their mounts and rode off to the north, the hoofbeats like thunder, leaving the main force watching them ride away.

"Now, we must move fast." The general reached into his inventory and pulled out a glass bottle, a pink liquid sloshing back and forth within. "All of you have potions of swiftness. It's time to drink them." He uncorked the cap and drained the bottle, then threw it aside, the rest of the monsters doing the same. "Now, we run. And soon, we'll fight for our skeleton warlord and for the safety of the skeleton kingdom. The Great War is again brewing on the horizon, but this time, the villagers will be surprised by the outcome. The monsters of the Far Land will be ready and will not be victims to the tyranny of the NPCs." He held his sword high over his head. "Now, my friends . . . RUN!"

The skeleton army became a white wave of bones and bows as they flowed through the forest at incredible speeds, every last monster thirsting for battle.

CHAPTER 10

The squawking sounds and fluttering noises surrounded Watcher as if he were in the middle of some kind of strange twittering maelstrom. Things shot past his face and moved around his body. He couldn't see any of them, but Watcher was able to feel the breeze caused by these things, or creatures, or . . . whatever they were as they shot past, just out of reach.

The fear that had thundered through his mind slowly dissipated as the tornado of squawking and growling things did no harm; they just moved near his body without attacking. Slowly, he reached into his inventory and grabbed the hilt of his sword, Needle. Instantly, the squawking things grew loud with agitation, the high-pitched zombie and spider sounds increasing as well.

But still, the creatures stayed their claws and held back their attack. Cautiously, Watcher drew Needle, just the smallest bit, from his inventory. As a portion of the blade emerged from his inventory, a faint purple glow spread outward from the enchanted weapon and splashed onto the floor. The mirror-like surface of the blade reflected his surroundings. He was standing on sandstone, a thick layer of dust obscuring the surface at spots. But as the glow from his sword pushed back on the darkness, Watcher could see tiny footprints in the dust, as if a hundred chickens had marched through recently.

The growl from what sounded like a hundred zombies floated out of the darkness masking the far end of the chamber. He drew Needle further from his inventory, the purple light growing brighter. Pale columns emerged from the darkness, the pillars made from chiseled sandstone, the face of a creeper etched into each.

Something flew past his face.

Watcher ducked instinctively, then pulled his sword all the way out. The squawking intensified as the shimmering light from Needle reached further into the chamber. The near wall came into view. It was built from polished sandstone, its glassy surface reflecting the rays to other parts of the room. A small ledge stuck out from the wall, a line of redstone running along its length.

A group of fluttering things blew past him, then settled on the ledge.

"Parrots!" Watcher exclaimed. "They were parrots."

Colorful birds stood on the ledge, then walked back and forth, their dark eyes staring at him warily.

"*Parrots.*" One of the birds mimicked in Watcher's voice, then fluttered its wings and flew across the room, revealing a lever mounted near the redstone.

Watcher stepped past the sandstone columns and flipped the switch. The redstone signal ran across the ledge, illuminating the parrots with a crimson glow from underneath, making them look a little threatening. Then the redstone reached its goal, lighting a series of redstone lanterns. The glowing cubes came to life all across the room, splashing a warm yellowish-orange glow on his surroundings.

The room was filled with birds of every color imaginable. They flew from side to side, weaving around the many columns that lined both sides of the chamber, their squawks, which was mostly monster impersonations and copies of Watcher's voice, filling the air.

He smiled. These animals, with their fabulous colors, were a treat to watch.

A pounding echoed behind him, causing the birds to fly quicker, clearly agitated. It sounded as if someone was trying to dig into the chamber; likely it was his friends, but it seemed as if they weren't making any progress. He wouldn't be surprised if this chamber was protected by some kind of enchantment.

Turning away from the noise, Watcher scanned the room. It seemed as if the structure was designed with one side being the mirror image of the other. The left and right sides of the chamber were each ornately decorated with different kinds of sandstone and redstone lanterns, but everything was exactly the same from side to side.

And then he noticed it . . . a small chest at the end of the chamber. Moving slowly through the maelstrom of colorful feathers flapping across the room, Watcher approached the chest. The edges of the wooden box glowed like Needle, the magical enchantments either on or within the chest leaking power into the outside world.

The banging on the doorway grew louder, the noise like a giant gong being struck by a blacksmith's hammer.

Putting away his sword, Watcher reached down and carefully opened the chest. Instantly, a burst of bright purple light shot out of the chest. The ball of iridescent light bounced around the chamber once, then split into two pieces, then each divided again, creating four balls of magical power. The glowing orbs streaked about the chamber, then shot to the ceiling and hit the stone surface, disappearing as if extinguished.

He was stunned at what just happened. *Did I just release something that should have remained sealed up?* he wondered.

Images of terrible monsters with equally terrible weapons burst into his mind as his always-overactive imagination filled in the blanks. He imagined massive armies of monsters storming across the Far Lands, destroying everything they touched. Fire blazed in his mind, scorching the forests and jungles of Minecraft, scouring the land and leaving it bare. Starvation and disease followed in his premonition, causing a single tear to trickle down his cheek.

"What have I done?"

"What have I done?" "What have I done?" "What have I done?" The parrots repeated his words in their squawky, high-pitched voices.

No, I will not give in to nightmares and daydreams. I'm here, in the now, and that's what I'm going to focus on, Watcher told himself.

Pushing aside the thoughts of what might happen, he knelt and reached into the chest. There was just a single item . . . a small stick. It was as long as one of Blaster's knives, and slightly crooked, like a lightning bolt. One end was capped with gold, but the other end was split down the middle, as if the wand was in the process of dividing into two, but frozen in mid-process. The two ends were also capped in gold, the rest of the stick colored an inky black with small sparkling crystals, almost too small for the eye to see, embedded throughout its length.

"That's it?"

"That's it?" "That's it?" "That's it?"

"Oh, will you shut up!"

"Shut up!" "Shut up!" "Shut up!" "Shut up!"

Watcher scowled at the birds, but his anger quickly evaporated as one of the parrots, a brightly colored red and yellow one, landed on his shoulder. The creature nuzzled his head against Watcher's neck, the bird's feathers tickling his skin. He laughed ever so softly, but enough to calm all the parrots.

Glancing around the chamber, he searched for additional chests, but saw none. There were no visible clues suggesting the presence of any hidden artifacts or weapons; the wand seemed the only thing in the chamber.

What does this thing do? Watcher wondered.

He pulled out a wooden shovel from his inventory and tossed it to the ground. He then aimed the wand at it . . . nothing happened.

"Maybe I need to flick it?"

Watcher waved the wand around over his head. He could feel a tingling sensation in his hand, as if tiny needles were poking into his skin. With a flick of his wrist, he tried to throw the sensation at the shovel. Another one of the glowing balls of light, like those that escaped from the chest, shot out of the wand and enveloped the shovel. At the same time, a stabbing pain shot through his body, then quickly faded. The light grew so bright he had to look away, the parrots squawking in complaint. When the glow subsided, Watcher found two shovels where only the one had been.

"Great, a way to make lots of extra wooden shovels." He said sarcastically.

"Great." "Great." "Great."

Watcher rolled his eyes.

The pounding on the door now grew frantic.

Watcher moved to the entrance and pressed the stone button, allowing it to swing open. Instantly, the redstone lanterns extinguished, plunging the chamber into darkness again. Cutter stood there with an iron pick axe in his hands, ready for another swing, but held it back.

"Are you okay?" The big NPC put away the pick and drew his diamond sword.

"Shut up." "Shut up." "Shut up."

"What did you say?" Cutter scowled at the boy.

"No, no, that wasn't me." Watcher pointed over his shoulder. "It was them."

"Them?" Cutter asked.

"Them." "Them." "Them." The parrot's voices deep and booming like Cutter.

The big NPC glared at the boy as if angry at a prank gone awry.

Watcher stepped out of the room and into the bright light of the rainbow-block room.

"There's a bird on your shoulder." Blaster sounded amazed.

"It's so beautiful." Planter crossed the multicolored floor, following the rainbow path.

She reached out to the bird. It ruffled its feathers, then flew through the air and landed on her shoulder, squawking excitedly.

Just then, the other parrots streamed from the chamber like a blast from a squawking confetti-cannon. They flew around the perimeter of the square chamber, their colors merging with those of the colored blocks, then streaked out of the room and into the long tunnel. The red and yellow parrot flew off Planter and landed again on Watcher's shoulder. It squawked once, then nuzzled its beak against the boy's neck and stayed put.

"Looks like you have a little friend." Planter held a finger out to the bird and stroked its feathery head.

"Maybe so," Watcher replied.

The boy reached for the strange split wand and was about to show it to the others when the parrots returned. But there was something different about them. Instead of squawking or imitating Watcher or the other villagers, the birds were making a strange sound that was difficult to identify.

"What are those birds doing?" Cutter asked as he stepped out of the sandstone chamber.

"I don't know." Watcher shrugged. "They aren't really saying anything, just making a noise like—"

"Like a bunch of sticks rattling together," Blaster said. The boy pulled on a set of gray-colored leather armor.

"Sticks rattling together?" Watcher was confused.

Blaster nodded as he pulled on the gray leather cap, his dark curls sticking out from the sides. "And that can mean only one thing . . . skeletons."

The other villagers gasped and pulled out their weapons.

"We need to get out of here." Cutter pushed through the crowd of villagers. "If we get trapped down here, we're doomed. Come on."

The big warrior charged out of the room and into the long tunnel just outside the chamber. The villagers followed Cutter, sprinting through the passages and up the stairs, then emerged into the desert temple.

"Everyone stay inside until we know what's going on," Watcher said.

The NPCs moved to the walls, some of them trying to peer out of the doorway. Some of them moved into the two towers that loomed over the entrance while others clustered around the main doorway. The sounds of approaching skeletons were easy to hear.

"You think the monsters are nearby?" Cleric asked. The old man looked scared.

Watcher shrugged. "Let's go up top and see."

With the parrot still clutched to his shoulder, the boy took the side passage and stairs that led to the top of the structure. Climbing the sandy blocks, Watcher stood on the top of the desert temple and scanned the surroundings. The clattering of skeleton bones rode to them on the winds, but the monsters were not yet visible.

"This is not good," Blaster said.

"Why?" Watcher gazed at his friend as he changed into a set of beige armor.

"If we can hear the skeletons, but not see them yet, then that means there are a lot of them coming." Blaster pulled out his knives, their keen edges gleaming in the afternoon sun. "I'll let you know where they are in a few minutes."

The boy quickly replaced his gray armor with something colored a pale yellow, then jumped off the temple and streaked across the parched desert. Blaster quickly disappeared, his armor matching the color of the dry sand.

"Er-Lan doesn't mean to interrupt, but . . ." The zombie stared up at Watcher.

"But what?"

"Why not use the birds?" Er-Lan said it as if it was the obvious solution. "The parrots can give the location of the skeletons."

"How will we know what the birds find?" Planter asked as she climbed to the top of the temple.

The zombie shrugged. "Just listen."

"You can talk to the parrots?" Watcher asked.

Er-Lan nodded, seeming confused. "Villagers cannot?"

Watcher and Planter gave each other a confused look, then turned their gaze back to Er-Lan.

"Tell them to go out and find the skeletons for us, if you can," Planter asked. "That would be really helpful."

The zombie nodded, then held his arms out. Instantly, four parrots flapped through the air and landed on his shoulders. Turning his head, he whispered something to the birds, his voice sounding like a series of short whistles. They flew off, squawking to their feathery brothers and sisters. Instantly, the rest of the birds flew from the temple and soared into the air, flying in all directions.

In minutes, a group of birds returned. Er-Lan held out his arms again, signaling the birds to land on him. Instantly, they squawked and screeched, some of them mimicking the sound of the skeletons.

The zombie's face grew pale. "They say there is a large group of skeletons heading this way."

Suddenly, a huge explosion detonated far from the temple.

"It seems Blaster found the monsters," Cutter said from the desert floor.

Watcher stared out into the pale landscape. A column of smoke climbed into the sky, likely the location of the blast. As he scanned the surroundings, a pale shape streaked across the sands, heading for the temple; it was Blaster. The villagers moved off the top of the temple and back inside the structure. Watcher stood at the structure's entrance and waited for his friend.

In seconds, Blaster stepped through the doorway, panting heavily. He removed the beige leather cap and ran his fingers through his curly, dark hair.

"How many are there?" Cutter asked.

"You mean after my little surprise?" Blaster smiled, then grew very serious. "Still a lot, and they're running really, really fast. My explosion slowed them down for a while, but it won't last long." He moved closer to Watcher and Cutter and spoke in a low voice. "We can't fight them out in the open—there are just too many of them."

"Then maybe we fight them down in the passages underground," Planter said. "If we set up some kind of trap to give us the advantage, then maybe we'll be okay."

"That's a great idea." Cutter nodded at her, drawing a smile from the girl. "Come on, everyone . . . into the tunnels."

The big warrior charged down the steps with the rest of the villagers following behind, leaving Blaster and Watcher in the temple, alone.

"Are you coming?" Watcher pulled out his bow and notched an arrow.

"In a minute." Blaster removed the rest of his armor, revealing his perpetually wrinkled red and white smock. "I want to make sure they know we're here, so they'll follow us into the tunnels." He put a hand on Watcher's shoulder. "Your job is to develop some strategy down there. You're the idea guy. Come up with some kind of brilliant idea so we don't get wiped out by a bunch of skeletons . . . you got it?"

Watcher nodded, then stared at Blaster's back as he walked casually out of the temple, shouting at the top of his voice. Turning, the archer followed the rest of the villagers into the subterranean passages. The clattering bones of the skeletons diminished a bit as he went further underground, easing his fears a little. But Blaster's comment made him more nervous.

"I'm supposed to come up with some kind of great idea that will save everyone?" The responsibility for everyone's safety felt like a punch in the stomach. Waves of fear rippled down his spine as he tried to come up with some plan that wouldn't get everyone killed.

CHAPTER 11

A tense silence hung in the air as the villagers huddled together in the empty chamber, packed tightly together, the small space not designed for so many occupants. They waited for the skeleton horde to arrive, not knowing how many they would face. But the NPCs knew there was no retreat or surrender; this threat had to be stopped for the sake of the Far Lands.

The room was pitch dark; all torches and redstone lanterns extinguished to retain the element of surprise. Watcher stood against one wall next to a group of diggers, while Cutter and the other swordsmen and swordswomen gathered near the chamber entrance, ready to charge toward the skeleton horde when they were near.

"I hope this works," Watcher whispered.

"Shhh," Planter replied. She placed a hand on his shoulder.

Watcher was shaking . . . he knew she could feel it, but her touch had a calming effect, as if having Planter there made everything alright.

This was my idea and I'm responsible if everything fails. The thoughts bounced around in his head, chipping away at his courage. Images of the terrifying skeletons filled his mind . . . their protruding ribs . . . their bony skulls . . . their lifeless eyes; everything about the monsters filled Watcher with an unshakable desire to curl up in a ball and hide. They reminded him of the awful, recurring nightmare he used to have as a kid. He'd think there were skeletons in his room, trying to attack him. He'd see them in his room and would quickly shut his eyes, hoping the dream went away. Only later, when he was older, did he learn the bigger kids were sneaking into his room and putting armor stands near his bed. He was furious, but the cruel prank had done its damage . . . skeletons terrified him to his very soul.

He went through the plan in his head . . . again, hoping to distract himself from the images in his mind; it didn't help.

"Squawk. Squawk . . . squawk." Some of the parrots were getting agitated in the darkness.

"Er-Lan, keep the parrots quiet," Planter whispered.

For some reason, Er-Lan had a way with the birds; he could get them to do anything he wanted, and right now, being quiet was critical. The zombie moaned something to the parrots. A few mimicked him briefly, then they all fell silent.

A rattling sound echoed down the long passage leading to their hiding place.

"They're coming."

Fear seemed to spread through the chamber like the ripples from a stone dropped in a cold, dark pool. Every time the rattling of bones drifted into the chamber, tiny square goosebumps spread across Watcher's arms; he was near to panicking.

Villagers shuffled about nervously, kicking up the ancient dust that covered the floor. It made Watcher want to sneeze, but he put a finger under his nose and suppressed the urge.

Scratchy voices came to their ears: "I know they're in here, I saw a villager run down the stairs." It was from one of the skeletons.

"Did you check all the rooms off this main hall?" another monster asked, his voice growing louder as they approached.

"Of course I did," a skeleton snapped. "They're all empty. The villagers must be at the end of this tunnel."

They were almost to the entrance of their room.

Cutter lightly tapped his armor once with the hilt of his sword. The warriors pulled out their shields. He tapped it again; they all moved to the doorway.

"You hear something?" one of the skeletons asked.

"No . . . I think you're going crazy," his bony companion answered.

They were right outside, in the hallway.

Cutter tapped his armor one last time, then charged through the doorway, yelling his battle cry as loud as possible. A flood of warriors followed the big NPC, each with his shield held up high, screaming as loud as they could. At the same time, diggers tore into the stone wall that separated this room from the adjacent. The warriors crashed into the skeletons driving them back. At the same time, someone lit a torch and held it high into the air.

As the warriors yelled and screamed in the passage outside their chamber, Watcher could hear arrows striking their shields. The shafts hit in rapid succession; it sounded like a hundred drums all playing at the same time. Many of the NPCs warriors shouted in pain as a barbed tip found soft flesh, but they held their ground, yelling at the top of their voices to cover the sound of digging.

Watcher moved back into the room and checked the diggers' progress. They had just finished digging through the wall, and were now tunneling into the next room. He peered into the newly formed passage. It was filled with dust as chips of stone flew in all directions, stinging his face as the jagged shards cut into his skin. He was just about to ask how much longer when one of the diggers cheered; they were through.

"Archers, follow me." Watcher pulled out his bow and ran through the new tunnel.

They emerged into the adjacent chamber. It was dark, with no furnaces or fire places to light the area. Someone placed a torch on the ground. The flickering light revealed a cobblestone floor, the remains of broken wooden furniture in the corners, an iron door marking the exit. The archers moved to the door and waited.

"Everyone ready?" Watcher asked in a quiet voice. The scared soldiers all nodded. "Here we go."

Watcher opened the door and moved silently into the passage. Before them stood a group of skeletons, all of them firing at Cutter and his soldiers. The defending villagers had their shields held together, forming a solid barricade of wood and metal, blocking the passage. But Watcher could see cracks across many of the shields; they weren't going to last much longer.

"Everyone, draw," Watcher whispered.

"Aim."

He stilled his body and aimed at a pale monster. His heart pounded in his chest. His throat was dry from all the dust . . . and fear.

"FIRE!" His voice echoed off the walls.

The villagers released their arrows. Their pointed shafts fell upon the skeletons, taking them by complete surprise. Drawing more arrows, the archers continued to fire as the confused monsters tried to figure out what was happening.

The bony creatures yelled out in pain and surprise. Turning to see what had just attacked, the skeletons snarled and growled, then advanced toward the archers. Watcher knew he was supposed to do something now, but he couldn't remember the plan; fear ruled his brain. An arrow streaked by him, the feathers at the end brushing past his ear.

"We have to do something," someone said nearby, then yelled out in pain.

"Give the signal," another called out.

"What?" Watcher was overwhelmed by the terrifying horde approaching their position.

The archers fired back, but many were yelling in pain as skeleton arrows found their targets.

"The signal," someone said again.

The signal . . . I need to . . . Watcher tried to drive the fear from his mind, and then he remembered.

"NOW!" Watcher yelled as loud as he could.

Instantly, the swordsmen and swordswomen lowered their shields and charged, shouting their battle cries again. The skeletons turned back toward the charging soldiers, allowing the archers to get another volley off before they too drew their swords and attacked.

Both groups of soldiers closed in on the skeletons attacking them from both sides. Watcher held Needle in his right hand, a dark blue shield in his left. He was pushed forward by those behind, moving closer to the nightmarish creatures. He wanted to fight, but he was so scared . . . he couldn't even think.

Just then, a pair of arrows struck the villager next to him. He cried out in pain, his HP dangerously low. The villager glanced at Watcher, terrified, then a third arrow struck him, taking the last of his health. He disappeared, a scared expression on his square face.

Watcher turned and glared at the NPC's killer. The monster turned his bow toward Watcher and pulled back on the string. A fury like he'd never known took over Watcher's mind. He charged forward, his sparkling, enchanted blade moving quickly, knocking aside an arrow Watcher hadn't even seen yet. The monster fired, but that shaft was knocked aside with ease. When he reached the skeleton, his sword was a shimmering blur. He slashed at the creature, quickly destroying the monster's HP, then turned and attack the nearest enemy. Swinging to the left then to the right, he knocked bows from skeletal hands, then tore into their HP. Using the edges of his vision, Watcher kept an eye on those near him, lending his blade to any needing help. He moved without thought, driven by rage, as if someone else controlled his motions.

A small handful of skeletons, those wearing armor, were equipped with swords, but most only had bows. In close quarters, the monsters' arrows were no match for the iron blades of the villagers. In minutes, the battle was over.

All across the floor, piles of skeleton bones and glowing balls of XP littered the passage . . . but so did the inventories of fallen villagers.

"What took you so long?" Cutter asked. "We heard you shoot, but then you didn't give the signal."

"I hesitated," Watcher said, lowering his gaze to the ground in shame. He saw the items from his fallen comrades and was overwhelmed with grief. "Some of the archers . . . are gone. I froze. I shouldn't be leading them."

"We'll see, Watcher, but for now, I'm in command of this army, and I've put you in charge of the archers." Cutter glared down at the boy. "So get over it, and get it done next time."

"You two having a nice chat?" Blaster asked with a grin. Both looked away. "I take that to mean 'No'. Okay then." He patted each of them on the back, then smiled again. "I think it best we get out of here before more skeletons show up. I saw their whole army, and this was just the smallest portion . . . likely just a bunch of scouts. There are more of them out there."

"I think you're right." Cutter put away his sword. "We need to get out of here."

"Where should we head?" Cleric asked.

Cutter looked at Watcher and raised his unibrow in question.

The weight of responsibility fell upon his shoulders again as more eyes turned toward him. "We need to find the next ancient relic before the skeletons find it." Watcher nervously wiped his brow.

"But we didn't find anything here, right?" Winger asked.

Reaching into his inventory, he pulled out the gold-capped wand with the split end and held it up for all to see.

"What does it do?" Cleric asked.

"I tested it in that chamber with the parrots. It seems to make a copy of whatever it's aimed at." Watcher held the wand up for others to see. He pulled it back when Blaster reached for it. "Just like with the zombie warlord's enchanted armor, this thing gets its power from the wielder; it hurts to use."

Mapper moved close and stared at the enchanted weapon, looking closely at the markings along its length.

"We need more information about all these enchanted relics." Cleric glanced at his old friend. "Do you recognize it?"

Mapper seemed uncertain. "I remember reading something about a split wand, but can't recall. I'll have to do some reading when we have a chance."

"This is great and all," Blaster said. "But let's focus on where we need to go next."

"To the east." Mapper's voice was scratched and aged, but filled with confidence.

"What's to the east?" Cutter asked.

"The book that gave us the location of this temple also talked about a great treasure that lies beneath the ocean on the other side of what it called the Creeper's Jungle," Mapper said. "That's the next closest relic. If the skeletons know about this place, then they likely know about the ocean as well."

"Right, let's get out of here and move as fast as we can to the east." Cutter bent down and picked up the bones that littered the passage. "Don't leave any evidence to let the skeletons know what happened here. Pick up every bone and gather the last arrow. We leave this place clean."

The other villagers snapped into action, scouring the passage.

"Come on." Blaster led the way out of the temple, putting on bright green armor as he ran up the stairs.

Watcher followed the last of the NPCs, thinking about the battle. He had totally frozen in the middle of the conflict, and his hesitation had gotten some of the villagers killed. His fear of the skeletons was almost too much to bear. But something about his fear seemed ancient, not just related to that terrible prank when he was younger. His fear went back further, from long before he was born. It made no sense.

It's like they're my enemy from ages ago, for some reason. Watcher pondered the thought. *But I've never really tangled with the skeletons before, so how could that be?*

It was confusing, but for some reason, this feud between him and the skeletons felt like it had been going on for hundreds of years . . . and that seemed ridiculous. It was as if he was remembering someone else's life, and that life was filled with great violence and destruction, much of it focused at him.

Watcher shuddered and shook his head, trying to dislodge the feelings, then followed the rest of his companions out of the temple.

CHAPTER 12

eneral Rusak gazed across the savannah landscape and toward the desert biome. He'd sent his fastest scouts ahead of the main force in hopes of catching the villagers by surprise. It was unlikely those monsters survived, but his goal had not been to destroy the NPCs; it had been just a delaying tactic. In the distance, the desert temple was just barely visible through the darkness, but a couple of the idiotic villagers carried torches as they exited the structure, making them easy to see.

"The fools, they fear the dark, but have no idea why." The skeleton chuckled, his jaw clicking together. "The skeletons will teach the villagers what they fear . . . soon, very soon."

"What did you say, general?" Captain Ratlan asked.

"Nothing." Rusak turned to his subordinate. "Did any of the advanced party return?"

"No sir," the captain replied. "I expect them back soon."

"Did you see those three villagers leave the temple?"

Captain Ratlan nodded.

"They're scouts for the villager army. They aren't retreating, they're getting ready to head toward their next destination." Rusak turned away from the desert temple and stared down at Ratlan. "Your advance party is likely destroyed."

"But that was twenty of our fastest skeletons," the captain protested.

"Not anymore," the general said. He turned and pointed at a group of monsters. "Bring in the scouts. I want everyone ready to leave at sunup."

The pale soldiers saluted, then ran off.

The general turned back to the temple.

"Do you think the villagers found anything in there?" the captain asked.

Rusak shrugged. "It was marked on our map, and Krael said there were powerful weapons at each of these ancient sites, and so far he hasn't been wrong. Krael's map led the skeleton warlord straight to the great Fossil Bow of Destruction. I'm sure we'll find more artifacts as we search these sites."

Ratlan nodded, showing his understanding, but the general doubted the skeleton really understood the significance of these ancient weapons.

"Eventually, the villagers are going to attack the monsters of the Far Lands." Rusak paused as another skeleton placed a chest at his feet. The general opened the wooden box and pulled out a handful of bones. Stuffing one or two into his mouth, Rusak chewed the bones, gaining nourishment and HP. "They've done it multiple times throughout history. Some say a great war raged across the Overworld, but with the Far Lands being so far away, we remained untouched by the conflict." More soldiers came close and listened. The general stuffed another bone into his mouth; he figured it was from a chicken or pig, and chewed noisily. "Eventually, the NPCs will find a strong enough leader to give them the courage and direction needed to attack . . . and then they'll try to invade our lands, destroy us and our families, try to exterminate the other monsters . . . they'll annihilate everything. That's all villagers can do . . . take and destroy."

Another skeleton reached into the chest and took a handful of bones. It munched on the dry bones, crunching them with its blunt teeth.

"Who do you think their leader will be?" Captain Ratlan asked. "Maybe the huge warrior I saw at the Wizard's temple who wears the enchanted iron armor?"

Rusak shook his head.

"Maybe one of the older villagers," another skeleton suggested. "Perhaps the NPCs value age and wisdom over strength and courage."

Again, Rusak shook his head.

"They're coming out," a monster shouted.

The general quickly turned and peered over the top of the hill that hid his skeleton army from any observers. Laying on his stomach, he crawled his way to the top of the hill, and peered down at the sandstone temple in the distance. A long string of villagers ran from the desert structure and into the night. It looked as if they were heading to the east, sprinting across the arid plains.

And then at the end of the column, a lone boy stepped out of the temple, a girl with long, blond hair at his side. The girl pulled out a torch and held it high in the air; it seemed she was checking to make sure there were not stragglers. In the flickering light, Rusak caught sight of the boy's hair. It was a reddish brown and cropped short. In his hand, he held an enchanted bow, an arrow already notched to the string. Even from the great distance, the general could see the villager held the bow like an expert, as if he'd been trained to do this for hundreds of years.

"There's their leader." Rusak's jaw clicked and he scowled in annoyance. "The boy with the bow is a descendant of the wizards."

"He's the one I saw at the Tower," Ratlan confirmed.

The general nodded. "We must not let that wizard beat us to any of the enchanted artifacts hidden away by the wizards and warlocks. Everything depends on us being faster and smarter than him."

"But what about the wizard . . . what do we do about him?" Ratlan's voice was hushed with uncertainty, and a little fear.

"When we get the chance, we attack him with everything we have." Rusak moved back from the top of the hill, then stood. "When any of you have a shot at that boy, you take it and you don't miss. We'll get only one opportunity. Likely he's incredibly brave and is already in charge of the army. That will mean he'll sacrifice the rest of the villagers to protect himself; we must be ready for that." His voice grew stern and the skeleton general scowled. "We show that wizard no mercy."

"No mercy," the other skeletons replied as if on cue.

"Everyone finish eating," Rusak commanded. "Eat as much bone as you can. We move out in five minutes and there will be no rest until we are victorious. Now eat . . . and prepare yourselves for war."

CHAPTER 13

At night, he thought the desert would have been cooler, but, like the guilt still burning within him over freezing in battle, the parched terrain continued to blast him with its relentless, scorching fist. Watcher wiped his forehead, again, trying to keep the square beads of sweat from his eyes . . . it didn't help. The salty moisture stung when it trickled past his unibrow and found his blue eyes.

Many of the villagers around him ran without armor, the metallic coatings still too hot to wear in the sweltering climate. Watcher kept his chain mail on as he ran, but not for the sake of being a good example for others; rather, it was fear that drove his actions; he was terrified a monster would leap out at him any minute.

"How are you doing, son?" Cleric ran next to him, his usually pristine white smock now stained with dust and sweat.

"Well . . . okay, I guess."

"You still bothered by that battle in the tunnels?"

Watcher nodded.

Ahead, Er-Lan glanced over his shoulder, stopped and waited for the young boy to catch up with him, then continued running at Watcher's side.

"Er-Lan knows the battle was terrifying, but Watcher did everything correctly." The zombie spoke as if sharing some universal truth.

"How can you know I did everything right?" Watcher's eyes grew sad. "I froze in the middle of battle. I didn't give the command to attack when I should have. Villagers lost their lives because of me."

"*Squawk.*" The multicolored parrot on Watcher's shoulder fluttered its wings.

Er-Lan nodded to the creature, then watched as the bird leapt into the air and flew in a wide circle around the army of villagers.

"Well . . . Er-Lan can . . ." The zombie lowered his gaze to the ground and his posture slumped; he was clearly uncomfortable discussing the topic.

"It's okay," Cleric said in a soothing voice. "You can tell us."

Er-Lan sighed. "The other zombies think Er-Lan makes this up to get out of work, or think Er-Lan is crazy."

Winger moved to the zombie's side and put a reassuring arm around the monster's shoulders.

"We don't think you're crazy," Watcher said. "You're part of our family. If you have a problem, then *we* have a problem. We're always there for each other, and that includes you too."

Raising his head, Er-Lan glanced at Watcher, then gave a strained smile.

"It started a long time ago, when Er-Lan was very young. At first, they were thought to just be strange dreams. But when the dreams started coming true, Er-Lan knew they were something else."

"Your dreams come true?" Winger asked. "Cool . . ."

The zombie nodded and looked at her, then shook his head. "But not just dreams . . . something more. Er-Lan can see them when awake." He glanced at Watcher again. "Er-Lan knew Watcher would hesitate, but also knew the battle would be successful."

"But a couple of villagers died in that battle," Watcher protested. "How can you call that successful? Maybe they died because of my hesitation." A frown spread across his square face. "You should have told me."

Er-Lan lowered his gaze to the ground again. "Watcher sounds just like Er-Lan's brother, Ko-Lan."

"What do you mean?" Cleric asked the creature.

"Er-Lan told of mother's death, remember?" the zombie said.

Watcher nodded. "You told me when we were chasing the zombie warlord a few months ago."

Er-Lan nodded.

"I didn't know about your mother, Er-Lan, I'm sorry." Cleric moved around to walk on the other side of the zombie. He placed a hand on his green shoulder. "Losing a mother can be difficult."

"Ko-Lan blamed Er-Lan for her death." The zombie closed his eyes as if reliving the painful moment in his mind. "It was when the spiders were feuding with the zombies, a few years ago. A large group of spiders were attacking."

"You mean they were trying to destroy your zombie-town?" Watcher asked.

Er-Lan shook his scarred head. "Not destroy, but take over. The spiders wanted to use it as their lair to hatch many eggs. Fresh water ran through the cavern, with good air supply and lots of room . . . it was perfect for zombies, and spiders."

"So what happened?"

"The spiders attacked the entrance to zombie-town. During the fighting, Ko-Lan accidently destroyed a stone block." The little zombie stopped speaking for a moment as his whole body tensed with anger. "It caused the ceiling to fall in, dumping sand and gravel across the entrance. Many zombies were trapped as well as the spiders, but a handful of the enemy made it into zombie-town." He grew quiet for a moment and frowned, the painful memory playing through his mind. A low growl sounded from deep in the monster's throat. "Zombies, like Er-Lan's mother, were defenseless."

The sky before them grew bright with an angry red glow as the sun slowly peeked over the eastern horizon. The crimson light seemed to add an additional fury to Er-Lan's words.

"Er-Lan's mother was killed in that attack." He looked up into the sky as if trying to commune with her spirit. When he lowered his head, small square tears tumbled from the corners of his eyes. "Many zombies blamed Er-Lan for not warning the others about the spiders, with Ko-Lan the loudest of the accusers."

"You can't be held responsible for what the spiders did," Cleric said. "You didn't kill your mother or those other zombies."

"But Er-Lan failed to act when it was possible to help," the zombie snapped.

"Did you know when the spiders were going to attack?" the old man asked.

The zombie shook his head no.

"Could you have stopped the spiders from attacking?" Watcher asked.

Again, the zombie shook his head.

"Then how could the other zombies hold you responsible?"

"Er-Lan saw the cave-in happen in a vision." The zombie paused to take a deep, wheezing breath. The expression on his face was that of incredible grief. "Er-Lan knew Ko-Lan would cause the cave-in, yet nothing was said."

"And the other zombies thought it was your fault?" Cleric's sympathetic voice did little to ease the zombie's grief.

"Ko-Lan was the first to point the claw of blame." The zombie's voice grew soft. "Ko-Lan said Er-Lan could have warned the zombies and saved everyone . . . saved mother." He sniffled and clenched his fists, trying to control his emotions. "Ko-Lan had said zombies that don't fight are more than useless; they are a threat to the zombie community. Er-Lan was said to be proof of that."

"That's not true, Er-Lan," Watcher said. "You and I both know fighting is not always the answer."

"Fighting might have saved mother, but instead, Er-Lan did nothing." The monster slowed his pace until he was barely walking, his clawed feet dragging through the sand.

"Why didn't you say anything about the attack?" Cleric asked.

The zombie looked up at the old man. "Just because Er-Lan can see a thing, it does not mean Er-Lan knows *when* that thing will happen. If warning would have been given, zombies could have done something to make matters worse. Changing the present has uncertain effects on the future. Sometimes, the current future is good enough."

"Even if you know your mother will die?" Watcher asked.

"What if warning would have caused all zombies to be destroyed?" Er-Lan asked. "Changing the present can have uncertain effects to the future, and once those changes are in place, they cannot be taken back. The present instantly becomes the past as time ticks by, and then it's too late to undo what has been done."

The zombie grew quiet for a moment. Watcher could tell a battle raged within the monster's mind, a battle between responsibility and guilt . . . something he understood quite well.

"Er-Lan, you cannot take responsibility for the future." He glanced up at the sun as it rose above the eastern horizon before them. The sky was painted with beautiful shades of red and orange. "That's too much for anyone. Sometimes, we must be responsible for our own actions. You didn't cause the avalanche, your brother did. You didn't kill your mother, the spiders did. Just because you think you can see the future, it doesn't make you the caretaker of the future."

"Having sight into the future can be painful." The zombie sighed. "Knowing a friend will die long before it happens brings much grief."

"Have you seen one of us in your visions?" Watcher asked.

Er-Lan lowered his gaze.

"You have to tell us if you see something like that."

"Visions of the distant future are difficult to see. Much is uncertain and the images are fuzzy and out of focus. Only when the event comes nearer do the premonitions grow clearer." Er-Lan looked up at Watcher with a single tear tumbling down his green cheek.

"You have seen something, haven't you?" the boy asked.

Er-Lan nodded.

"What is it? Who is it?" Watcher grabbed him by the shoulder and shook the zombie as if trying to dislodge the answer.

Er-Lan put a hand on the archer's shoulder, calming him.

"It is not certain; the image is unclear. Many people will be underwater. They might drown, or they might not . . . their fate is still uncertain."

"Why can't you tell what's going to happen?" Winger asked.

"When those linked to the event are uncertain of their choices, then the future is uncertain." The zombie glanced at Winger, then back to Watcher and closed his eyes. "I see many outcomes, all at the same time. It is very confusing . . . and disturbing."

"We understand," Cleric said softly.

"No, we don't!" Watcher snapped. "I need to know what's gonna happen. Who among us is gonna drown? What can I do to stop it?"

Er-Lan opened his eyes, then shook his head. "Too much is uncertain. The visions are too painful. This ability is a curse. Er-Lan wishes it would go away."

The zombie sighed and lowered his gaze again.

Watcher could see his friend was in pain. Reaching out, he wrapped an arm around his shoulders and pulled the zombie to him, holding him tight. "We'll see this through, together, you and I, for we are like brothers. I promise you, Er-Lan, I'll always be there for you."

The zombie looked up at Watcher, but there was a great sadness lurking in his dark eyes. The monster was still holding something back, and it was important enough to cause him great grief.

"There's the jungle!" someone shouted.

Watcher dropped his arm, then ran to the small sand dune up ahead. Before him, a thick green wall of soaring trees stood at the edge of a jungle biome, each with vines hanging down like long tangles of unkept hair. Thick layers of leaves and shrubs covered the ground, creating an image of an impassable verdant wall of growth. The bright green of the plant life stood out in sharp contrast to the pale landscape of the desert; it was a welcome relief to the eyes.

The sun climbed higher into the morning sky, separating from the horizon, but the tall junglewood trees blocked it from sight. Long shadows stretched across the ground, reaching deep into the desert. It was almost as if the jungle was stretching out its arms and welcoming the intrepid explorers into its embrace . . . or trying to ensnare them.

"That's it?" Watcher asked.

Mapper nodded. "Yep. According to the map, that's the Creeper's Jungle."

"I don't really like that name of that place," Planter said. "I hate those creatures."

"You mean creepers?" Blaster asked.

Planter nodded.

Blaster laughed. "I love 'em. Creatures that explode and give you gun powder . . . that's a monster I understand." Blaster smiled. "I can't wait to say hello to them."

"Careful what you wish for," Cleric said.

Watcher glanced at Planter out of the corner of his eye. Every time he looked at her, he noticed something different: the way her eyes sparkled, the tiny little dimples in her cheeks when she smiled, her soft, almost radiant skin . . . everything about her seemed to be changing . . . or was it Watcher who was changing? For some reason, Planter was looking more and more like a beautiful girl instead of his childhood friend; it was confusing.

Watcher stood there, dumbfounded, watching the way her glorious blond hair swayed back and forth as she walked, the other villagers cresting the hill and heading for the jungle, passing him by.

"I see you finally noticed how pretty Planter is," Winger whispered in his ear.

Watcher turned and found his sister standing right next to him, a huge smile on her face.

"What . . . ahhh . . . I don't know what you're talking about." Watcher could feel his cheeks getting hot; he knew he was blushing.

Winger laughed, then grabbed her brother's shoulders and turned him so they were facing each other. Watcher tried to turn his head away, but she put both hands on his red cheeks and pulled his head toward her. "It's okay to like her . . . Planter is terrific," Winger said.

"I don't know what you're talking about." Watcher pulled away from her grip and stormed away, heading for the jungle tree line.

What if Winger says something to Planter . . . she'll know! What if Planter rejects me . . . I couldn't handle that.

Fear pulsed through his veins as if he were battling with the fiercest monster; or was he battling with himself?

"This is too confusing," he whispered.

"Too confusing." "Too confusing." "Too confusing."

The group of parrots flew past his head, their mimicry fortunately getting lost amongst the many squawks that surrounded the army. The parrots circled the villagers, returning from the forest after feasting on fruit and cocoa seeds. Some of them had been flying high overhead, watching the landscape for movement. Now, each bird found a shoulder on which to land, the magnificent creatures fluttering their feathers as they settled for a rest. A bright red creature landed lightly next to Watcher's ear, then nuzzled its beak along his neck. The animal then turned its dark eyes to Er-Lan, who stood nearby and gave off a series of squawks and squeaks.

The zombie nodded. "A large party of skeletons follow across the desert, and there are many creepers in the jungle."

"I still can't believe you understand them," Watcher said.

The zombie didn't respond.

"What do you think we should do?" Watcher asked the green monster.

Er-Lan shrugged. "Much is uncertain."

The young boy sighed, then glanced back across the parched desert landscape. The skeletons must be too far away to be seen, or were trying to remain unseen. He turned and stared at the jungle.

"I think the enemy before us is better than the one behind," Watcher said. "Let's get through this jungle as quickly as possible. We must find this ancient structure in the ocean before the skeletons do."

"Agreed," Cleric said, nodding. "Lead on."

Pulling out his enchanted bow, Watcher notched an arrow, then sprinted toward the Creeper's Jungle.

CHAPTER 14

The villagers all ran through the jungle, everyone glad to be out of the sweltering dry heat of the desert. Though it was not as hot, the jungle was incredibly humid, making it feel just as uncomfortable as the previous biome.

Watcher continued heading to the east, but with the tall jungle wood trees obscuring the clouds and sun, it was difficult to tell which way they were heading. He glanced at his father. "I'm afraid we're gonna get lost in this jungle."

"To reach your goal, it's important to not only know where you're going . . . but why." Cleric gave his son a knowing smile. "To know your true goal, you must first know yourself. Only then, can you point the way for others."

"What?" Watcher was confused.

"Here, use this." Blaster tossed him a dark object.

Snatching it out of the air, Watcher stared down at the object . . . it was a compass. He looked up and flashed a grin at Blaster, then gave Cleric a wry smile. "Sorry Dad, but a compass is much easier to use than one of your philosophical riddles."

"We'll see," his father replied.

Watcher held the compass out, then headed east. Blocks of leaves and thick shrubs blocked their progress, and at times it was necessary to use axes to cut through the undergrowth. Glancing around, he saw the villagers were becoming scattered, the difficult terrain forcing many to choose alternate paths around the frequent obstacles.

"This is not good." Watcher searched for Cutter. He found the big NPC chopping through blocks of thick leaves, creating a path for the wounded. Motioning with his bow, he gestured for him to come near. "We need to keep everyone together. I suspect this is called the Creeper's Jungle for a reason."

"I know," the big warrior said. "I'm trying to—"

BOOM!

An explosion rocked the jungle. The ground shook and leaves fell from the towering trees, creating a leafy rain that made it difficult to see for just an instant. Cutter stared down at Watcher with fear in his wide eyes.

He's deathly afraid of creepers, Watcher realized. *But he doesn't want anyone to know.*

"Archers, form a perimeter around me!" Watcher yelled as loud as he could. "Everyone, come to the sound of my voice." He glanced up at Cutter. "Bang your sword on that armor of yours . . . make some noise."

The villager glanced around at the green blocks that surrounded them, his head moving from place to place in a panic. Watcher drew Needle from his inventory, then smacked Cutter across the chest with the flat of the blade. The warrior turned and glared down at the boy, his hand reaching for his own sword.

"Bang on your armor and get everyone's attention. We need the army together, in one place." Watcher smacked his chest again, lightly. "Do it!"

Cutter shook his head, as if trying to dislodge his fear, then pulled out his huge diamond sword and another piece of iron armor. He banged on the metal plating as if it were a gong, the clanking drifting out into the jungle.

"Everyone, move to the sound," Watcher shouted. "Come together . . . here, with me and Cutter."

Villagers moved toward them, their eyes darting about, eyeing the green surroundings with suspicion. As soon as Watcher had enough archers, they fanned out into a large circle. Next, he sent the woodcutters to clear out some of the brush so they could see each other without having to look around shrubs or large clusters of leaves.

Psssss . . . BOOM!

Another creeper detonated, but this time, the explosion was punctuated with a terrified scream that was suddenly cut off.

I hope my friends are okay, he thought. Just then, a terrible image came to Watcher's mind.

"Where's Planter?" Watcher said, panicked, as he searched frantically for his friend.

"I'm here." Her voice was like the ringing of a perfect bell. He took a breath and allowed the stress that had built up to seep slowly away.

The villagers were beginning to set up defenses, placing blocks of dirt on the ground to make it difficult for creepers to approach. Swordsmen pulled out shields and blades, ready for any monster attack.

"I think we have everyone together now," Blaster said, his green leather armor merging with the background. "I'm going to the treetops with some other scouts. We'll try to find the creepers. When we do, we'll let you know where they're at."

"How will you let us know where the monsters are hiding?" Winger asked.

"Don't worry . . . you'll know." The boy smiled.

"Wait . . . take these." Winger handed him four pair of Elytra wings. "They might make it easier for you to get back to the ground."

Blaster took the shimmering gray wings, then ran to the largest junglewood tree with three other villagers following close behind. Using blocks of dirt, he built a set of stairs that spiraled around the trunk of the looming tree until they disappeared into the foliage high overhead.

A hissing sounded off to the right.

"Creeper!" one of the archers yelled.

The twangs of bowstrings filled the air as a group of warriors fired on the creature. In seconds, a cheer rang out, signaling the monster had been destroyed.

"Watcher," a voice said from high overhead. "Keep moving to the east. There's a large group of creepers sneaking up from behind. Get moving!"

Cutter turned and looked behind the group, but the only thing visible was the thick jungle foliage. The creepers could have been right there, but their mottled green and black skin merged perfectly with the foliage. He put his diamond sword back into his inventory, then pulled out an axe.

"That's a good idea." Watcher smiled up at the big warrior. "Swordsmen, take out axes. We're cutting through the jungle as we head for the ocean. Archers, keep your eyes open for creepers. Use your ears . . . their hissing will give them away." He glanced around at the army of NPCs. They were scared; he could see it in their eyes. But now, his friends and neighbors were looking for him to lead them to safety.

Maybe I can *do this.* Watcher found Planter and gave her a smile, then pulled out his enchanted bow and notched an arrow to the string.

"Everyone forward!"

The army moved through the jungle to the sound of chopping. The soldiers tore into the leaves and shrubs as if they were cutting through an army of monsters. As they attacked the jungle with their axes, the archers stood guard on the perimeter, ready to silence any creeper that might be foolish enough to approach.

An explosion detonated high in the treetops, far to the north.

"That must be the signal from Blaster," Cleric said. "There are creepers to the north."

Another explosion rocked the jungle to the south.

"More creepers," Cutter said, his voice lacking its normal confident, booming edge.

"Come on, everyone . . . we need to move faster!" Watcher put away his bow and pulled his own axe out, lending the iron tool to the effort.

The army of NPCs moved through the jungle but it was slow going. The growth of shrubs, trees, and vines was thick, and almost seemed to be getting denser as they delved deeper into the biome. Sweat rained down from Watcher's forehead as he hacked at the blocks of leaves before him. He could just imagine the mottled green creatures sneaking up on them from the three sides, the strange, four-footed monsters wanting to end their lives by destroying as many of his friends as possible. It made him shudder with dread.

Just then, an explosion punctuated through the sounds of the jungle high in the treetops ahead of them. Then more blocks of TNT went off behind and to the left and right . . . the creepers were closing in from all sides.

"We're surrounded," Cutter said, his voice shaking.

Watcher put away his axe and glanced around at the members of their army. Everyone had stopped cutting through the jungle and were just staring at him, terrified expressions on their faces . . . all except Er-Lan. The zombie seemed to be staring off into the distance, listening to the animals of the jungle. The faint growls and howls of ocelots could be heard through the foliage, the spotted cats elusive and difficult to tame.

"What I wouldn't give for a clowder of cats right now," Watcher muttered.

"Clowder of cats?" Er-Lan asked.

"Yeah, clowder means group of cats. Creepers are afraid of cats." Watcher turned in a circle and surveyed their surroundings. He glanced at Cutter and could tell the big NPC was paralyzed with fear. "Here's what we're gonna do. Everyone pull out blocks of dirt or stone or whatever you have. We're building our own little castle right here in the jungle." He pulled out his enchanted bow. "We aren't gonna let any creepers get close to us without paying a price."

A few villagers cheered . . . but very few.

"I know you're all scared, but we can get through this if we work together." Watcher held his bow high over his head. "This is not the end . . . it's only the beginning of our defense against the monsters of the Far Lands."

Just then, a whistling sound filled the air. Behind him, Er-Lan had two fingers in the corner of his mouth and was making a piercing sound that cut through the noises of the jungle. Instantly, parrots descended upon the circle of villagers. Colors beyond anything Watcher could imagine floated down to their clearing, all of the birds heading toward the zombie.

The decaying creature held his arms out, allowing many of the creatures to land. They bobbed their heads up and down, squawking and squeaking. Er-Lan said something to those nearest, then flung his arms upward, sending the parrots into the air. The feathery creatures squawked to each other, then dispersed out in all directions.

"What was that?" Watcher asked.

Er-Lan smiled. "Clowder means a group of cats." His grin grew larger.

"I think the zombie is losing it," Cutter said.

Watcher spun around and saw the big warrior approaching. "You okay?"

"Yeah . . . sorry. Creepers are not my favorite monster."

"I know, I'm afraid of them too," Watcher said.

"Who said anything about being afraid?" Cutter snapped.

"Ahh . . . well, I . . . umm." Watcher looked for something to say, but found no words that would help.

"And who put you in charge?" The big NPC glared

at Watcher. "I'm leading this army, not you. You're just leading the archers; everyone does what I say. You got that?!"

Watcher nodded and took a step back. The angry edge to Cutter's voice was a little frightening.

What did I do? I was just trying to help, the boy thought.

Notching an arrow to his bow string, Watcher moved to the perimeter and watched for the green monsters. Villagers all around him were building barricades of dirt and stone. Swordsmen were clearing away shrubs beyond the impromptu barricade, making it easier for the archers to find their targets. Archers built tiny towers of dirt, then attached wide platforms on top able to hold four defenders, allowing them to shoot over the walls at any approaching monsters.

The defenses came together quickly, but Watcher suspected they would not be enough. He knew if one creeper made it to their wall, it would detonate, tearing open their defenses. The monsters would then pour into the clearing. Their explosive lives would destroy every last member of their army until no one was left.

I've led everyone into a trap, and their deaths will be my fault, Watcher thought. *I can only hope I don't survive; I don't think I could bear this guilt.*

"They're coming!" a voice said from high overhead.

Four figures jumped out of the trees overhead, then leaned forward, causing their Elytra wings to snap open. The gray wings allowed the villagers to fly in a wide circle around the perimeter of their formation, slowly floating toward the ground. They landed gracefully, then removed the wings and replaced them with armor.

"Thanks for the wings," Blaster said to Winger. "They got us down so we wouldn't miss the fun."

"What do you mean?" Winger asked.

Blaster sighed. He removed his leather armor, and replaced it with thick iron.

"You can't run very fast or hide in that," Watcher said.

"I don't think we're going to do much running or hiding." A sad expression came across the boy's face.

He reached out a hand to Watcher, the archer doing the same. The clasped each other's wrists, a sign of greeting and parting. This time, Watcher knew it meant the latter.

Panic suddenly flooded through him. *Where's Planter?* Watcher glanced around, looking for his friend. *I must make sure she's safe.* And then he saw her. She was organizing the archers along one of the walls, placing villagers so they'd have the clearest field of fire while at the same time staying near the children, ready to protect them with her bow. Watcher's heart swelled as he watched her, but was then filled with panic when he heard the next words.

"Here they come," an archer shouted from his perch. "Oh no . . ."

"What?" Watcher stared up at the villager, who stood on a tall watch tower built out of dirt. The archer looked down with a resigned expression on his face and just shook his head.

Pulling blocks of dirt out of his inventory, Watcher jumped into the air and placed the block under his feet. He repeated this six times, then slowly turned. Emerging from the jungle were countless creepers, their dark eyes filled with hatred. Some of the monsters sparkled, with electric sheets of energy hugging their bodies; these were charged creepers . . . and they were very dangerous.

He tried to count the monsters, but there were just too many. The creepers were packed together, shoulder to shoulder, with more ranks of monsters pushing through the underbrush. They probably outnumbered the villagers ten to one . . . it was impossible.

Watcher gazed down at his companions.

"Well?" Planter stared up at him.

Her green eyes and long blond hair had never looked so beautiful to Watcher. And then, suddenly, Watcher realized what he'd been feeling toward Planter: he liked her, not just as a childhood friend . . . but something more. And now, he'd never get a chance to experience this emotion with her . . . that is, if she felt the same way about him.

"What do you see?" she asked.

What should I say . . . that I see everyone's death? It's hopeless.

He said nothing, just stared down at Planter and tried to burn her image into the back of his mind so that it'd be there at the end.

"Here they come!" another villager shouted.

Watcher turned toward the tree line as hundreds of creepers charged toward them. It was the end.

CHAPTER 15

Bowstrings sang as the archers fired upon the creepers, but there were just too many of them. The pointed shafts did little to slow the green wave of destruction.

"Keep shooting!" Cutter glanced up at Watcher, expecting the boy to do something.

But all Watcher could do was watch in horror as the monsters drew closer and closer.

Suddenly, the villagers were enveloped in a fluttering storm of color. Hundreds of parrots descended upon their position. The birds landed on the ground or clung to the trunks of trees. Many landed on Er-Lan's outstretched arms, the creature now smiling a toothy grin that would have looked terrifying coming from any other zombie. The parrots squawked and howled as if each bird were competing to see which could be the loudest. The cacophony was terrible, forcing many villagers to put their hands over their ears.

And then the strangest thing happened.

All of the birds grew silent. A tense hush spread across the jungle. The creepers, unsure what was happening, stopped their advance. No one spoke and no one fired a weapon. Every NPC stood completely motionless, afraid to disturb the silence.

And then one of the birds made a noise that sounded like that of a cat meowing. Another made a meowing sound, followed by an angry feline growl. More of the parrots joined in, each mimicking the sound of the jungle ocelots, the mortal enemy of the creepers. The sound slowly percolated through the jungle, reaching the ears of the creepers. At first, the monsters held their ground, but then the parrots walked across the ground, moving closer to the hastily constructed barricade. They meowed and growled and howled louder, the replicated cat sounds becoming fierce.

Watcher saw the first creeper turn and run. One of the charged creepers tried to shout some kind of command, but as soon as the others saw one creeper retreat, it broke the horde's courage. The creepers' fear of the cats far outweighed their lust for destruction. The monsters turned and fled as the parrots screamed their performance louder and louder.

Finally, only one creeper remained; it was the biggest of the electrified monsters. The charged creeper glared up at Watcher with such hatred in its eyes, it almost hurt to stare back.

"Next time the villagers invade my jungle . . . the outcome will be different," the monster said.

"We aren't invading, we're just passing through and . . ." Watcher stopped speaking; the monster was gone. Glancing down at Planter, he smiled, then shouted, "They're gone!"

The villagers cheered and hugged each other in joy.

Watcher used a shovel and dug up the blocks beneath his feet, slowly lowering himself to the ground. When he was two blocks from the ground, he jumped to the jungle floor and ran for Planter. But before he could get there, Cutter gathered her up in his arms and gave her a giant hug, a huge smile spreading across the big

NPC's square face. Skidding to a stop, Watcher stared at his friends, his joy slowly deflating.

Planter released Cutter, then turned to Watcher and smiled. "We're safe."

She reached out and pulled Watcher into her arms, but the boy was still confused at what he'd just witnessed. He glanced at Cutter just as the warrior turned and headed for the barricade.

"Everyone, let's move out." Cutter used a pick axe to dig into the blocks of dirt that formed their defenses. "We need to hurry before those creepers come back."

The villagers gathered their belongings and dug up their fortified wall, then continued to the east, toward the still-unseen ocean. As they moved past, Watcher approached Er-Lan.

"I know you saved all of us." He put an arm around the zombie. "Did you see that trick with the birds in your vision?"

Er-Lan shook his head. "The premonitions come when they come, there is no control of what is seen."

"Then how did you know to have the parrots mimic the ocelots?"

"All zombies know creepers are afraid of cats. Don't villagers know that?"

"Well . . . I guess . . . I was pretty scared and just didn't think about having the parrots mimic their meows."

Er-Lan nodded. "At least no creatures of the Far Lands had to perish."

"Agreed." Watcher pulled out an axe. "Let's catch up with the others. I bet it's not a good idea to be on your own in the Creeper's Jungle."

The zombie grunted his agreement, then followed his friend through the dense vegetation. They caught up with the rest of the army. Watcher ordered the archers to the edge of the formation with arrows notched and ready. Parrots flapped overhead, diving amongst the branches, their ocelot mimicry still being blared into the jungle.

"You smell that?" Planter said.

Watcher stopped for a moment and inhaled. "I don't smell anything."

"Try again."

Drawing in a huge breath through his nose, he closed his eyes for just an instant . . . and then he smelled it.

"Salt!"

Planter nodded, smiling. "We're close to the ocean."

This raised the spirits of the villagers, causing them to chop through the brush faster. Many of the archers now pulled out axes; the flock of parrots were more effective at keeping creepers away than their arrows. The NPCs moved faster through the jungle, the scent of the salty air pulling them forward.

And then they chopped through the last of the thick leafy blocks that marked the edge of the jungle biome, revealing a sandy beach. Just beyond was the deep blue ocean. When they stepped onto the beach, the hot and humid air instantly vanished, replaced by a cool, salt-air breeze. Some of the villagers ran to the water and dove in, washing away the last of the jungle heat from their bodies.

Cutter pointed to Mapper. "Where do we go now? We're at the ocean . . . what did your book say?"

The old villager looked confused. "All it said was, 'a great treasure lies under the ocean.' I'm not really sure what that means."

"We can't really search the entire ocean floor," Cutter said. "Where do we go? We can't just stand here; eventually the creepers will find us again. I doubt they'll fall for that trick with the parrots again."

Mapper knelt on the beach and placed the linked ender chest on the sand. Opening it, he leafed through the book that sat in the companion chest, hidden in the Wizard's Tower.

"I know where we need to go," a voice said from high overhead.

Everyone looked up at the tall junglewood trees that

loomed along the edge of the beach. Standing atop one was a figure clad in bright green armor; it was Blaster.

"What do you see?" Cutter shouted to the treetops.

"I see our destination," Blaster replied. "Mapper said the next relic was under the ocean, right?"

"That's right," the old man replied, closing the ender chest. "Do you see an ocean temple?"

"Nope."

"What about an underwater chest?" Watcher asked.

"Nope, nope." Blaster smiled.

"We don't have time for games," Cutter muttered in a low voice. He glared up at Blaster. "Then what do you see?"

"To the north, at the end of that peninsula, I see a hole in the ocean." Blaster pointed with one of his curved knives.

Everyone turned toward the peninsula that jutted out from the shoreline like a sandy finger. There seemed to be nothing in the ocean, just water. Watcher was confused and glanced back up at the boy. Blaster smiled, then leapt off the top of the tree into the open air. Opening his Elytra wings, he flew gracefully through the air. Banking to the right, he soared northward, descending as he glided. He landed on the base of the peninsula thirty blocks away, then motioned for the others to join him.

"Come on everyone," Blaster shouted. "We have a hole in the ocean to explore!"

And without waiting, Blaster ran to the end of the peninsula and dove into the waters. Then the strangest thing happened: Blaster stood up on the ocean, the gentle waves caressing his ankles. He smiled, then walked casually across the water, heading out into the open ocean, and then disappeared under the waves, a chuckle escaping from his mischievous lips.

CHAPTER 16

The skeletons sprinted after their prey, the threat of retribution from their general motivation enough to make them ignore their fatigue. A group of the pale monsters stopped to catch their breath when they reached the edge of the desert. Some stared up at the morning sun with angry eyes as the heat beat down on them mercilessly.

"What are you doing?!" Rusak bellowed.

He pulled out an enchanted iron sword and smashed the nearest skeleton, ripping into its HP. After only two hits, the monster crumbled into a pile of bones.

"The rest of you, keep running," the skeleton general growled.

Those that had stopped instantly sprinted into the dense jungle, climbing over blocks of leaves and veering around the looming junglewood trees, anxious to get out of arm's reach of their commander.

"You can see where the villagers cut through the jungle," Captain Ratlan said.

General Rusak nodded. "The fools leave an easy trail to follow."

The captain grinned. "Where do you think the villagers are heading?"

"They seem to be heading for the eastern ocean. And that can only mean those idiotic NPCs know about the Submerged War Room. The wizard with them must be drawing on ancient memories from his ancestors. How else would they know where to go?"

"That wizard is more dangerous than we thought," Ratlan said.

Rusak nodded. "I have no doubt now, the boy-archer with them must be a wizard returned from the dead, somehow. It is even more important he is destroyed."

The skeletons ran through the carved path left behind by the villagers. The sounds of life in the jungle enveloped them from all sides. The catlike growls of the ocelots were everywhere, as were the moos of cattle and the clucks of chickens. But there was a new sound; it was of some kind of multicolored bird General Rusak had never seen before.

"Do you have a plan for when we catch up to the villagers?" Ratlan asked.

"They will, without a doubt, reach the War Room before we do," the commander said. "This was a place built by the monster warlocks and we cannot let them defile it. They must not be allowed to leave alive."

A group of creepers approached from the left. When the mottled green monsters saw it was skeletons, they held back their attack.

"Why are they heading for the monsters' War Room?" Ratlan asked. "We've searched that structure many times and found nothing."

"The boy-wizard must know where our ancestors hid some powerful weapons." Rusak swung his sword at a cluster of leafy blocks that barred his path. The blocks instantly crumbled into dust. "We cannot allow those villagers to touch any of our sacred artifacts. Those ancient weapons belong to the monsters of the Far Lands, not to the puny villagers. All they can do is steal and destroy. They must all be exterminated."

"We will do as you command, of course," the captain asked. "Tell us what to do."

"I'll go in first with a company of skeletons and confront them. Even with the boy-wizard with them, they will be no match for our forces. We have far more skeletons than they have NPCs." General Rusak laughed a harsh, hacking sort of laugh, his jaw clicking together with each chuckle. "I will drive the villagers into the main tower, and that's where you'll be waiting with a little trap. After we spring our trap, the NPCs will be doomed. You and I will listen to them beg for their lives as they are slowly destroyed." He smiled. "It will be a great battle and a great victory."

"But what if the boy-wizard has started to uncover his powers?" Ratlan said, sounding worried. "He may have some tricks of his own."

"Are you afraid of this wizard?"

Ratlan nodded. "I saw him shoot his bow back in the Wizard's Tower; he's a deadly archer." The captain swerved around a tall junglewood tree. For some reason, there were blocks of dirt attached to the side of the trunk, as if someone built a spiral staircase around the trunk. "But if he has also learned to work some of the enchanted weapons from the past, he could be a very dangerous adversary."

Rusak punched the captain in the bony arm. "You worry too much, Ratlan. This child might be a wizard, but he's still a child who can be easily crushed. Our bows and arrows will be enough to destroy them. And if not, we can always call for reinforcements from the skeleton warlord, Rakir. There are hundreds of skeletons in the Hall of Pillars, and only one boy-wizard. His destruction is assured."

Captain Ratlan smiled and nodded, but the general could still see there was doubt in his subordinate's dark eyes. It didn't make a difference. General Rusak would make certain the boy-wizard and his companions never left the Submerged War Room alive.

CHAPTER 17

Watcher ran along the shoreline, heading for the long sliver of land that extended out into the cool blue waters. At his side, Er-Lan ran in lock step, the zombie concerned about their mutual friend. When they reached the base of the peninsula, they waited for the rest of the NPC army.

"Did Blaster drown?" A concerned expression covered the zombie's scarred face.

"No way, he's an expert swimmer." Watcher walked to the end of the peninsula as the rest of the villagers arrived, Er-Lan still at his side. "I've gone swimming with him many times in the lake near our village. He couldn't have drowned."

Suddenly, Blaster's head popped up above the ocean surface about twenty blocks away from where he had jumped in. "What are you all doing . . . come on, you won't believe what's down here."

"What's he doing?" Winger asked, confused. "It doesn't look as if he's swimming."

Blaster then rose out of the water as if he were somehow walking up a flight of stairs. Getting higher and higher, he eventually stood, ankle-deep, on the ocean's surface.

"There's an invisible path," the boy shouted. "Just walk out straight toward me."

Watcher moved to the end of the sandy beach, then stepped hesitantly into the ocean waters. But instead of sinking in to his waist as he would have expected, he found a solid surface underfoot. Moving cautiously along the path, the archer walked across the watery layer, stunned by what was happening.

He walked along the path, heading straight for Blaster. A few times, his foot slipped off the invisible path, but he was able to keep from falling in the water. When he reached Blaster's side, Watcher stared at him, confused. "How is this possible?"

His friend shrugged. "The wizards must have created some kind of invisible block. Maybe we can call it a barrier block."

"We don't know if it was the wizards responsible for this." Cleric said.

Watcher turned and found his father standing directly behind him and a line of villagers standing on the invisible path as if waiting to enter a theater.

"It could have been made by the warlocks instead," Er-Lan said.

Both Watcher and Blaster nodded.

"Come closer and look down." Blaster pointed to the ocean surface.

Before them, a huge area was blocked off by the transparent barrier blocks; it stretched from above the ocean surface all the way to the ocean floor. Blaster moved to the end of the invisible path, then stepped up onto the invisible structure, his feet no longer touching the water. "It's okay, come closer."

Watcher moved to Blaster's side and stepped up onto the transparent barrier. It felt as if he were standing on a normal stone block, yet it was completely transparent, as if made of air.

Glancing down at the invisible structure, he found the ocean water pressed against the transparent wall, the structure wrapping around in the shape of a huge cylinder until it closed itself off. Water hugged closed to the outside of the barrier, unable to get through, but on the inside of the enclosure, it was just air. The whole thing looked as if someone had scooped out the water, all the way to the ocean floor, leaving behind an empty and dry region.

On the dry ocean floor, a massive structure was built, stretching to the edges of the barrier blocks, then extending through the barrier and into the water. Angry-looking designs made of black coal blocks and redstone cubes decorated the walls and roofs of the buildings, with sweeping blood-red arches marking the entrance. Near the far end of the hole in the ocean, a tower made of obsidian stretched from the sandy floor to sea-level, the dark blocks hidden by the blue waters, making it invisible from the beach. Part of the tower touched the barrier blocks, the wall of the huge turret holding back the waters from flooding into the structure.

"Let's go down." Blaster ran down a line of dark stairs leading to the bottom, toward the not-so-inviting red arch.

Watcher moved carefully down the steps, the rest of the villagers following. Parrots flew around them, squawking loudly. He wasn't sure if their loud calls were those of excitement . . . or warning. Regardless, Watcher knew they had to continue.

When they reached the bottom, the villagers gathered around the bottom of the stairs, uncertain about the wall of water surrounding them, the invisible blocks holding back the flood. Fear was painted vividly on the square faces of the villagers as they stared up at the waters; each of them knew that if one of those barrier blocks were to break, the crushing flood of water would destroy them all.

"Well . . . are we going in?" Blaster pointed to the red-and-black structure.

Watcher stared at the huge entrance. It was a wide, curved opening rimmed with blocks of redstone and coal spaced along the edge. The dark cubes resembled black teeth along the edge of a prehistoric leviathan's mouth, the great maw waiting to swallow those foolish enough to enter. It brought a trickle of fear that spread through Watcher's body. Instinctively, he put on his chain mail, hoping the metallic layer would somehow protect him from the dangers circling about in his mind. He shuddered just as his parrot landed gracefully on his shoulder. It startled Watcher, but when he felt its beak nuzzling his neck, he smiled.

Somehow, Watcher sensed danger within this structure. He wanted to warn everyone, though he had no idea as to the peril. Before he could speak, Cutter spoke.

"Let's go. I'm sure there are hidden weapons in there. We must find every one of them." The big NPC glanced at Mapper. "Any idea what we're looking for here?"

The old villager just shrugged. "The book didn't really specify what was here, but it did say something."

"What?"

"Well, it was sort of a hint, I guess, for where to look." Mapper said. "The book said, 'Search the tip of the sword.'"

"What's that supposed to mean?" Blaster asked.

Mapper just shrugged.

"You're a big help." Blaster removed his green armor and replaced it with black. "Come on everyone, let's look for a sword."

The villagers moved into the gigantic structure, the dark stone walls blocking out the rays of the sun. Many of them held torches high over their heads to light the shadowy passages, but the darkness of the place seemed oppressive, as if the shadows were somehow seeping into their souls. A strange, ancient feeling seemed to fill the place, as if they'd all just gone back in time. The refreshing salty air from the beach was now replaced with stagnation and dust. A layer of grime covered the floors and walls; it was as if this place had been deserted for hundreds of years.

Deep in the back of Watcher's mind, a memory tickled his awareness, letting him know it was there, but too insubstantial to be recognized. Like seeing someone's face he recognized, but not being able to remember their name, the memory nagged at him, but stayed just out of reach. All he knew for sure was something bad happened here a long, long time ago.

Watcher stayed at Planter's side; he wanted to make sure she stayed safe. With his enchanted bow and her enchanted golden axe, a circle of shimmering light followed them through the structure.

"Check the side passages for monsters." Cutter pointed to a few dark corridors that extended away from the main hallway.

Small groups of villagers explored those passages, planting torches as they moved through the ancient building. Watcher glanced down one of the side passages and could tell much of the ancient structure actually extended out of the dry hole the ancients had carved into the ocean somehow. These extensions off the main tunnel were completely surrounded by water, with moisture dripping from the walls and ceiling. If someone accidently broke a block, those passages would quickly fill; they had to be careful.

The villagers returned from the corridors that stretched off the main passage, reporting they were all empty and devoid of any furniture or items. They continued down the wide hallway, everyone looking for pressure plates and tripwires on the ground.

Far away, at the end of the huge corridor, a strange purple glow could be seen painting the walls and floor.

"What do you think that is?" Planter asked.

Watcher shrugged. "I don't know, but I don't like it. Unexpected things are never good."

She nodded, then gripped the handle of her axe tight.

They moved down the stone-lined hallway with archers walking along either wall, swordsmen and the infirm in the center. Their footsteps echoed off the cold walls and dusty floors, making the group sound like they were a troop of a thousand, and not just a few score.

The hallway finally ended at a large room, the walls and floors bathed in a soft, purple light, some of the iridescent glow leaking into the dusty passage. Watcher poked his head into the glowing chamber and scanned it with his keen eyes. The chamber was filled with wooden furniture, book cases, crafting benches, and a line of furnaces along one wall, all cold and silent.

"Where's Er-Lan?" Watcher asked.

Shuffling forward, the zombie moved to the boy's side.

"Can you send in a couple of parrots and have them look for any hidden monsters?" Watcher glanced up at the bright red parrot that was still perched on his shoulder.

Er-Lan moved his green head next to the bird and whispered something to the creature. Instantly, the bird leapt off Watcher's shoulder and took to the air. Flapping its wings, the parrot flew up near the ceiling, around ornate chandeliers made of redstone blocks and across the massive room. A couple more parrots shot into the glowing chamber, banking in opposite directions. Squawking as they flew, the creatures flew around the chamber multiple times, then landed on the chandeliers that hung from the ceiling. The largest parrot made a series of long and short squawks, then ruffled its feathers.

"The birds say all is safe," the zombie said.

"Great," Watcher said, slapping the zombie on the back. "Come on."

Moving cautiously into the glowing chamber, Watcher scanned the surroundings. The chamber was circular in shape, with a high ceiling of netherquartz. Obsidian cubes were intermixed with the red and white netherquartz, forming elaborate patterns in the surface high overhead.

"Everyone, watch out, I'm going to flip this switch," a voice said from the far side of the room; it sounded like Blaster.

There was a click, then lines of redstone dust along the walls grew bright, giving off a crimson glow. The glowing lines crisscrossed the walls and climbed up to the ceiling until they reached the chandeliers high overhead. The redstone lanterns in the intricately designed hanging structure came to life, generating a warm crimson radiance that filled the chamber.

"That's better," Blaster said with a smile.

He waved at Watcher and was about to say something when his mouth fell open in awe. The boy pointed at the floor of the chamber. Glancing down, Watcher too was stunned. The floor had a wide stripe stretching across it, from one wall to the other. The stripe was a bright blue, the surface polished to a glassy sheen. Watcher reached down and ran his hand across the light blue surface, stunned at what he was seeing.

"These are diamond blocks." Watcher was amazed. He stared down at the stripe; it must have been a dozen blocks wide.

He ran along the diamond stripe from one wall to the other. The stripe narrowed to a single block at one end; the other fanned out wider for a few blocks, then suddenly ended, a single line of dark, obsidian blocks stretching from the diamond to the opposite wall. The cyan stripe glowed with a faint purple glow; it was incredible and likely worth a fortune. Near the end of the diamond stripe, an iron door stood closed, embedded into the wall of the chamber.

"Everyone, search the room." Cutter's commanding voice boomed off the stone walls.

"What about all this diamond?" someone asked.

Blaster pulled out an iron pick and swung it down upon one of the blocks. He swung it again and again, but the shining cube refused to show a single crack.

"Don't waste your effort." Cleric pointed to the

faint, purple glow that wrapped around the glistening blocks like a protective cocoon. "Can't you see? They're enchanted. Likely the ancients put some sort of spell on the diamond blocks to keep people from stealing them."

Blaster nodded, then put away the tool.

"Anyone find anything?" Cutter said.

The villagers all shook their heads.

"You mean to tell me there's nothing here?" one of the villagers complained. "We trudged through that terrible jungle for nothing?"

"Maybe this place had already been raided," Mapper suggested.

No, this isn't right, Watcher thought. *There must be more here.* He looked up at the chandelier. A blue parrot looked down at him from the light fixture, then squawked and flew into the air.

"I wonder what the room looks like from up there," Watcher whispered to himself.

Glancing around at the room, he imagined how the chamber would appear from high overhead. Moving to one end of the room, he stood on the line of obsidian blocks at the end of the diamond stripe. With his head down, he walked along the stripe again, noting the section that was very wide but abruptly narrowed to the dozen-block-wide stripe. As he walked, he could see the light from the magical enchantment leaking out from between the blocks. When he neared the opposite wall, the stripe grew narrower and narrower until it ended with a single block. From above, that single block would look like a point . . . *or a tip!*

He turned and looked down the length of the stripe.

"It's not a stripe," he said.

"What?" Planter asked, confused.

But Watcher was lost in thought and never heard her question. He stared at the far end. The blocks of obsidian would look like a handle and the wide section a hand guard.

"What are you looking at, Watcher?" His father came next to him and stared in the same direction. "It's just a wide stripe."

Watcher shook his head. "No, it's not a stripe, it's a picture of a huge sword."

Cleric turned and looked at both ends of the stripe, then smiled and nodded his head. "Search the tip of the sword . . . that's what the book said."

Watcher nodded. He drew an iron pick axe from his inventory and moved to the single block of diamond at the tip of the stripe. He swung his tool down onto the cube, striking it hard. His pick rang like a bell as the shock of the impact vibrated through the handle and into his arms. He smiled . . . there was a faint crack in the cube.

"Look, there's no purple light leaking around this cube," Watcher said. "It's not protected."

He swung his pick down onto it again and again. A spiderweb of cracks spread out farther and farther until they reached the edge of the cube. After six strikes, the diamond cube shattered and floated, in miniature, off to the side.

Dropping the pick, Watcher reached down into the hold and grabbed a wooden chest covered in dust. He set it onto the ground as the other villagers gathered near.

"Well . . . open it!" Blaster exclaimed.

Watcher grabbed the lid and lifted. The cover screeched as the rusty hinges complained about the many centuries that had passed. Inside was just a single item. It was a helmet made of some kind of metal, but the surface was mirror smooth, reflecting the faces that stared down at it. Along the top of the helmet, precious gems studded the perimeter, one of each kind found in Minecraft. The silvery helm reminded Watcher of his sword, Needle. They both reflected the surroundings, almost like mirrors. It was as if they were made by the same materials.

Reaching in, he pulled it out and held it over his head. The instant he touched the shiny object, it seemed to make a connection with something in his inventory . . . his sword. Somehow, this helmet and Needle were linked. Maybe it was because they were made from the same material . . . or maybe they were made by the same wizard, or warlock. He wasn't sure, but there was a clear connection; Needle could now feel the presence of that helmet, and the sword transmitted that feeling to Watcher.

Everyone in the chamber was stunned at the sight; it was the most beautiful thing they'd ever seen. The helm gave off the characteristic purple glow of magical enchantments, but this artifact pulsed with power, as if it had a heartbeat. Watcher realized the object's pulse was synchronized with his own, as if they were somehow linked.

Suddenly, the clattering of bones echoed down the long passage.

"Skeletons," Cleric whispered, a look of fear in his eyes.

"They're coming down the main hall," one of the warriors said. "We're trapped."

Suddenly, an arrow flew into the room and embedded itself into the far wall. It was followed by twenty more deadly projectiles.

"What do we do?" Mapper asked.

"Form lines on either side of the doorway," Cutter said. "We'll get them in a crossfire when they enter the room." He glanced at Blaster, then pointed to the door near where the chest had been found. "Get that door opened; we're too exposed in here. We'll hold them off as long as we can."

Blaster nodded, then ran to the iron door and began searching for levers or buttons that would cause it to open.

The rattling of bones grew louder and louder as the monster horde moved closer. Villagers ran about the chamber, looking for a safe place from which to fire, but there were no safe places . . . they were trapped. Suddenly, the rattling was joined by a harsh, malevolent laugh, a clicking sound accompanying each chuckle.

And then, the largest skeleton Watcher had ever seen stepped into the chamber. The monster wore a full suit of iron armor and held an enchanted broadsword that glowed with evil-looking magical power. The monster stared straight at Watcher, then pointed with his massive weapon. The young boy reached into his inventory and pulled out Needle, the silver helmet still in his left hand.

"Wizard . . . I am General Rusak, the skeleton warlord's second in command, and I have come for you," the gigantic skeleton said ominously, his jaw clicking together with the words. "You will not leave the warlock's War Room alive."

A chill settled across Watcher's soul as fear permeated every fiber of his being. This skeleton was the most terrifying thing he'd ever seen, and his violent hatred was pointed straight at him. He was petrified, too scared to move, and all Watcher could do was stand there and shake in terror.

CHAPTER 18

The huge skeleton charged straight at Watcher at the same instant that a large company of bony monsters flooded into the room. A couple of NPC archers fired arrows at the skeleton commander, but somehow he was able to deflect the shafts with his massive sword.

The skeleton moved closer, knocking aside pointed shafts as if they were insignificant bugs. The rest of the skeleton horde attacked, forcing the NPCs to turn their bows away from the hulking monster and toward their charging foe.

The armored skeleton commander stared down at Watcher's weapon and laughed. "You call that a sword . . . boy?" He laughed again, then glanced at the helmet. "I see you're planning on stealing something that doesn't belong to you." The battle raged around them, with skeletons and villagers all firing upon each other; it was as if they were in the eye of a violent hurricane, shouts of pain and fear revolving around them. "That artifact belongs to the skeletons. Give it to me, and I guarantee your destruction will be painless."

Watcher said nothing and just shook his head; he was too scared to speak. Slowly, he backed away as the battle raged around them, but the two combatants seemed separated from the rest of the fighting. None of the skeletons seemed anxious to attack Watcher, and certainly none of the villagers were interested in tangling with the massive skeleton.

Gripping the relic in his left hand, Watcher just stared up at the monster, silent and afraid.

"Very well," the monster said. And with a bellowing scream, the iron-clad skeleton charged, swinging the massive sword at Watcher's head.

Before the blade could reach him, Needle came up and deflected the blow. The two enchanted blades clashed together, causing sparks to burst from their keen edges. The force of the impact vibrated down Watcher's arm, making it numb for just an instant. He backed away, frightened of the gigantic skeleton, but not just this skeleton . . . *all* skeletons. Watcher was terrified at being close to the creatures; something about the bones and skulls . . . it was like a living nightmare for him. He could shoot at them with his bow from far away, but when they were within arm's reach, Watcher was petrified with fear. This was something no one else knew about him.

"What's wrong, wizard, aren't you going to fight?" The huge skeleton swung his blade at Watcher, and again, Needle came up just in the nick of time, barely deflecting the blow.

Watcher continued to retreat, his mind nearly petrified with fear.

Suddenly, one of the NPCs, a big villager by the name of Builder, stepped in front of the boy, his iron armor and sword lacking the enchanted glow of the skeleton's. "You leave him alone!"

"Or what? Are you going to stop me?" Rusak laughed a loud, hollow laugh, his jaw clicking together, then without warning, he charged at the NPC.

Builder stepped to the side, allowing the overhead strike to slice down, cutting only air, then swung his iron blade at the monster. It hit the skeleton's armor and bounced off, doing no damage. Rusak laughed, then attacked again, this time feigning to the left, then attacking to the right. The monster's glowing blade cut deep into the villager's armor, tearing out huge chunks of Builder's chest plate.

"Watch and learn, boy," Rusak said to Watcher. "This is how you will be executed . . . soon, very soon."

The skeleton blocked an attack by Builder, then charged at the villager, his enchanted sword moving faster than Watcher thought possible. He struck Builder over and over again, the villager frantically trying to block the attacks, but to no avail. The skeleton's blade tore into the NPC's armor, tearing it to shreds until it fell to the ground in pieces. He then continued the attack, striking the doomed NPC again and again until his HP was exhausted. The expression on Builder's face struck Watcher to his soul; it was a visage of fear and uncertainty and overwhelming sadness . . . and then the NPC disappeared, his inventory clattering to the ground.

"Now, boy . . . it's your turn."

The skeleton attacked, swinging the massive broadsword in a savage overhead strike. Needle came up, moving on its own volition, deflecting the blow, but not fast enough. The gigantic blade caught part of Watcher's shoulder, tearing a huge gash into his chain mail and finding soft flesh underneath. Pain exploded through his body, his left arm growing numb. He dropped the shining helmet, just as the monster attacked again. This time, Watcher knew Needle would not be fast enough to block the weapon. Everything seemed to go into slow motion, the skeleton's sword streaking toward his head, Needle trying desperately to come up in time to stop the lethal blow; it was like watching a nightmare slowly unfold.

But then suddenly, a shining blue sword blocked the skeleton's attack . . . it was Cutter. His diamond blade stopped the skeleton's attack before it could reach Watcher.

"You look like you could use some help." The big NPC smiled.

"Begone, villager," the skeleton growled. "This is between General Rusak and the wizard."

"Look around you, *General;* your forces have been defeated." Cutter pointed around the room with his sword.

For the first time, Watcher surveyed the chamber. The skeletons were slowly being destroyed. NPCs from all sides of the chamber were firing on the monsters as they huddled at the chamber entrance. Most of the skeletons had now been defeated, but at the cost of many NPC lives. Now, the villagers slowly turned their bows toward the skeleton general, ready to fire.

"You think you've won?" the skeleton said, then laughed a hollow, clicking laugh, then shouted at the top of his voice. "NOW!"

Just then, more skeletons streamed into the chamber. There were at least eighty of them, easily outnumbering the villagers. There was no way they could survive this assault.

"Quickly, everyone this way!" Blaster shouted. He'd gotten the iron door open and was now sprinting into the dark passage.

The other villagers saw the open door and followed Blaster. Cutter reached out and grabbed Watcher by the arm and ran for the passage, ignoring Watcher's complaints.

"The ancient relic . . . we must go back for it!"

"Be quiet and run if you wish to live," Cutter said.

More skeletons were moving into the chamber, but for some reason, they were not firing. The monsters were allowing all the NPCs to escape through the dark passage. It felt wrong to Watcher, but there was little he could do about it.

Once all the surviving and wounded villagers entered the passage, Watcher sealed it up with blocks of cobblestone. That instantly plunged the tunnel into darkness.

Someone up ahead pulled out a torch and placed it onto the wall, letting Watcher see his surroundings clearly.

The passage was made of obsidian and extended for maybe thirty blocks, then opened into a huge cylindrical chamber, also made of the same dark blocks. A faint purple glow shimmered from behind the dark cubes, just like with the diamond blocks in the previous room; likely the obsidian was also unbreakable.

The villagers gathered in the center of the chamber, their voices echoing with fear and panic off the dark, shimmering walls.

"What kind of place is this?" someone asked.

Watcher moved into the chamber. Along the walls, wooden tables and chairs stood in disarray, many of them crumbling due to the ravages of time. Groups of bookcases stood along the opposite wall, following the curve of the cylindrical room, the shelves empty and covered with dust. It had the look of some kind of meeting chamber, though it was clear it had not been used for centuries. The villagers quickly searched the room for another exit, but found none.

Just then, that terrible hollow laugh floated down to them from high above. Watcher glanced upward and found Rusak staring down at them from a single hole high up in the cylindrical wall, near the cobblestone ceiling.

"Well, well, well . . . it seems we've caught a bunch of thieves." The skeleton general laughed again, his jaw clicking. "Do you know what we do with villagers who try to steal from the warlocks' War Room?"

None of the villagers spoke.

"We drown them." Rusak laughed again. "Feel free to try and break the obsidian walls. Sadly, I think you'll find they are enchanted and indestructible. To think I get credit for destroying a wizard . . . it's a great day, a great day indeed." The skeleton glared down at Watcher. "Oh, and one more thing: thank you for this enchanted relic." He held the mirrored helmet before the small opening so all could see it. "I don't know what it does, but I'm sure it'll bring great power to the skeleton nation. Good bye, villagers. Ha ha ha . . . Come on, skeletons. We must return to the Hall of Pillars, to present our new treasures to the skeleton warlord."

The skeleton's face disappeared from the hole, then water came gushing from it. The liquid fell down the wall of the chamber, then began filling the room. The level slowly crept higher and higher.

"What do we do?" Mapper asked. "The water level is getting higher."

"Maybe the water will stop," Planter said. "Maybe it'll run out."

Cleric shook his head. "No, this is ocean water . . . I can taste the salt. That monster has opened that block to the Eastern Ocean. It will fill this chamber all the way to the top."

"What do we do?" Mapper asked again.

Cutter moved to the walls of the chamber with his diamond sword in his hands. He swung the blade at the dark wall with all his strength. The diamond edge hit the dark cube, causing a shower of sparks to fly out in all directions, but when he ran his fingers over the face of the block, he just shook his head.

"Not even a scratch." Cutter put away his sword and pulled out an iron pickaxe.

Watcher held up a hand as others began pulling out their pick axes. "Don't bother, iron tools cannot hurt obsidian, only diamond." The boy pushed through the water, it had now reached his waist, and tables and chairs floated off the ground and circulated around the chamber as the currents pushed everything about. He too ran his hand across the obsidian; the surface was perfectly smooth . . . not even a dent.

"We can't break these walls," Watcher said.

Cutter used his diamond sword on the walls again, this time swinging harder.

"It won't help," Watcher said, but the big NPC ignored the boy and kept swinging until he was exhausted.

"What do we do?" Planter asked. "We can swim as the water level goes up, but when it gets to the ceiling, we'll drown."

"If only the water were solid, we could just stand on it and we'd be okay," Blaster said with a smile, trying to lighten the mood.

"Stand on it . . . of course." Mapper grabbed Watcher by the sleeve and tugged him close. "Those diamond boots we found in the Wizard's Tower. Put them on . . . fast!"

Watcher was confused, but did as the old man asked. He leaned over and removed his leather boots, and replaced them with the shining diamond boots. They were cold to the touch and instantly numbed his fingertips.

"Now, stand on this table." Mapper pointed to an old table floating off the ground.

Watcher stepped up on it. Instantly it became covered with an icy sheen.

"Now walk."

The old man gave Watcher a sudden shove. Instead of falling into the water, the water underfoot froze instantly, allowing him to walk across the sheet of newly formed ice. Other villagers moved onto the frozen surface, but it quickly melted as Watcher moved away.

"We need more people with these boots," Mapper said.

Watcher quickly distributed four more pair of the Frost Walker boots. Planter, Winger, Cleric, and Mapper all donned a pair of the shining boots and ran around the chamber, freezing the water under their feet. The other villagers quickly climbed up onto the icy layer. As the water rose, the new level was quickly changed to ice, keeping everyone from drowning.

"This is great and all," Cutter said, "but we're getting closer to the ceiling. It's only cobblestone and I'm sure we could dig through it, but not fast enough to save everyone from drowning . . . or freezing in a block of ice." Cutter glanced at Watcher, an expression of uncertainty on his face. "Somehow, we need to make a big hole in that ceiling."

"You say we need a big hole?" Watcher asked.

Cutter nodded.

"I know just the person who can do that." Watcher turned to Blaster and gave him a smile.

Blaster gave him a devious grin and nodded.

As the water level rose closer to the ceiling, many of the villagers appeared scared. They jumped to the new level of ice when it appeared but kept a wary eye on the cobblestone overhead.

"We're only four blocks away from the ceiling," someone said. "I'm getting scared."

"It's okay," Watcher said. "Blaster will take care of us . . . right, Blaster?"

"Yep," came Blaster's reply.

"Inspiring speech," Winger said with a sarcastic smile.

The boy just shrugged.

They were three blocks from the ceiling now. Blaster pulled out a pick axe and cut a single hole in the ceiling. He then positioned himself directly beneath the hole. With a block of cobblestone in his hands, he jumped upward and placed the stone under his feet on the frozen surface. With his head through the hole, he drew a block of TNT from his inventory and placed it on the ceiling. He jumped off the cobblestone and landed on the slippery frozen surface with a flint and steel in his hands. Flicking the tool, he lit the TNT. The cube instantly began to blink, growing brighter and brighter.

"Everyone get to the walls!" Blaster sprinted away toward the walls.

Some of the ice melted when Watcher and the others stopped running around the room, but no one cared. They all knew the water would protect them from the explosion. The water was now only one layer from the ceiling, the edge of the room ringed with heads bobbing above the surface.

"Did you light it?" Watcher asked. "I don't think it is going to—"

BOOM!

The TNT exploded, tearing a huge hole in the ceiling, allowing the sparkling stars in the clear night sky to shine through the jagged gap.

"Quick, everyone swim to the center and climb out." Watcher was able to get the last words out before the water reached the ceiling.

Pushing off from the ceiling, he swam for the hole in the center of the obsidian tower. Watcher climbed out of the tower, then turned and helped others climb onto the roof of the structure. Villagers crowded the opening, each desperately trying to climb out before they ran out of air. Working frantically, he pulled person after person from the watery trap, grabbing a young girl and pulling her from the water as she took damage, but he couldn't help them fast enough. Some of the villagers flashed red as their oxygen was exhausted and their HP slowly disappeared.

Getting to his knees, he reached down and tried to grab a woman who was flashing red over and over again . . . she didn't have long. She was far from the opening in the ceiling, her arm outstretched; it seemed as if she were pointing to him for some reason. Watcher stuck his head into the water and reached down for her. Grabbing her arm, Watcher pulled her upward, but she disappeared before reaching the air, her HP finally consumed.

"Mother!" A young girl wailed with grief, then collapsed to the ground.

Watcher pulled himself out of the water and sat back, stunned at the feeling of the woman's wrist in his grip at one instant, then gone the next. She had perished in his grasp; he hadn't done enough to save her.

"How many did we lose?" Watcher asked.

Planter moved to his side and placed a gentle hand on his shoulder.

He looked up at her, angry and sad. "How many?"

"Well . . . we lost a dozen people in the fighting, then another four in the water," she answered gently.

"Sixteen?"

Planter nodded.

Those were my friends and neighbors, Watcher thought. *They're all here because the skeletons think I'm some kind of wizard. And now sixteen people have perished . . . for what . . . me?*

Guilt raked through his soul like a hot knife. Glancing at Planter next to him, Watcher realized it could have been her who died, or his sister, or his father or . . . it didn't matter who it could be; he wasn't worth more than the life of another. *How many more would die because of me?*

"This was my fault," Watcher said, his voice growing weak. "I led those people to their deaths. I've failed again."

"There's no time to assign blame," Cutter said. "Right now, we need to get off this tower and get somewhere safe, and anywhere is safer than this terrible . . . what did that monster call it?"

"The War Room," Blaster said.

"Right, the Warlock's War Room . . . it's no place for us." Cutter reached down and helped Watcher to his feet. "Right now, we need someplace safe to figure out what we're gonna do, and I think that beach over there is a better place than on top of this tower."

"I think you're right," Planter added. "Come on, everyone, let's swim for the shore."

She put a hand on Watcher's arm, trying to reassure him, then turned and leapt off the tower, landing with a splash in the Eastern Ocean. The others followed her example and jumped off the tower, then swam for the shore, until he and Er-Lan were the last to leave.

"Guilt is a difficult burden to bear," the zombie said. "Er-Lan learned that with the passing of mother. But Er-Lan knew mother would not want this zombie to just give up. And those who were lost here believed in Watcher, and would also want Watcher to continue the fight. Giving up dishonors their memory."

And with that, Er-Lan jumped off the tower and swam for the shore, leaving Watcher atop the obsidian tower. He glanced back at the hole in the ceiling. The image of that woman disappearing as he held onto her wrist haunted his mind. He just wanted to curl up and die, but he knew he had to move. There were people on the beach who were relying on him, and he couldn't let them down like he did the sixteen NPCs in this tower.

He glanced toward the shore. Many of the villagers struggled in the water. Some swam toward the line of barrier blocks and climbed up on the invisible path while others just swam for shore. The silvery face of the moon shone down upon the landscape, bathing it in its lunar glow. It was slowly dropping behind the tall junglewood trees, settling in for the evening; it would be morning soon. Maybe things would seem better then.

With a sigh, he jumped into the water and swam to the shore, the ocean water mixing with his tears.

CHAPTER 19

The skeletons trudged behind their general, knee deep in the ocean waters. Their bony footprints could be seen in the soft sand, but quickly disappeared as the gentle waves washed them away.

Rusak gazed down at the temporary footprints and smiled. "Let's see if any of the NPC survivors from the War Room can follow us now." He smiled to himself, proud of his cleverness.

"What?" Captain Ratlan asked. "Did you say something?"

"Be quiet," Rusak said. "I said nothing to you."

"Yes sir," the captain replied. He cleared his throat, then spoke again, this time tentatively, as if expecting to be punished. "Ahh . . . sir . . . may I ask . . . umm . . ."

"What is it, Captain? Spit it out."

"Well, the other skeletons were wondering . . . umm . . . where are we heading?" Ratlan glanced around and found the other skeletons had moved back, leaving the captain the only one within arm's length of the general.

Rusak glared at his subordinate, a scowl growing across his bony square face, but then he noticed the other skeletons skulking behind the captain and looking away. He growled at the soldiers, then slapped Ratlan on the shoulder and laughed, impressed with the captain's courage.

"You should always speak with courage, Captain Ratlan. Never act from a position of weakness, for others will lose respect for you." Rusak glared at the other soldiers. "These pathetic skeletons were afraid to stand with you, and for that, they will all do extra duty when we get back to the Hall of Pillars."

"But our home is not to the south, it's to the southwest." Captain Ratlan looked confused. "Where are we going?"

The general reached into his inventory and removed the map given to him by the skeleton warlord, Rakir. "This map was given to our warlord by the wither king, Krael."

"Yes, general, I know."

"Then you'll know many of the ancient structures built by the wizards and warlocks are marked on this map."

Ratlan nodded.

"To the south is a sacred warlock building called the Swordsmith's Workshop." Rusak pointed to a bright red spot on the map. "The warlocks of old constructed many weapons in this structure. Most of them are hidden away in the Great Weapons Vault, the location of which has been lost to time. But Krael thinks there is still a great weapon hidden there. We will find that weapon and bring it back to the skeleton warlord."

"What does it say around this Workshop?" Ratlan asked.

Rusak examined the map. "It says 'Bad Lands'. That's the area around the Workshop. The stories say the great enchantments used by the warlocks to construct weapons in the Workshop were so powerful, they actually cracked the surface of the Far Lands. The ground is now shattered, with rivers of lava and pools of poison covering the landscape."

Ratlan smiled. "Sounds fantastic."

The skeleton general nodded.

"Do you think that wizard survived?" the captain asked.

Rusak pondered the question for a moment. "I suspect the wizard used some kind of enchantment to take the HP from his companions, so he'd stay alive while the others perished. The NPC wizards from the Great War had no honor and attacked the warlocks for no reason other than greed. They wanted to take the Far Lands for themselves and exterminate the monsters. If the warlocks hadn't been there to resist, we'd likely have been wiped out. I'm sure this wizard will try that again. Me and the skeleton warlord aren't gonna let that happen. We're going to destroy any other wizards we can find before they can even think about gathering an army."

A squid swam into the shallow water, curious about the creatures walking through the water. Rusak pulled out his bow and fired three quick shots at the creature, erasing it from the Far Lands.

Ratlan smiled and congratulated his general, but Rusak ignored the false praise.

"You saw all the villagers with that boy-wizard . . . right?" the general asked.

"Sure."

"My fear is there might be more descendants of the wizards amongst the villagers. These young wizards of the Far Lands might be awakening to their power and will start forming their armies. If we don't gather all these ancient weapons from the past, we may be too late to stop them. Wizards only understand one thing . . . and that's power. If we have greater weapons, then they'll keep their heads down and hide until they have their own ancient weapons."

"We must stop that," Ratlan said.

"Of course. But while those idiotic villagers are hiding their wizards, and pretending to be peaceful, the skeleton nation, led by our great skeleton warlord, Rakir, will lead the charge. We'll destroy every last one of them before they even know what's going on. This time, the Great War will have a different ending, and no villagers will be left alive to tell anyone what happened."

The general laughed, then Ratlan smiled and joined in.

"Soon, the Far Lands will belong to the monsters, and be ruled by skeletons!" Rusak glanced to the west as the moon moved behind the foliage of the jungle and began setting behind the western horizon. He wished for more darkness to hide his trail, but the inevitability of sunrise was something he couldn't avoid. "I just hope we've seen the last of that boy-wizard."

The monsters continued trudging through the water, too far away from the War Room to see the villagers leaping off the roof in the darkness and swimming for the shoreline.

CHAPTER 20

Watcher moved onto the beach and stared into the terrifying Creeper's Jungle, his keen eyes trying to pierce the foliage and find the explosive denizens that were likely watching him. Light from the rising sun barely leaked through the blocks of leaves and tree trunks, creating a green background and slowly brightening red backdrop. Under different circumstances, it might have been beautiful, but with what just happened in the obsidian tower, Watcher saw little beauty in the scene.

Drawing Needle, Watcher took a step closer to the treeline as more villagers moved out of the chilly ocean water, their weapons drawn as well. A rustling sound could be heard in the jungle, as if creatures were moving about behind the tall trees and thick bushes, but the sound grew quieter; the creepers were apparently prepared to wait for a more advantageous time to attack.

With a sigh of relief, he turned to watch the rest of the villagers step out of the surf. As he swung around, Needle grew bright when it pointed to the south. *That's strange*, Watcher thought.

"I think everyone's out of the water now." Cleric

glanced at Cutter, then to Watcher. "Which way do we go now?"

"The skeleton said they were heading for the Hall of Pillars." Cutter turned to Mapper. "Any idea where that's located?"

The old man knelt on the sand, then pulled out the linked ender chest from his inventory. Carefully, he opened the lid and opened one of the books. Paging through the ancient tome, he finally smiled when he found what he sought.

"This book shows a map of the Far Lands. We're here, at the War Room. It shows the Hall of Pillars to the southwest." Mapper took out a compass and looked down at it, they pointed into the jungle. "The skeletons should have gone that way." He pointed into the jungle, then closed the map, then opened another book. He ruffled through the ancient pages, searching for something, a concerted scowl across his brow.

"Mapper, what are you doing?" Watcher asked, intrigued.

The old man wasn't listening, his concentration was completely focused on the text before him. He flipped through a couple more pages, then stopped and read.

"Mapper . . . what are you doing?" A rustling of leaves came from the Creeper's Jungle. Watcher took a step toward the sound, his sword held at the ready. A bright-yellow ocelot walked out of the thick undergrowth, growled at him, then disappeared back into the jungle.

"Oh no." Mapper sounded worried . . . no, terrified.

Watcher moved back to the old man.

"What is it?" Planter asked, kneeling at his side.

"Look." Mapper pointed at the book lying within the shadowy interior of the ender chest.

Planter stared into the chest, her delicate lips mouthing words as she read, then her eyes grew wide with shock. She looked at Mapper and the old man nodded, both seeming terrified of what they had just read.

"What is it?" Watcher asked, worried.

Planter looked up at him with her bright-green eyes, fear behind the emerald orbs. "That helmet thing the skeleton took from you . . . this book describes what it is."

"It's called the Helm of Calling," Mapper explained, his voice low, as if he were afraid of being overheard. "That skeleton can put it on and call monsters to his side, growing his army."

"How many monsters can he gather with this . . ." Watcher turned to Mapper. "What's it called?"

"The Helm of Calling."

"Right . . . how many monsters can he gather, a hundred? Two hundred?"

Mapper took a nervous swallow and cast his gaze around their company, then brought it back to Watcher. "All of them."

"What do you mean, all of them?" Now Watcher's voice was getting softer.

Mapper closed the book, then carefully closed the lid to the ender chest. "The Helm of Calling can bring all monsters to his side, not just from the Far Lands, but from all of the Overworld, too."

"So, you're saying that skeleton could call just a couple hundred monsters right away?" Blaster asked. "But he could also bring thousands and thousands of monsters to his banner, and all he'd have to do is wait for them to arrive?"

The old man nodded.

A strained silence spread across the company, each NPC glancing at the other with expressions of panic and fear on their square faces.

Watcher thought about that woman he held in his grasp when she disappeared. As the memory filled his mind, he was surprised to notice there had been a look of gratitude on her square face just before she disappeared. And then he realized, right before grabbing her wrist, Watcher had helped her daughter out of the water. The mother had been pushing her daughter to the surface, and Watcher had pulled her out. He'd saved the girl, but at the cost of the woman's life . . . and the mother had been grateful, and somehow, Watcher knew she had faith in him.

Maybe I can help these people, he thought. *If in her dying moment, that mother had faith in me, then maybe I could have faith in myself as well. Maybe there's a way to stop these skeletons.*

"We need to run and hide before the monster horde gets here," one of the villagers said.

"Hide underground . . . we could hide in caves."

"No, we could go to the Nether."

"Or hide in the deserts."

"Or maybe we could—"

"We can't hide," Watcher said, his voice weak. "Running from our problem is not a solution. Problems always have a way of finding you, no matter how much you hide from them. We must face this . . . everyone is relying on us."

"This is impossible," Blaster said. "That monster could put on that helmet and have an instant army. They already outnumber us, but with that Helm of Calling . . . we have no chance."

"Then why didn't he use it when he took it from me?" Watcher turned his gaze on the boy, then turned and stared at Cutter. "You fought him, Cutter, as did I. That was a seasoned warrior, used to doing his duty, right?"

Cutter nodded thoughtfully. "I could tell by the way he moved and spoke, he was a soldier and a leader."

"But a soldier first," Watcher said. "He's trained to take orders, and I bet he was ordered to bring these magical relics to the skeleton warlord."

He thought about the gratitude in that woman's eyes again. Was she thanking Watcher for saving her daughter . . . or for saving everyone? Maybe she knew something about Watcher he didn't fully realize. He found

Cleric in the crowd and moved so he stood directly in front of him.

"Think about it, Dad, if that skeleton general used the Helm of Calling, he could probably take control of the entire skeleton nation. The warlord would never trust this task to someone who might betray him. That general was trusted to find these relics, then bring them back without using them."

"I don't know, son. You're making a lot of guesses in your theory . . . guesses that could get a lot of people hurt if you're wrong," Cleric said.

The image of that woman in the tower appeared in his mind. She was pointing at him again, a thankful expression on her face. But then, dreamlike words came from her mouth and echoed throughout his mind.

Watcher, you were meant for greatness. The words sounded as if they were coming from a hundred miles away, or maybe from a hundred years ago . . . he wasn't sure which. *You can do this, as long as you are true and face that which must be faced.*

The skeleton warlord.

The image of the woman nodded her head. *Have faith in yourself and in those around you. Your friends will not abandon you in your hour of need.* And then the strange voice disappeared from his mind.

"Watcher . . . are you okay?" Planter was shaking him, her face concerned.

"What?" Watcher glanced around and found everyone looking at him.

"You just stopped moving and stood there, as if you were paralyzed." There was worry in Planter's voice. "Are you okay?"

Watcher nodded, then turned and glanced at everyone around him. "I know it seems like I'm asking the impossible, but that Helm cannot make it back to the skeleton warlord." He saw the young girl whose mother had died in Watcher's grasp and put an arm around her. She wept and buried her face in Watcher's still-wet smock. "I cannot stand aside and watch that monster destroy everyone that's important to me. I must catch that skeleton general, no matter the cost. For if I don't stop him . . . who will?"

"But son, this is an impossible task. Those skeletons already outnumber us, even if the general doesn't use that magical helmet." Cleric seemed scared for his son. "And besides, we don't even know where they went. Do you see any footprints in the sand? It's like they disappeared."

"I know it seems impossible, but it's not." Watcher glanced at Planter and smiled; her presence gave him courage. "There are two things what will help us to be victorious."

"What's that?" Cutter asked, the big warrior standing close to Planter . . . a little too close. He looked doubtfully down at Watcher.

"First, that skeleton general thinks we're all dead. If he thought we might escape from that drowning trap, then there'd be skeletons here on the shoreline, waiting to finish off the survivors. So, we'll have the element of surprise on our side."

"That's great, but we don't even know where they went," Cutter said.

Watcher smiled, then drew Needle and held it high over his head. He pointed it toward the ocean, then slowly turned to the north. The villagers backed away and watched the boy, confusion evident on their faces. He continued to turn until the tip of his blade was pointing westward, toward the Creeper's Jungle. Turning more, he felt the blade vibrate slightly in his grip, as if anticipating something. When it was pointing to the south, the blade lit up with a bright purple glow. The villagers gasped in surprise.

"Needle and that Helm are connected, somehow," Watcher said. "I can't explain it, but this blade will point us in the right direction. So, we have the element of surprise, *and* we know where they're going; the skeletons went to the south. They probably walked in the water to hide their footprints."

"But what's to the south?" Planter asked.

"There's another ancient structure in that direction," Mapper said. "But we don't want to go there."

"Why's that?" the villager asked, moving closer to the old man.

"It's in the Bad Lands," Mapper explained.

"What are the Bad Lands?" Winger asked.

"The books I've read have many theories, but most agree the land has been broken by great magical powers." Mapper looked at Watcher, an expression of sympathy on his face. "These lands are covered with lava rivers and poison streams. One of the books suggests there is an ancient castle at the center of the Bad Lands that protects a great weapon. That's probably what the skeleton general is after." The old man glanced around at his companions. "In general, it's a pretty terrible and dangerous place."

"Sounds lovely," Blaster said, then smiled.

"So, you want to chase after a skeleton that can call hundreds of monsters to his side, and follow him into a biome that has been shattered by magic," Cutter said.

Watcher nodded. "I don't *want* to go after this monster, but I know I must."

The big warrior shook his head and lowered his gaze to the ground. Watcher looked at the rest of the villagers; they were all stepping back, their eyes focused away from Watcher. He stared at Planter. His friend looked back with her bright green eyes, but then shook her head and stared down at her feet. Only one pair of eyes would return his gaze, and they belonged to Er-Lan.

"I know I can do this . . . I know I can." Watcher put a finger under Planter's chin and gently lifted her head so they were looking eye to eye. "I know I'm terrified when those skeletons are up close and within arm's reach, but I can't quit."

Just then, the sun rose above the jungle's treeline, painting the villagers with its warm, yellow glow. The light shone down upon Planter's blond hair, making it appear as if it were liquid gold spilling down her shoulder. He reached out and took her hand in his.

"I know this seems impossible, but I know we can do this if we work together."

Planter just sighed, then pulled her hand back and lowered her gaze again.

Watcher was stunned. He was sure she'd be with him, but now he felt totally alone. "I understand. This seems insane, but it must be done, and I'll do it alone. All of you should hide somewhere, just in case I'm not successful at stopping that skeleton general from reaching his warlord. Maybe you'll be able to live a full life before the monsters reach your door."

Slowly, he backed away from his friend, but bumped into someone standing behind him. Turning, he found Er-Lan standing there, his gaze fixed on Watcher's.

"Watcher will not be alone," Er-Lan said. "A hero doesn't have to be big and strong, like Cutter. A hero can be the smallest and weakest person, yet do great deeds if people believe in them." The zombie put an arm around Watcher, his razor-sharp claws sparkling in the morning light. He stared into Watcher's square face. "Er-Lan believes in Watcher. This zombie will be at his side, no matter how much danger or fear. Family sticks together . . . no matter what. Watcher taught that to Er-Lan, and it will always be remembered."

Watcher's bright red parrot flew down and landed on his shoulder, followed by another and another. In seconds, a half-dozen birds were perched on Watcher's shoulders, an equal number on the zombie. Overhead, the flock of brightly colored creatures flew in a circle around the party, their voices squawking the zombie's words, *"Watcher will not be alone . . . Watcher will not be alone . . . Watcher will not be alone."*

Watcher looked up and smiled, then patted the zombie on the back and started walking to the south.

"Wait," a voice said.

Watcher turned. Planter looked up at the birds, then whistled and held out a hand. One of the parrots flew down and landed on the girl's palm, then scurried along her arm until it stood on her shoulder. She drew the enchanted golden axe, then walked toward her friend.

"You aren't going without me," she said. "Family sticks together."

Watcher nodded gratefully and choked back a tear.

Another whistle pierced the air. Cleric stepped forward with a dark-green bird on his shoulder, his eyes filled with hope. "Family," was all the old man said.

More whistles cut through the squawking cacophony as villager after villager stepped forward, a bird on every shoulder.

"Family stays together . . ."

"We're with you, Watcher . . ."

"Family is everything . . ."

Their words filled Watcher with courage.

The daughter of the drowned mother then stepped forward, a blue parrot on one shoulder, a yellow on the other. "My mother would want me to help. You didn't give up on her, so I'm not giving up on you."

Finally, tears of gratitude, or hope, or released guilt escaped from Watcher's eyes.

Lastly, Cutter gave off the loudest and most shrill whistle of them all. A handful of birds all soared down to him and landed on his shoulders. He turned his head and scowled at the parrots. "I don't like birds!" He shook his shoulders, trying to dislodge the animals, but they refused to leave. The villagers laughed, only to receive a glare from the warrior. "But I'll still be at your side, boy. These people believe in you, and I do as well. You brought us together when we were ready to give up. That makes this your army now and you're in command. Give me an order and I'll do whatever you say."

Watcher glanced at his companions . . . no, his family, and smiled as small cube-shaped tears tumbled down his cheeks. He was about to say something when a voice from farther down the beach yelled to them.

"Come on, we have some skeletons to catch!" It was Blaster, wearing multi-colored armor, the chest plate, pants, boots and helmet all from a different color set. He seemed to merge with the many-hued birds that clung to the leather.

"He looks like one of the birds," Cutter said with a smile.

The rest of the army laughed.

"Come on, everyone, Blaster's right," Watcher said. "We have a skeleton to catch and we can't do it standing around here. It's time to run!"

Instantly, all the parrots took flight as the family of NPCs sprinted to the south, chasing their terrible and dangerous prey.

CHAPTER 21

The skeletons trudged through the stagnant waters of the swamp. The murky water reached up to their bony knees, making it difficult to walk. A family of green slimes was bouncing cautiously out of bow range, watching the invaders but unwilling to come near. All creatures knew to be wary of skeletons and their arrows.

"General, the villagers are following," a skeleton shouted. It was one of the scouts sent back to watch for anyone following.

"What?" Rusak bellowed in disbelief.

The skeleton was out of breath, having sprinted to catch up to the company of monsters. He looked cartoonishly small next to the hulking form of the general. But that was what made this monster such a great scout; with his diminutive size came the ability to hide easily, as well as great speed.

"Tell me what you saw."

The scout slogged through the mire, moving closer to his commander. "The boy-wizard leads a group of villagers. There are many warriors there, but elderly NPCs as well." The scout stopped to take another breath. "I thought they had all been destroyed."

"As did I." Rusak stopped walking and considered the problem.

"How did that wizard do it?" Ratlan asked, shocked. "He must have used powerful magic to get out of that trap."

"Perhaps." General Rusak stared at the scout. "I'm more curious as to how they found our trail."

"Perhaps that wizard is stronger than we thought." Captain Ratlan sounded scared. "He must have great powers."

"Indeed," Rusak replied, then focused on the scout again. "Did they see you?"

"No, General. I hid in the water, then moved to islands filled with vine-covered trees." The tiny little skeleton stood tall, though he was still dwarfed by his commander. "They did not see me, and I ran as fast as I could. They are only a few hours behind us."

"Excellent, go back to your position as forward scout. I don't want to stumble into any surprises up ahead."

"Yes, sir." The lithe skeleton took off, running much faster than a normal skeleton.

"That was a clever idea to send that skeleton back to see if we were being followed," Captain Ratlan said.

Rusak scowled. "I don't need your approval."

"I'm sorry, sir." Ratlan took a step back.

The general relaxed a bit. "I've learned to never assume an enemy is gone, even if it seems impossible. I have no idea how they escaped that trap in the War Room. I would have figured all the villagers would have drowned. That boy-wizard's magical powers must be growing. He is indeed dangerous and must be destroyed."

The captain nodded his agreement.

Glancing at their surroundings, Rusak considered how he would use this terrain to their advantage. Small islands dotted the shallow waters, with oak trees standing tall on the tiny chunks of land, each draped with long, hanging vines. Lily pads floated on the still and stinking waters, allowing the skeletons to occasionally step out of the waters and check their surroundings. Off to the left stood a witch's hut, the building standing atop four legs.

Rusak smiled. "Did you see that old hag's face when she saw our warriors?"

Ratlan nodded, remembering. "She tried to defend herself by throwing poison on our skeletons . . . what a fool."

"She was obviously ignorant about the undead," Rusak said. "Poison has no effect on skeletons. If the hag had used potions of healing on our skeletons, then she might have done some harm . . . NPCs are such fools. Our warriors enjoyed destroying her."

"Was there anything useful inside her hut?" the captain asked.

"Just a few bones and some bone meal. It will feed a couple of our soldiers, but not many."

"What do you want do about the villagers that are following us?" Captain Ratlan asked.

"We're going to set a little trap for the NPCs. You see those two steep hills up ahead?" He pointed to a pair of hills covered with trees, long, stringy vines hanging from the branches.

Captain Ratlan nodded.

"We're gonna lead them through that pass. When they're knee-deep in water and between those two hills, your two squads of archers will step out from behind the vines and open fire." Rusak reached up and scratched at the scar that ran down his face and across his red and useless eye. "You'll destroy as many as possible, and slow them down while the rest of the army continues toward the Swordsmith's Workshop. The villagers have been finding some important relics, like this Helm of Calling, here." He pointed to the shining, silver helmet under his arm. "Perhaps there are more at the Workshop."

"But what if the villagers won't slow down?" Ratlan

asked, an uncertain look on his pale face. "What if they attack us? We are outnumbered."

Rusak grabbed the skeleton by the collar of his iron chestplate and yanked him close. "They will be in the water, fool. How fast do you think they can move?"

"Well . . . I mean, what if—"

"I don't care about 'what if's'. If you're too afraid, let me know and I'll find another to promote to Captain."

"No sir, I'm not afraid." Ratlan stood tall, bony chin held high. "We will stop them."

"You better. If those villagers get through that pass without slowing down, and you are still alive, I'll be most displeased." Rusak leaned forward and leered over the captain.

The captain shrunk back, intimidated, and lowered his gaze to the ground. "We will not fail you."

"Very well. Take your archers and get onto the hills. I'll leave a trail for the villagers to follow."

"Yes, sir." The captain saluted, then trudged through the knee-high water, motioning to his squads to follow.

While the soldiers veered off and headed for the hills, Rusak put the Helm of Calling into his inventory, then put away his bow and drew his long, iron broadsword. It sparkled with magical enchantments, producing a purple glow and giving the general the faintest splash of color.

"You, private," Rusak boomed, pointing at one of the skeletons.

The monster turned toward his general, then pushed through the muck to reach his commander. "Yes, general."

"Turn around and face away from me."

The skeleton did as he was instructed, for to disobey the general meant instant death. In this case, it didn't really matter if he obeyed or not; the fate was the same. Raising his blade high in the air, General Rusak brought it down upon the skeleton, tearing into the monster's HP. He hit him again, destroying the defenseless skeleton. A handful of bones, along with his bow and arrows, fell to the ground, floating on the surface of the water.

"Thank you for volunteering, private. You are the beginning of the trail that will draw the villagers into our trap."

The general smiled, then pushed onward through the smelly swamp water, driving the skeletons faster and faster, occasionally finding more volunteers to keep the trail easily visible.

CHAPTER 22

Watcher plodded through the knee-deep water, the putrid smell of the swamp making him want to gag. He stepped up onto a lily pad, then jumped to a block of dirt, then leapt to another lily pad, glad to be out of the muck for a moment. The army moved slowly through the swamp, but they knew it was the right direction. Needle kept glowing as it pointed toward the ancient relic carried by the skeleton general.

"Are they still heading in the same direction?" Cutter was at the front of the formation, his diamond sword in his strong hand.

The big warrior stopped and waited for Watcher to catch up.

"So far, they're still heading south." Watcher turned to the east. Needle dimmed, then grew bright again when he brought it back to their original direction.

"Maybe they're actually running from us," Cutter said with a smile.

Planter laughed and slapped the big NPC on the back. He glanced at her and placed a hand on her shoulder for just a moment.

I hate the way she laughs at his jokes, Watcher thought. *He's not that funny.*

This had never bothered Watcher before, but for some reason, it really got to him now. And then he saw it: Cutter placed a hand on Planter's shoulder.

Did it linger there a bit too long? Did he brush his fingers down her arm like Cleric used to do with Watcher's mom?

"I don't like the way he looks at her," Watcher whispered to himself. "I wonder if he likes her . . . does she like Cutter?" Icicles of fear stabbed into Watcher's soul . . . *am I too late?*

He felt angry, but it was something different . . . something he hadn't experienced before. Watcher knew he didn't hate Cutter, but right now, he couldn't stand looking at the warrior.

He jumped back into the muck and pushed his way through the swamp, turning away from the pair as Planter giggled again, then stepped up onto a nearby lily pad, happy to get his feet out of the murky waters. He glanced back at the army, Planter and Cutter at the edge of his vision.

Focus, Watcher, check on the people who are counting on you. Watcher's internal voice was angry, but now it was focused at himself. The army was strung out in a haphazard formation, with no thought given to how they marched and their defenses.

"I don't like how exposed we are out there," Watcher said.

"What?" Cutter asked.

Planter had moved off to walk next to Winger.

"I said I don't like how exposed we are out here."

"What do you suggest?" Cutter asked.

The young boy rubbed his square chin and he thought. He glanced at the two hills that seemed to be in their path, the trail leading between them. "I want to put the archers on the outer edge of the formation. If the skeletons attack, it will be with bows first."

Cutter nodded, but said nothing.

"I remember seeing some of the skeletons with swords. When they get close, they'll use their blades instead of bows, but I suspect they aren't very good with them. That's where we'll have the advantage; the skeletons can't compete with your swordsmen up close."

Cutter smiled, silently accepting the compliment.

I hate that I just complimented him. . . . Focus, Watcher . . . focus.

"We'll have the archers on the outer edge, then your swordsmen behind them. Also, I'm gonna distribute the Frost Walker boots, as Mapper calls them, to our best fighters. We have about ten pairs in total; I want to use them effectively. The elderly, sick and wounded should be at the center where they can be protected. Right now, they're all just spread out in no particular order. We need to be prepared."

"But I don't see any skeletons nearby," Cutter said. "Why does it matter right now?"

"The problem isn't with the skeletons you can see," a voice said from behind. "Rather it's with the ones you cannot see."

Watcher turned and found his father, Cleric, smiling up at him.

"Always prepare the battlefield before the battle starts; that's what a wise commander does," his dad said.

Watcher nodded.

"But there isn't a battle going on," Cutter said.

"Not yet," Cleric added.

Cutter considered the words, then nodded. "Watcher, you're in command. This army is following *you* to the Bad Lands, not me. Give the command, and the warriors will do as you say. If they don't, they'll have to answer to me."

Watcher gave the warrior a scowl. *Why is he being so nice?* He jumped off the lily pad and landed with a splash in the mire, some of the murky water splashing on Cutter's ornate armor. Watcher smiled spitefully, then moved to the archers and told them where to go, then collected the weaker villagers and put them at the center of their formation, surrounded by swordsmen. Watcher put Winger in command of the right flank of archers, while he and Planter would be with the left. As he positioned the troops a voice shouted out from in front of the army.

"I found bones up here." A villager suddenly stood, his grayish-green armor making him difficult to distinguish from the swamp.

Watcher moved toward the individual. As he drew near, he saw a huge grin form on the NPC's face; instantly, he knew it was Blaster, their forward scout.

"It looks like skeleton bones," Blaster said when Watcher and Cutter reached his side. "I found them just floating here with the monster's bow and arrows."

Watcher took the weapon as Blaster threw the bones aside.

"Why would they just leave these bones here?" Winger asked as she approached. "It doesn't make sense. They knew we'd see them."

"Maybe the skeletons don't know we're following them," Planter said.

"They know, alright." Blaster removed his leather cap, allowing his black tangle of curls to spring outward as if trying to take flight. He scratched his head, then replaced the cap. "Every now and then I see a skeleton hiding in a tree or lying low in the water. They know we're here, and they're probably watching us right now."

They all glanced around as if hoping to spot a skeleton.

Blaster laughed. "*You* won't see them. These skeletons are crafty and careful; they've been trained well."

"If they're watching us, then let's give them something to be afraid of." Cutter glanced at Watcher. The boy gave him a nod. "Everyone, we're gonna speed up . . . it's time to run." He turned back to Watcher and the others. "We're gonna put some pressure on the skeletons. If they want to watch us, fine. They're gonna watch us getting closer and closer. Eventually, they'll make a mistake, and we'll be there to catch them."

"So, your plan is to charge forward?" Winger asked. Cutter nodded.

"Clever idea," she said, a sarcastic tone to her voice.

"Let's all get back to our positions," Watcher said. "Cutter is right. We need to close the distance so we can see where these monsters are going. They must be heading for that ancient building in the Bad Lands. And being in that terrible-sounding place, I bet it's not a wizard's tower, but it will be a monster place, built by the warlocks."

"I'm not sure I like the idea of the skeletons reaching a warlock building first," Cleric said.

"Then we better hurry up." Cutter moved forward, running as best he could through the shallow bog.

Watcher and Planter took up their positions on the left side of the army. As they trudged through the muck of the swamp, he looked up at the two hills on either side of them. Scanning the hillside, he looked for threats, but all he saw were thick vines hanging from the branches of oak trees.

Suddenly, ghostly white shapes emerged on both sides. Skeletons pushed through the drooping foliage and took aim at the villagers, their pointed shafts notched and ready to fire; the group was under attack from both sides.

"It's a trap!" Watcher shouted as fifty arrows took flight and rained down upon them like deadly hail.

CHAPTER 23

"Everyone, hold something over your head," Cleric shouted.

The old man pulled an iron chest plate and held it over his head. Others used pieces of armor or blocks of stone or dirt; anything to shield them from the arrows that were about to strike.

Watcher stood there, staring at the arrows, terrified beyond the ability to think. Planter rushed to his side and knocked him into the water, then pulled out a wooden shield. Holding it over her head, she protected both of them as arrows thudded into the wooden rectangle.

"Get up." Planter reached down and grabbed Watcher by the collar and pulled him to his feet. "We need to do something, fast."

"Yes, do something." Watcher glanced around at the army.

The archers and swordsmen were all looking to him, waiting for him to give some command. Even Cutter was waiting for him. The big warrior glared at Watcher for a moment, expecting him to do something, then stopped waiting and gave his own commands.

"Swordsmen, get ready to—"

"No! I know what to do," Watcher shouted.

He placed a block of dirt onto the soggy ground, then stood on it so as to have a good view of the battlefield. "Archers . . . ready . . . FIRE!"

The villagers returned fire just as the skeletons launched another volley.

"Every other archer . . . protect, just as I taught you."

Half the archers pulled out pieces of leather armor, then held them over their companions, the two soldiers hiding under the makeshift shields. The arrows struck the armor instead of hitting the villagers.

"Fire again." Watcher turned to the swordsmen. "Those with Frost Walker boots, put them on and get to the shore as fast as you can. The rest of the swordsmen, move to the archers and protect them."

Ten swordsmen and swordswomen put on the Frost Walker boots. Instantly, the water beneath their feet froze solid, allowing them to run across it. Half of them headed for one hill while the rest moved toward the other. As the warriors ran, the archers continued their attack on the skeletons. With a constant rain of arrows falling upon them, the skeletons were forced to remain under cover.

"Archers, advance to the hills." Watcher pulled out his enchanted bow and drew back an arrow. His keen eyes sought out anything white amidst the hanging vines. When he spotted something, he fired, then drew and fired again.

The frost walkers made it to the shore quickly. Now, with swords drawn, they charged up the hill, shields held at the ready. The NPC archers drew closer to the hills, continuing their barrage of arrows as they advanced. When the swordsmen drew near, the archers ceased fire and charged to the shore. The sound of fighting emerged from beneath the branches of the oaks. Shouts of pain, from skeleton and villager alike, filled the air. Watcher knew his friends were getting hurt, but there was only so much he could do from here.

Putting away his bow, he drew Needle and charged up the hill, moving behind what he figured would be the skeletons' position, Planter and a group of archers following behind. Some of the archers drew swords, but most kept to their bows. They pushed through the bushes and ferns until they came upon the enemy formation. Skeletons were standing in an arc, trying to shoot at the swordsmen and swordswomen in front of them. The NPC soldiers kept their shields held high, blocking the nearly constant flow of arrows, just as Watcher had instructed. Some of them had their shields right next to each other, forming a continuous surface of wood and iron, making it impossible for the skeletons to hit any part of their body. But that didn't stop the monsters; they kept firing, unaware of what was creeping up from behind.

Watcher was terrified. All these skeletons, right there in front of him . . . it was like living through a nightmare. He didn't know what to do; his fear of these terrible monsters was overwhelming his mind.

One of the swordsmen yelled as a pointed shaft found a small gap between shields. The warrior dropped to one knee, flashing red as he took damage. The skeletons focused on the gap and all aimed at the wounded villager. The other warriors closed the gap, protecting their friends, but more arrows made it past the barricade, striking the warrior again and again . . . he was close to death.

"NO!" Watcher yelled.

The skeletons suddenly stopped firing and turned toward the sound. Their hateful gazes all fell upon Watcher and his archers.

You aren't gonna hurt my friends, he thought as fury bubbled up from within his soul.

"ATTACK!" With a firm grip on Needle's hilt, Watcher charged, his mind now overwhelmed with rage.

The archers opened fire as Watcher sprinted toward his foe. The skeletons notched arrows and drew back, all of them aiming at the advancing boy, but before they could release, the other swordsmen and swordswomen fell on them from behind. The battle quickly went from a carefully planned set of moves to complete chaos.

With Needle in his hand, Watcher smashed into the skeletons, his enchanted blade streaking to the left and right, faster than the monsters could react. A skeleton attacked to his left, but was suddenly silenced by three quick shots. Glancing over his shoulder, he saw Planter smiling, her enchanted bow in her delicate hands. Before he could thank her, she drew and fired again, hitting another skeleton.

"Come on, let's get this done," a voice said to his right. Watcher turned to see who it was, but only saw a green blur streak through the battlefield, two curved knives reflecting the sunlight; it was Blaster.

Charging after him, Watcher reached the young boy's side. Fighting back to back, they pushed against the skeleton horde, their razor-sharp blades slashing at any creature foolish enough to come within arm's reach. Meanwhile, the archers fired upon the monsters at the edges while the swordsmen and swordswomen slashed at them from behind; the skeletons didn't stand a chance. In minutes, it was over. The last remaining skeletons were given the option to surrender, but none accepted the offer. They fought until the last monster was wiped out.

"We need to keep moving," Watcher said in a loud, clear voice when it was all over. He felt good; his strategy with the Frost Walker boots and archers and shields had worked.

"Why move so quickly?" Blaster asked. "We need a rest."

"The skeleton commander knew these monsters couldn't win this battle." Watcher picked up some arrows dropped by one of the enemy. "He tried to delay us for some reason, and his plan worked. We can't help his plans by staying here longer. We must keep moving.

The skeletons are up to something and we need to do the unexpected."

"And that's continuing to follow them?" Planter asked.

Watcher nodded. "We're gonna sprint along the land for as long as we can, then keep trudging through the swamp. Eventually, we'll reach solid land, and then we'll be able to catch our prey."

"Unless the skeletons are leading us into another trap," Blaster said.

"Possibly," Watcher admitted.

"Come on, everyone," Cutter said in a loud voice. "Listen to Watcher. It's time to run."

Putting away Needle, Watcher pulled out his enchanted bow and sprinted down the hill. He waved to the villagers on the other hill and motioned for them to run as well. With the army split in two, they ran across the sloping ground, slowly gaining on the skeleton army.

But something Blaster said nagged at Watcher's mind.

The skeleton general knows we're following him. Maybe he is leading us into another trap. But without seeing it, I can't figure out what to do . . . what if my plans fail? The thoughts circled through his mind, the doubt and uncertainty slowly chiseling away at his courage. But he knew they had no choice; they had to continue chasing the monsters. The skeletons couldn't be allowed to keep the Helm of Calling. If the skeleton warlord got his hands on that magical relic, it could mean the end for all the villagers of the Far Lands, and maybe for all of Minecraft as well.

CHAPTER 24

General Rusak listened to the distant sounds of battle.

"It seems the villagers fell into our trap." The zombie laughed a deep, guttural laugh that sounded more like the growl of some great prehistoric beast. "I want scouts to go back and see what happened to the villagers. You and you." He pointed with the end of his huge bow. "Get me information and return. Don't get caught and don't be seen . . . understood?"

The two skeletons nodded their heads, expressions of fear on their pale white faces.

"Then go!" Rusak yelled.

The two monsters turned and took off running, sloshing through the shallow water.

"The rest of you, come on, we're heading to the great workshop of the warlock swordsmiths. If the villagers are able to find ancient relics so easily, then we should be able to find some as well."

"Sir, you already have a relic, why not use it and see what it does?" The question came from an archer Rusak didn't know. He was a new addition to the army and the General hadn't learned his name yet.

"What is your name?"

The skeleton looked surprised. "Me? Umm . . . my name is Rassa."

"Do you know anything about ancient relics, Rassa?" The general glared down at the monster.

The skeleton shook his head.

"When the great warlocks made these awesome weapons, they designed them so that the life force of the wielder would power the enchantment. The stronger the weapon, the greater cost to the wielder." He pulled out the Helm of Calling. "Do you want to try this on and see how much of your HP it consumes?"

Rassa shook his head and glanced down at the ground.

"I thought so, but thank you for volunteering to test the next artifact we find."

"But I didn't—"

Rusak raised his hand, silencing the objections. "Come on, everyone, the workshop is just on the other edge of the swamp, in the Bad Lands." The general glared at his soldiers. "Everyone move fast or be left behind as a trail for the villagers to follow."

The monsters instantly moved forward, pushing through the swamp water as fast as they could. The smell from the stagnant waters was terrible, even by skeleton standards, but as they approached the edge of the biome, an aroma of sulfur and ash mixed with the rotten odor.

In the distance, the general could see a strange glow, as if the landscape were on fire. Even the bright afternoon sun could not push back the glow. Many of the monsters in his army also saw the glow and grew concerned, but a glare from their commander was enough motivation to keep trudging through the murky waters.

When they reached the end of the swamp, Rusak smiled. He was tired of walking through the knee-high muck and was glad to have solid ground under his feet again. But before him stood the most depressing and terrifying landscape he'd ever seen: the Bad Lands.

The ground looked as if a giant had smashed it with a hammer as large as a mountain, shattering the surface of Minecraft and leaving behind a spider's web of cracks. Lava filled each of the cracks, some of the boiling streams only a block wide, some much wider. Intermixed with the bright orange tributaries were pools of black, poisonous water covering wide areas of the terrain. An acidic smell rose from the toxic lakes, making it hard to breathe when passing nearby. Rusak made sure he avoided those deadly waters.

The air had a smoky-gray color to it as ash and soot floated up into the air from the rivers of boiling stone. The haze made it difficult to see, but the general knew their goal was at the center of the Bad Lands.

Running through the cracked and broken landscape, Rusak looked for places where they could cross the lava without too much risk. He didn't want to lose any skeletons to the lava if it wasn't necessary. He wove his way around a huge, noxious pool, only to be stopped by a wide river of lava. Pulling blocks of dirt from his inventory, he placed one in the middle of the river. Fortunately, the lava wasn't very deep, and the top of the block stayed above the boiling stone.

"Jump from the bank to the block of dirt," the skeleton commander yelled. "Don't be an idiot and fall in!"

The general jumped to the block of dirt, then sprang to the other side and continued running.

"General Rusak, where is this place you seek?" one of the skeleton lieutenants asked.

"In the Bad Lands, all lava leads to the lake of fire, and that's where we'll find our goal." The huge skeleton pointed to the burning river that cut through the landscape. The lava that bubbled and boiled within its banks slowly oozed along the sinuous channel. "Follow the lava."

The skeletons moved along the edge of the glowing river, the heat of it almost too much to bear. The glow from the molten stone painted each of the pale creatures with an orange hue, making them seem to glow in the afternoon light. Many of them stared down at the deadly liquid with expressions of fear on their bone-white faces.

"Hurry, you fools," Rusak growled. "I want to be at the workshop before nightfall."

He glanced up at the sun. Its bright square face tried to shine through the gray pall that covered the afternoon sky, but all it managed was a faint fuzzy glow that barely managed to penetrate the smoky mist overhead.

"We must go faster." The general shoved one of the skeletons forward.

The monster stumbled and fell to the ground, his bow falling out of his bony fingers and falling into the lava filled stream. The weapon instantly burst into flames.

"Keep moving, all of you, or a bow won't be the only thing that lands in the lava," Rusak growled.

The skeletons moved quicker, scurrying as fast as their pale legs would go. They followed the glowing river, careful to stay beyond arm's reach of their general, crossing narrow tributaries that fed the wide river of fire.

Slowly, a building emerged from the haze. It was a massive castle built from the various colors of stained clay that made up the Bad Lands. Watchtowers sat at the corners of a fortified wall that hugged the castle, their dark and silent windows staring down at them like lifeless eyes. Tall arcs of dark stone jutted up into the air from the imposing wall, curving high up into the open air and out from the barricade like curved blades. The tip of each curled structure glowed bright orange as lava fell from the tip of the arc and splashed down upon the scorched ground, then flowed into the wide Lake of Fire surrounding the structure.

Orange light from the many rivers feeding the Lake of Fire shone upon the fortress, but there was also a faint purple glow to it as well. Magical enchantments, cast many centuries ago, protected the structure from both the ravages of age and the scorching heat of the lava.

The skeleton general approached a bridge that spanned the boiling lake. Two looming towers stood at the far end, daring them to cross. Rusak was unafraid; this was a monster place, and they belonged here. He moved across the bridge and headed into the courtyard, his troops following close behind. Narrow lines of lava flowed underfoot, creating geometric patterns that stretched across the courtyard. Over the glowing channels, cubes of glass kept the molten stone contained and the inhabitants of the castle safe from the lava's burning kiss.

"Search all the rooms. Look for hidden passages, pressure plates, or buttons. We need to find any relics that are here." General Rusak glared at his soldiers. "Break the walls if you must, but find me the magical artifacts that have been tucked away for us."

The general drew his enchanted iron sword, the keen edge nearly glowing in the light of the setting sun. As the skeletons dispersed through the many doorways and passages that opened to the courtyard, General Rusak walked into the main hall. Long tables and chairs lined the edges of the room, with a huge fireplace built in the center. Flames perpetually flickered within the bedrock-lined structure; they'd been burning for as long as any skeleton could remember.

"I will find the secrets that lie within these halls, even if I must destroy every block. There must be a weapon here left behind by the warlocks that can aid us in our quest to control the Far Lands."

Pulling out the Helm of Calling, he stared at the object, the fire at the center of the room painting the reflective helmet with delicate, curved flames. The gems that ringed the top of the object seemed to glow with magical power, something he hadn't noticed before . . . unless they hadn't initially been glowing.

"You know something's here, don't you," the general said to the mirrored Helm. "Perhaps you can help me find my prize."

Staring down at the jeweled armor, Rusak walked slowly through the castle, staring down at the gems at they grew brighter and dimmer, trying to tell the skeleton something he couldn't quite understand . . . yet.

CHAPTER 25

The villagers trudged through the swamp, running across blocks of dirt or lily pads whenever possible, trying to catch their distant prey. But no matter how hard they sloshed through the mucky waters, they never saw the skeleton army.

"I see some of their scouts up ahead." Watcher was standing atop an oak tree that stood on a small island of grassy blocks. The parrot on his shoulder squawked, then flew off to search the land. "There are two of them out there, trying to hide behind some shrubs. I'm sure they see us."

"No reason for us to hide," Cutter said. "They obviously know we're here, or they wouldn't have set that trap for us back on those hills."

"Maybe they're trying to see if any of their skeletons survived the battle." Winger's dark brown hair fell across her face as she glanced at the others. She pulled the rebellious strands back behind an ear and continued. "They probably figured some of the skeletons would have survived. There's no way they knew what we were going to do when we were attacked."

"That's for sure," Planter added, then glanced up proudly at Watcher in the tree.

He looked down at her and smiled, her blond hair glowing bright in the afternoon sun. Planter had morphed from the child he'd made mud pies with when they were little to the beautiful girl she was today. Her smile seemed whiter and her green eyes brighter. He'd never noticed it before, but those green eyes had a magical pull, making him want to just stare into them and never leave their emerald embrace. And then he remembered his father saying something about his mother's brown eyes, how they were like melted chocolate . . . or something like that. It was a long time ago, before she died, but it was something he enjoyed about the woman who was the love of his life.

Is that it? Watcher thought. *Is this love? But what if she doesn't feel the same way?*

Icicles of fear stabbed into him, chilling him to the bone.

Someone said something, but Watcher didn't hear.

Just then something banged on the tree trunk beneath him. It snapped Watcher out of his daze. He stared down at the ground and found Cutter glaring up at him, Planter at his side. They stood close together . . . way too close for his liking, but what could he say? Anger bubbled up within him again, an anger focused at Cutter, though he didn't hate the warrior. In fact, the big warrior was supposed to be his friend.

And then he understood . . . it was jealousy. *I'm jealous of Cutter. Does he like Planter? And does Planter like him?*

This was getting much too confusing. Just being friends was much easier than all these emotions.

"Get down . . . we need to hurry," Cutter said. "I don't like being out here in the swamp at night. The last thing we need is to run into a bunch of slimes . . . or worse."

"I agree," Planter said, nodding.

Watcher scowled.

Mapper moved to the big NPC's side, near a block of dirt. He placed his ender chest on the ground and opened it, then flipped through the book that was, technically, still in the ancient library in the Wizard's Tower. Glancing up at Watcher, he motioned him to come down. The boy quickly moved to his side, then motioned for Cutter to come as well.

"Watcher, Cutter . . . this book shows a map from that ocean structure to the swamp. You can see those two hills where the skeletons attacked." Mapper pointed to the page in the book. "They named the hills the Twins. It says they were named because of two wizards that—"

"We don't care why they're named the Twins," Cutter snapped. "Just show us where we're at."

Mapper pointed at the map, careful not to touch the ancient document. "The Twins are here. We're here in the swamp, and south of us are the Bad Lands."

"Why are they called the Bad Lands?" Winger asked.

"It's said that during the Great War between the wizards and the warlocks, the monsters cast such powerful spells that they actually cracked the world around them. The Bad Lands were once full of lush forest and grassy plains, but now they're charred and damaged, the soil actually baked into different colors of clay. Rivers of lava stretch across the land, making travel precarious."

"What's that?" Watcher asked, pointing to a pair of crossed swords in the middle of a lava lake.

"It says 'Swordsmith's Workshop.' The markings suggest there is an ancient relic there, but I'm not sure about that. It's a warlock place, but it's said to have sunken into the lava. No one goes there anymore; it's far too dangerous."

Watcher glanced at Cutter. "I bet that's where they're going. Maybe the Workshop didn't sink into the lava. The skeleton commander is probably going there looking for an ancient relic."

"We aren't gonna let that happen, are we?" a voice said from behind. Blaster stepped forward as he changed from his gray-green leather armor to his favorite, black.

"Let's catch up with the rest of the army," Cutter said. "The only place the skeleton general could be heading is toward that building in the middle of the lava lake, if it still exists. I say we head straight for it."

"Agreed." Watcher glanced up at the sun. Just then, his parrot squawked overhead and descended, landing gently on his shoulder. "It'll be dark soon. The lava in the Bad Lands will help us to see, but we need sharp eyes around us. I'll ask the archers to keep a watch out for monsters."

"You don't ask . . . you command," Cutter said.

The warrior's statement felt like a rebuke, but Watcher knew Cutter was right. He was in command, and he needed to act like it. Watcher nodded, still not used to being in charge.

They marched for another hour. Many of the birds flew high above the swamp, likely glad to be in fresh air instead of the stagnant and odorous air that clung to the swamp. By the time the sun had reached the horizon, the villagers had made it to the edge of the swamp and the start of the Bad Lands.

"Look at all the smoke and soot in the air," Winger said. "It's sunset, and the sky is gray with barely any color to it. I love sunset, but I hate this place."

Watcher glanced to the west. The horizon was taking on a grayish-red smear that appeared more like a stain across the sky than a beautiful sunset. The sad display made everything seem a little more hopeless.

"This land earned its name well," Cleric said. "Many tales have been spun about the Bad Lands. The few who sought it out never returned."

"Well, that's a cheery thought," Blaster said.

"The zombies had a name for this place," Er-Lan said, a faint quiver to his voice.

"What was it?" Cleric asked.

"Land of Death," the zombie answered, his dark eyes filled with fear.

"Well . . . that's another happy thought." Blaster

slapped Er-Lan on the back, then put an arm around him and stepped into the Bad Lands.

They walked across the brown, hardened clay, heading toward a thick column of smoke in the distance. Rivers of lava cut through the terrain, making the path difficult at times. Frequently, they had to build bridges out of cobblestone to get around some of the wide, boiling tributaries. At times, they found blocks of dirt or cobblestone already placed in the middle of a river, letting them jump across safely. Many of them found this strange, but they were grateful for the safe route.

Watcher coughed as he inhaled, the smoke and ash biting the back of his throat. The orange glow from the rivers of lava illuminated the smoky haze, making the air appear to glow as if it were aflame. The sight made him nervous.

As the sun sat farther behind the western horizon, the land drew darker, allowing the light from the molten stone to dominate the landscape. Everything took on an eerie, orange glow, the smoke becoming too thick to see through. Imaginary beasts lurked in the back of Watcher's mind, waiting to emerge from the thick, smoky haze. It made him shudder.

Suddenly, a warm hand settled itself on his arm. Turning, he found Planter smiling at him, her golden axe held at the ready.

"You okay?" She smiled.

It felt as if the fear and worry and anger were suddenly swept away by her radiant beauty. That's what Planter did to him; it was like she filled the empty little spaces within him, where he was incomplete.

"Yeah . . . just a little nervous."

"We all are, Watcher."

He nodded, then slowly curved around one of the dark pools of water, a toxic smell rising from its surface. None of the villagers ventured close to the poisonous liquid, the choking gasses floating up from the surface too terrible to bear.

Should I say something to her about how I feel? Watcher thought.

He steeled himself for that terrible moment, but before he could speak, someone shouted, "I think I see a footprint!"

Watcher moved to the voice and stared down at the ground as others passed him by. A narrow set of prints were visible on the ground; a bony foot had brushed away some of the ash, leaving a red stained-clay block visible underneath.

"There's something over here," another shouted. The NPC lifted a wooden stick into the air, the ends charred. A long string hung from the piece of wood, its end also burned. "I think it's a stick or tree branch."

"No . . . it's a bow," Cutter said as he took the item from the villager. The big NPC stared down at it for a moment. "It's the remains of a skeleton bow. One of the creatures must have dropped it in the lava."

Watcher nodded, then motioned everyone forward. They continued through the scorched terrain, following the faint hints of skeleton footprints when they could. They moved slowly and carefully, making sure there were safe places to cross when streams of lava intersected their path. As they walked, Watcher stared at the back of Planter's head, her blond hair now taking on a crimson hue in the orange light. Winger moved next to him and elbowed him in the ribs.

"What?" Watcher asked.

His sister just smiled at him. "Well?"

He shrugged, pretending to not understand what she was asking . . . but he knew exactly what she was asking: Had he told Planter how he felt?

"Winger . . . it's just that—"

"There's something up ahead," a voice said from the haze.

Slowly a dark shape emerged from the ashen fog; it was Blaster wearing charcoal-gray leather armor that seemed to melt into the smoky background.

"It's a huge castle with a giant moat of lava surrounding the structure." He stopped and waited for the others to reach him.

Cutter ran to him across the landscape. The perpetual east-to-west breeze suddenly increased, blowing the landscape momentarily clear. The mysterious castle came into view, with its hardened clay exterior, magma blocks, and tall flows of lava falling from its heights. It was something that would have looked more at home in the Nether than in the Far Lands; its very presence brought feelings of trepidation and fear.

The NPC army approached the castle and stood before the dark, sparkling bridge that spanned the boiling moat. Watcher stared up at the watchtowers that loomed overhead, his enchanted bow notched and ready; he expected guards to attack at any moment, but the stone sentinels remained silent and empty.

Before them, the massive wall of baked clay loomed high into the air, towers dotting the barricade at its corners. Just beyond the obsidian bridge, massive iron gates stood open, daring them to enter. Watcher stared at the gates and felt a tickling warning of fear in the back of his mind. There was something strange about this place, something unnatural and evil. But there was also something alluring to it, as if the ancient structure was whispering to him, the words unintelligible, but tantalizing. It felt as if the castle was trying to draw him into its dark halls and shadowy passages, past the burning fires and glowing magma blocks. But would this enchanted structure allow any of them to leave?

Watcher knew they had no choice either way . . . they must enter and pursue their enemy at any cost.

CHAPTER 26

Sweat trickled down the back of Watcher's neck as he crossed the obsidian bridge. The parrot on Watcher's shoulder ruffled its feathers, then jumped into the air, squawking, apparently not enjoying the heat either. Many of the birds flew in lazy circles overhead, some settling on the fortified walls while others stayed close to the villagers. Er-Lan had them scanning the building for monsters, but they gave no indication of seeing anything.

Lava bubbled beneath the bridge throwing ash and smoke into the air, making breathing difficult. As Watcher moved across the bridge, an eerie chill trickled down his spine; *Was that some kind of magical warning?* he wondered.

Stepping off the bridge, Watcher bolted across the rusty, baked ground until he reached the entrance to the castle. The huge iron gates seemed to be rusted in place, forever open, but not inviting. Next to the opening, lava spilled off the high, fortified wall, falling to the ground and flowing into the moat that ringed the structure. The heat was unbearable.

"Come on, everyone, we need to find those skeletons." Cutter drew his diamond sword. "They must be

stopped from finding any magical artifacts or weapons."
He turned toward Watcher. "What's the plan?"

The boy peered through the haze and into the courtyard that stood within the fortified walls. Footsteps
could be seen on the ash-covered ground . . . a lot of
them. Orange light glowed through the thin layer of soot
as streams of lava moved beneath the floor of the castle. Cubes of glass kept the boiling stone contained, but
Watcher was worried; he knew how fragile those transparent cubes could be.

Dark passages stood empty along the edges of the
courtyard. Some were narrow hallways, just a block or
two wide, while others spanned a dozen blocks or more.
They all led into the terrifying depths of the massive
castle.

"They didn't leave any skeleton bones behind,"
Blaster said at Watcher's side, "so at least we know the
monsters aren't trying to lure us into some kind of trap."

The other villagers nodded. The young boy turned
and cast his gaze across the villagers. Fear and uncertainty covered each face. They could all feel the ancient
and terrifying power of this fortress; each of them knew
there'd be dangerous things lurking in the shadowy
tunnels.

"Whatever the skeletons are looking for in this fortress, it must be denied them." Watcher pulled Needle
from his inventory, the purple glow pushing back the
light from the lava and raising their spirits. "We'll split
up into small groups and go into each passage. As soon
as any of you find the skeletons, come back to the courtyard and wait for others. If you don't find any monsters
in five minutes, come back here anyway."

He turned to Cutter, hoping the big warrior would
validate his plan. Cutter just nodded, then patted
Blaster on the back and headed off into one of the passages, a torch in his hand.

The other villagers broke into groups of five to eight
and chose different passages.

"Come on, Watcher." Planter tugged at his chain mail. "We're searching this one."

He turned and followed her with Winger and Er-Lan at his side, Cleric and Mapper following close behind. They moved through a large doorway. Above the opening, two item frames were placed on the wall, each with an anvil mounted in the center; that seemed strange.

The passage was dark, the light from the many lava channels being blocked by the stone walls. It gave a welcome relief to the heat, but the darkness was anything but reassuring. Overhead, magma blocks ran down the center of the passage, the glowing cubes lighting the ceiling, but doing little to brighten the corridor. Watcher pulled out a torch and placed it on the wall. It cast a flickering glow, illuminating the passage and making the ground—and any possible tripwires or pressure plates—visible.

The corridor turned left, then right, then plunged downward, heading deeper under the terrifying castle. They seemed to descend forever; the rocky stairs extending off into the darkness and disappearing. Watcher thought they might hit bedrock, but then the passage leveled out and opened to a long tunnel that stretched out farther than they could see. Iron doors dotted the walls every dozen blocks or so. Picking one with the flickering light of torches coming through the iron door's window, Watcher pressed his ear against the metal surface and listened.

"You hear anything?" Planter asked.

Watcher shook his head. "Let's go in and look around."

Before anyone could respond, Watcher reached for the lever next to the door and flipped it up. The door squeaked open. Instantly, Watcher's parrot jumped into the air and flew around the chamber. Other birds joined the first, searching the room for dangers. They quickly returned and nuzzled the necks of the villagers.

"The birds think it is safe." Er-Lan stroked the

feathery crown of the royal blue parrot on his shoulder, his clawed hand moving gently down the animal's back. "Care is still advised."

Watcher nodded. "I think you're right; everyone watch for tripwires or pressure plates. This feels like a monster place, and who knows what kinds of traps they've left behind."

He stepped into the chamber and surveyed the room. At the center, a large fireplace built from red brick dominated the chamber. A fire burned within the hearth, painting the walls and floor with a flickering yellow light. Along the walls, crafting benches of different sizes stood next to enchanting tables, the two surrounded by shelves of books. Tiny, almost transparent symbols floated from the bookshelves and streamed into the open book that sat on the enchanting table, adding to the power of the magical device.

Chests stood along one wall, all with their lids already flung open. Their contents: stone tools, books, clothing, stone blocks . . . all lay discarded on the ground.

"It looks like this place has been searched recently." Cleric pointed to the chests.

Mapper quickly picked up the books that floated on the ground, then moved to the bookshelves and inspected the writing on the spines. He was like a child looking at new toys.

Watcher put away his bow and moved to the fireplace. He could see blocks of netherrack beneath the fire, the rusty red cubes fueling the flames for eternity.

Suddenly, something snapped on the far side of the room. Spinning, Watcher drew Needle and pointed it toward the noise. He found one of the parrots walking through the discarded items from the chests, munching on some seeds that were strewn across the ground.

"I don't think there's anything here," Winger said.

Watcher turned toward his sister. To his surprise, Needle grew bright as it passed by the fireplace.

"You see that?" Planter's voice was filled with excitement. "The sword lit up for a moment."

Watcher nodded, then slowly turned with the magical blade extended. When it neared the fireplace, the weapon gave off a bright purple light. "There's something in that fireplace."

Planter moved up to the flames, then used a shovel to put out the fire. Instantly, the room was plunged into darkness. Cleric pulled out a torch and held it over the cooling netherrack blocks.

"You see anything?" Mapper asked.

Cleric shook his head.

"It would be under the netherrack," Watcher said. "Use a pick axe."

Planter gently pushed Cleric out of the way, then brought a pick axe down upon the netherrack blocks. With two quick hits, she shattered one of the blocks, then broke the other and gasped in surprise. Beneath the second block was a wooden chest.

"Open it . . . open it," Mapper said.

As Planter put away her pick axe, Winger leaned into the hole and opened the chest. Reaching into the darkness, she lifted a bow and stacks of arrows, then set them on the ground.

"Look at the bow, it's glowing," Planter said in awe.

Winger picked up the weapon. "I can feel heat coming from the bow."

"I bet it's a fire-bow," Mapper said. "There were many made during the Great War. Be careful where you shoot; you could burn down an entire village if you weren't careful."

"Look at these arrows," Planter said.

She picked up a stack and handed them to Watcher. Some of them had tips which were blue and wet to the touch, another group seemed to smolder with some internal heat, a thin line of smoke escaping from their tips, while a few were colored ruby red and dripped as if some potion were contained within their sharp points. Watcher put away Needle and pulled out his bow. He fired one of the glowing arrows into the far wall. Instantly, the shaft caught fire, then lit the stone wall ablaze. Quickly, he fired one of the blue arrows. When it hit, a stream of water was formed, covering the far end of the chamber and extinguishing the flames.

"Fire arrows I understand," Watcher said. "But water arrows?"

"Good for irrigating crops, I think," Mapper said.

Watcher nodded, then brought the third kind of arrow to his nose and sniffed, then let a drop of the liquid land on his skin. "Healing arrow."

Instantly, Er-Lan stepped back, afraid. "Healing things are poisonous to the undead." He took another step backward. "Keep it away."

"Don't worry, Er-Lan, I'll keep it safe." Watcher stuffed it into his inventory. He glanced at his father. "Maybe would could use it on some of the villagers."

"Or maybe use it on a skeleton," Winger said. "They're undead . . . right?"

Er-Lan nodded.

"Hmmm . . ." Cleric was lost in thought.

Watcher gathered up the rest of the arrows and handed some to Winger, then put the rest into his inventory.

"There's something else in the chest." Planter reached in and pulled out an enchanted shield, the front colored blood-red, with three black skulls decorating the rectangle. "I could use a new shield." She glanced at Watcher and smiled. "You broke my last enchanted one . . . remember?"

"I *was* fighting a wither at the time," Watcher replied, grinning.

She shrugged, then put the glowing rectangle into her inventory.

"I think we should search some other rooms, son," Cleric suggested.

Watcher nodded and headed for the door.

They moved back into the long hallway and checked the next set of doors. Some were burning hot, the metal doors almost too warm to touch. Others had smoke billowing from the doorframe or bright lava light streaming from the barred window set in the middle of the door. None of these seem likely candidates. Further down the passage, they found a door that was cool and lacked any smoke or lava. Watcher stepped up to it and smiled.

"Let's see what's inside." Winger reached for the lever that was set into the wall.

"Wait," Er-Lan whispered. "Noises from within."

Watcher held up a hand, stopping his sister, then stepped to the door and pressed his ear against its cold, metal surface. As he stilled his mind, he could hear the bubbling and hissing of the magma blocks high overhead, the lava circulating about within the cube. Bats squeaked off in the distance. Water dripped from a ceiling, somewhere. Silverfish scurried through the shadows. But then he heard it . . . a sound like two dry sticks being rubbed together.

"Skeletons," Watcher whispered.

He drew an arrow from his inventory and notched it to his bow. "It doesn't sound like very many. Let's peek inside and see what they are doing."

"Er-Lan heard Watcher instruct the others to go back if they find skeletons." The zombie's eyes darted to the door, then back to Watcher. "There are skeletons in that room."

"I know, but it only sounds like a few." Watcher placed a reassuring hand on the zombie's shoulder. "We need to know what they're doing. If there's an ancient relic in this room, we need to take it from them."

Gently, he moved Er-Lan out of the way, then pushed on the lever. The iron door swung open, revealing a large chamber, the walls and floor lined with stone bricks. At the end was a huge fireplace, with furnaces surrounding the blaze, the light from the flames casting a yellowish glow throughout the chamber.

Two skeletons were visible in front of the fire, each with a bow in their hands, but no arrows notched to the bowstrings. Watcher quickly fired three arrows at the right skeleton while Winger and Planter fired on the left. Their shafts took the monsters by complete surprise, destroying their HP before they even had a chance to turn around.

"You see, Er-Lan, I told you it would be easy." Watcher put away his bow and stepped into the room.

Just then, a harsh laugh filled the room. It was accompanied by a strange clicking sound, as if someone were tapping together a pair of stones.

"Easy, indeed," a familiar voice said.

Just then, the skeleton general, replete with iron armor, stepped out from behind the massive fireplace. He was surrounded by at least fifty skeletons. In his hand, he held an iron sword, the blade glowing with a strange blue light. Sparks danced around the keen edge, some of them falling to the ground like the glowing embers of a firework.

"This castle belongs to the warlocks, and you are not welcome here," General Rusak said. "It is time for you to pay the price for your foolishness."

The monster glanced about the room, his gray eye glowing ever so slightly in the light from the fireplace, his other eye remaining black as coal.

"Skeletons, let none survive. . . . ATTACK!"

CHAPTER 27

Watcher stared at the skeleton general, his body frozen in terror. Arrows were flying toward him, fired by skeletons emerging from behind the monster. Something in the back of Watcher's mind screamed at him to run, but he was overwhelmed with fear at the sight of the huge skeleton holding that sparkling weapon.

Suddenly, a large rectangle appeared in front of him. The *thud-thud-thud* of arrows filled the air with a percussive rhythm as the shafts embedded themselves into the shield.

"Come on, Watcher, we need to get out of here." Planter grabbed his chain mail and gave him a strong tug.

The jolt shocked him out of his panic. Turning, Watcher ran for the door, right behind Planter. When he stepped into the hallway. Watcher placed a block of cobblestone just on the other side of the door. That would slow the skeletons for a moment and allow them to sprint down the passage and get out of range of their bows. But who knew if they were beyond the reach of that sparkling sword.

"You're too late, villager," the skeleton general yelled from within the room, his jawbone clicking as he bellowed. "I have what you came to steal. This is Lightning Blade, and soon, I'll show you what I have gained and you have lost."

The monster's words bounced off the walls of the passage, creating multiple echoes that blared at them over and over; it was like the sound from some kind of nightmare.

"Faster!" Winger shouted. "Everyone run!"

His sister streaked down the hallway, with Cleric and Mapper following as best they could. The parrots squawked and screeched, some of them mimicking the skeleton general's harsh laugh; that didn't help anyone's nerves.

Planter ran past Er-Lan and moved next to Mapper, ready to help the old man if necessary. Behind them, the sound of pick axes digging into stone echoed through the passage.

"The skeletons must be slowed," the zombie said, then skidded to a stop.

"Er-Lan, you can't fight them . . . there are too many of them." Watcher stopped at the monster's side.

"This zombie is not going to fight. Er-Lan is waiting for Watcher to give an idea."

"An idea?" Watcher asked, confused.

The zombie looked at Watcher, waiting for some kind of clever strategy to save them. An arrow zipped over their heads and clattered to the ground.

"They're out of the room," Watcher said. "We need to run."

"Idea first," Er-Lan said. "Those skeletons thirst for violence. They must be slowed."

"Thirst . . . water . . . of course! Er-Lan, you're brilliant." Watcher pulled out one of the water arrows as the zombie looked at him, confused.

He couldn't see the skeletons, but he could hear their bony feet on the stone floor. Aiming for the sound, he fired one of the water arrows, then fired another and another. Instantly, the sound of rushing water filled the passage, followed by shouts of frustration. Watcher placed a couple of cobblestone blocks across the passage, then pushed Er-Lan toward the exit and ran. Arrows bounced off the walls, the skeletons randomly firing in hopes of hitting the intruders.

Watcher and Er-Lan sprinted through the passage, slowly catching up to the others. They climbed the steps as fast as their legs would carry them until they reached the courtyard again. Many villagers were just standing about, their search of the many tunnels unsuccessful. Watcher knew why: the entire skeleton army was chasing them.

"Everyone get to cover . . . skeletons!" Watcher notched an arrow and spun, firing it into the passageway without aiming. "Run!"

The villagers sprang into action, some out of training, some out of fear. They found places behind clay structures, a wall here, a doorway there, and readied their arrows. Watcher moved to what had been a fountain at one time, the water having evaporated long ago. He notched two arrows and took aim at the doorway, expecting the horde of skeletons to emerge any instant. Seconds ticked by, but no skeletons stepped out of the passage.

Cutter and another group of villagers emerged from a side corridor. They saw the state of their army and instantly readied themselves for battle . . . but still no skeletons stepped out of the darkness.

"You think they ran away?" Cleric asked, he was standing at Watcher's side, his eyes filled with fear.

"I don't know. They might have—"

Just then, laughter emerged from the passage. The huge skeleton general emerged from the dark corridor, the shimmering sword in his hand. Sparks leapt off the blade and fell to the ground, some of them bouncing off his iron armor first.

"You pitiful little villagers think you have us outnumbered . . . ha ha ha." He glared about the courtyard, then his eyes found Watcher. "I see a red-headed wizard amongst you." The creature pointed the electrified blade at Watcher. "See what the warlocks created that your wizard ancestors could not."

He waved the sword in a wide circle, then pointed at a group of villagers. Instantly, bolts of lightning jumped from the blade and struck the NPCs. The energy shattered the cubes of hardened clay and evaporated the blocks of glass that sat over the narrow streams of lava. Some of the villagers fell into the molten stone while others simply disappeared, their HP destroyed in an instant.

"NOOOOOO!" Watcher moaned.

"Behold, one of the greatest creations of the warlocks: Lightning Blade." He pointed again, and more bolts of electricity sprang from the weapon and hit villagers, destroying many, but wounding many more. The glass over the lava cracked all throughout the courtyard as the ground shook with the blast.

"Everyone get off the glass," Cleric shouted.

Watcher glanced down at the glass beneath his feet, then moved sideways onto the hardened clay just as the transparent cube shattered.

"Archers . . . FIRE!" Watcher's voice ached at the volume of his shout, but he was filled with such rage he could hardly contain it. He fired as fast as he could at the skeleton, but a sheet of electricity formed around the monster, hugging him tight from head to toe. Arrows struck the charged coating and just vaporized as the enchantment from the shimmering blade made the monster indestructible.

The skeleton held the blade up high over his head and swung it in a circle again. The electrified coating around the monster's body disappeared for just an instant, then he threw more bolts of lightning at the villagers.

"Watcher, we must do something or that monster's gonna destroy everyone," Winger said desperately.

"Watcher, help them," Planter pleaded.

He turned back to the skeleton general and stared in horror as he swung the blade high over his head and threw more sheets electricity at his friends. As soon as the bolts of lightning left the blade, the electrified coating hugged the skeleton again, protecting him from any of the villagers' pointed shafts. The monster laughed and glanced over his shoulder. "Come, my friends . . . give me a hand with these pathetic villagers."

A flood of skeletons surged out of the passage, each with a bow or sword in their hands. The whole scene was surreal. But something about the skeleton's words bounced in the back of his mind: *Give me a hand . . . give me a hand . . . give me a hand . . .*

Watcher smiled. He had it, he knew what to do . . . but would it work?

Drawing only a single arrow, he waited and took careful aim. Watcher would only get one shot at this; it was their only chance. If he missed, they'd likely be destroyed. He pulled the arrow back, then pulled the string a little tighter until the bow was about to snap . . . and waited.

And then the skeleton general did it again; he raised Lightning Blade high over his head, above the shield that wrapped around his body. That was the moment . . . the instant when Watcher would either save his friends, or doom them to destruction. Stilling his breathing and his mind, Watcher released the arrow.

CHAPTER 28

His arrow seemed to fly through the air in slow motion. Everything around Watcher grew deathly silent, as if he and the skeleton general were the only two present. He knew other fighting was going on, but the sounds of battle had been muffled out by his fear.

Every last ounce of his attention was focused on the arrow. It soared through the air in a graceful arc, aimed at where he thought the skeleton's hand would be. It flew closer . . . and closer . . . and closer, then it struck. The arrow pierced the skeleton general's hand. Screaming in shock and pain, the monster dropped the blade, his electric shield instantly evaporating.

"Aim for their general!" Watcher shouted.

Lightning Blade clattered to the ground, bouncing off the hardened clay, then fell into one of the streams of lava, its glass covering shattered minutes ago.

The archers all turned their bows toward Rusak and fired. The monster reached over and grabbed another skeleton and used it for a shield, allowing the doomed monster to take all the shafts as he backed down the passage. The arrows struck the poor creature, tearing into his HP while a look of complete terror filled the doomed monster's face.

Rage bubbled up from within Watcher. That skeleton general was now hurting his own kind with no remorse showing in his black and scarred-red eye. It was clear the monster didn't care who was hurt or why . . . he just wanted to destroy.

"Skeletons . . . attack for your general and for your warlord, Rakir," the general yelled.

Anger pushed aside his fear as Watcher thought about his friends. He saw Planter out of the corner of his eye; she was hunched down behind a column of dark blocks, an expression of fear etched across her beautiful face. This skeleton commander would wipe every one of them out, whether they were a threat or not, just because he could . . . Watcher wasn't going to allow that to happen.

"I'm not gonna let her get hurt," Watcher said in a low voice, his eyes burning with anger. He drew Needle from his inventory and glared at his enemy. "I won't let any of my friends get hurt!"

The general threw aside the handful of bones after the skeleton in his grip perished. Drawing his bow, he fired at Watcher as he moved into the passage. Needle flicked the shaft aside, then knocked more of them away as other skeletons took aim at him. The blade moved of its own volition, without Watcher giving it any thought. He was completely focused on the skeleton general, their eyes locked onto one another.

Screaming as loud as he could, Watcher charged into the army of skeletons, slashing at the bony creatures as he pushed through their ranks. Arrows streaked toward him, but Needle flicked them aside, his fear of skeletons now supplanted by an overwhelming rage. The other villagers saw Watcher's charge and shouted their own battle cries, then advanced, firing as they closed the distance. Screams of pain from friend and foe alike filled Watcher's ears with guilt, but he knew he had to set it all aside and focus on the brutal skeleton general . . . he was the key here, and had to be stopped.

One of the skeleton warriors attacked Watcher with an iron sword. Needle knocked the blade aside, then slashed at the monster's HP. The creature howled in pain, then charged at the boy, but suddenly, a golden axe streaked through the air and crashed into the bony monster, taking the last of its HP. Planter cheered, then attacked another skeleton trying to sneak up behind her friend. She fought like a seasoned warrior, her enchanted golden axe tearing through their attackers like golden fire. Cutter appeared at her side, slashing at a skeleton archer with his diamond blade. The two fought back to back, making sure none would attack Watcher.

Turning, he pushed his way through the rest of the skeleton army . . . but the general had fled. A hidden passage lay propped open in the wall, something they'd missed in their search. Watcher entered the narrow tunnel cautiously, following the twisting turns until he found it ending at an open doorway in the fortified wall of the castle. A line of stone blocks were placed across the boiling moat, marking where the terrible monster had fled, the last few blocks in the narrow bridge destroyed, making pursuit impossible.

Scanning the terrain with his keen eyes, Watcher searched for the monster, but saw nothing, just the gray haze that hugged close to the scorched landscape; the general had escaped.

A scratching sound echoed off the stone walls. Watcher turned quickly, Needle ready to attack, but found only the concerned face of Er-Lan staring at him.

"The general escaped?" the zombie asked, disappointed.

Watcher nodded. "What happened with the battle? Are our friends okay?"

"The skeletons stopped fighting together when their general ran away and fought for themselves, ignoring comrades that needed help. Your villagers are in the process of destroying them."

"*My* villagers?" Watcher said softly.

Er-Lan only shrugged.

"What about that enchanted relic, the Lightning Blade?" Watcher moved past his zombie friend and retraced his steps to the courtyard.

"The lava swallowed it. That weapon is gone."

"Good, something that powerful would be dangerous in anyone's hands."

Er-Lan nodded.

They reached the entrance to the secret passage and stepped carefully into the courtyard. It was eerily quiet, as if everyone had been destroyed. But when he stepped out into the open, the air erupted in cheers. Villagers patted him on the back while others embraced him in jubilant hugs.

"We won . . ."

"We defeated the skeletons . . ."

"They're destroyed . . ."

The NPCs shouted in joy, their excitement filling Watcher with confidence. But then he saw a pile of items floating off the ground near one of the narrow streams of lava. There were other piles distributed throughout the courtyard, swords and armor and tools mixed in with skeleton bones.

Watcher realized what this battle had cost them. His smile turned to a frown as he lowered his gaze. Slowly, he raised his hand, fingers spread wide in acknowledgement for those that sacrificed everything; the salute for the dead. It was something done in Minecraft since the Awakening, since the first villager opened their eyes as a living creature. Cutter saw this and stood next to him, raising his own hand, his steely glare silencing the celebration. More hands raised until all of them held their arms straight up into the air. As one, they clenched their fingers together, crushing the anger and rage and sorrow into shaking fists, then lowered them to their sides. Some wept as they picked up the items dropped by fallen comrades while others seethed in rage, stomping on skeleton bones as if it would bring loved ones back.

Watcher placed a block of dirt on the ground, then stood on it and faced the NPCs.

"We lost many friends today."

"The skeletons paid dearly for it," someone shouted.

"That is true, but it will not bring any of our comrades back, nor does it lessen our grief."

The villagers nodded.

"You all saw the terrible damage that ancient relic wrought upon us. That was only one skeleton with one of the warlock's weapons. If they have more, they could destroy many villagers. The threat from the skeleton nation is not gone . . . they can still do great harm."

"But how can they without their skeleton horde?" one of the NPCs asked. "We destroyed their army here, in this courtyard."

Watcher shook his head. "I saw the size of their army when we were at the Capitol a few months ago, rescuing many of you from the clutches of the Wither King. There's a larger plan at work here, and I fear the Withers have a hand in it. But I know this was just the smallest fraction of their army."

"The Helm of Calling!" Mapper shouted.

All eyes turned to the old NPC.

"That's right." Watcher nodded. "The skeleton general still has the Helm of Calling, and he's carrying it to his warlord." Expressions of shock and fear covered the mourning faces that stared up at him. "The skeleton warlord cannot be allowed to use that relic. If he does, it will mean the destruction of every villager in the Far Lands." He drew Needle and pointed it to the southwest. The enchanted weapon blazed bright purple, shading the faces around him with an iridescent glow. "We know where he's going. I'm sure that general is traveling faster now that he's alone, but we must catch him."

"Then why are we standing around here, gabbing, when we should be running?" Blaster pushed through the crowd, then held his long knives in the air. "I say . . . it's time to sprint!"

"Yeah!" the villagers cheered.

"Follow me!" Watcher said, then jumped off the block of dirt.

With the villager army—*his* army—behind him and a huge flock of parrots squawking overhead, Watcher sprinted out of the castle and through the Bad Lands, heading for an army that was many times their size. The night sky was dark, devoid of stars because of the gray cloud of smoke that forever lingered over the landscape. A pale circle of light tried to pierce through the haze; it was the moon, but it shed little light. Fortunately, the many streams of lava gave enough light to see.

Watcher felt nervous as he ran. He knew this upcoming battle would either be a complete victory or a stunning defeat, depending on his strategy. He was risking all of their lives . . . even Planter's life, and the thought of losing *her* made him quake with fear. He glanced at her from the corner of his eye. Her blond hair streamed behind her like a flag of gold, a confident expression on her beautiful face.

I have to keep her safe, he thought. *Somehow, I must come up with a plan that will keep them all safe.*

The problem was . . . he had no idea how to give his comrades an advantage so they wouldn't be wiped out as soon as they set foot in the Hall of Pillars. Yes, that was tomorrow's problem, but tomorrow was approaching, fast.

CHAPTER 29

Rusak sprinted through the smoky terrain, the light from the boiling lava making it easy to see, though the night sky was pitch black. When he reached the end of the Bad Lands, the skeleton darted into a birch forest that hugged close to the fractured landscape and hid behind a tree. Glancing around the trunk, he checked to see if anyone was following.

"I can't believe that boy-wizard shot Lightning Blade from my hand." He looked down at his bony fingers, one of them noticeably shorter.

The gray haze, lit from underneath by the many lava rivers, glowed a soft orange as if the air itself were on fire. Everything appeared still, with no movement visible.

The skeleton breathed a sigh of relief. "Maybe my warriors destroyed them."

Reaching up, he wiped his sweaty skull with a bony hand. Just then, something glowing a soft purple emerged from the smoky background. As it neared, it grew brighter and more defined; it was a sword.

"He's still following," the general growled, frustrated. "That can only mean all my skeletons are destroyed." Rusak scanned the forest, making sure no one was trying to sneak up on him, then turned back and glared at his pursuer. "That little runt never gives up! Well, let's see how fast he can run."

Reaching into his inventory, Rusak pulled out a set of leather boots. They were colored a dark, dark black, as if made of shadows. A subtle purple hue sparkled around the edges of the boots, the magical enchantment held within the thick shoes making them glow.

He slipped the boots over his pale feet then stood and wiggled his boney toes.

"I knew I'd need these enchanted boots eventually. The wizard that made these would be horrified to learn they were being used by a skeleton instead of an NPC." He laughed a dry laugh, his jaw clicking together and adding a percussive beat to the chuckle. "Let's see if the Swift Boots are really as fast as the ancient books say."

Rusak glanced at the boy and his glowing sword. More NPCs were emerging from the haze with weapons in their hands; far more had survived the battle than he would have thought. The red-headed boy held a slim blade before him and turned to the left and right as if searching for something. The sword glowed a bright purple when it was directed at Rusak. Pointing, the villager walked across the baked landscape, straight toward Rusak's hiding place.

"So, you want to follow me . . . perfect. I'll lead you straight to the Hall of Pillars and into the arms of the skeleton warlord. He has a massive army just waiting to meet you." Rusak laughed, his jaw clicking. "Let's see how you fare against Rakir and the great Fossil Bow of Destruction."

Turning, he took off running, the magical enchantment in the boots letting him dash across the landscape with incredible speed. Rusak sprinted through the birch forest, the white trunks passing him in a blur. When he reached a small lake, the Swift Boots allowed him to run across the surface as if it were made of stone, his speed keeping him aloft. The leaves swayed and rustled as he zipped past, many falling to the forest floor. They would likely show his path, but Rusak didn't care. He *wanted* these villagers to follow him . . . to their doom.

He sped through the forest in a few minutes, a trek that would normally have taken an hour, moving into an extreme hills biome. Tall, steep mountains loomed high into the evening sky, many too steep to climb. A group of three tall peaks stood out in the distance, their profiles blocking out the sparkling stars . . . the Triplets; he was almost home.

Suddenly, he stumbled and fell as the magical power in the Swift Boots was finally exhausted. The dark leather no longer had the sparkling purple hue . . . now they were just boots. Pulling them off his feet, the skeleton cast them aside, then stood.

"You served your purpose well," the skeleton general said to them.

Slowly, he walked along the well-traveled path that led deeper into the hilly biome. The trail wound its way around steep mounds of stone and dirt, heading toward the three largest mountains up ahead. The smell of smoke nibbled at the edges of his senses. Soon, a wide crevasse came into view, the glow of lava and clouds of ash spilling out of the rift and filling the air. A waterfall spilled down one of the tall peaks, crashing around trees and blocks of stone until the liquid splashed into the deep crevasse, freezing some of the lava into cobblestone, with the occasional dark cube of obsidian formed where the lava source had once existed. Rusak easily leaped over the gap and continued toward his goal.

A stick broke off to the right, as if it were stepped on by something . . . or someone. Rusak pulled out his bow and notched an arrow, just to be safe, then continued his route. It eventually led him to the three tall peaks. Directly between the rocky mountains was a wide hole. It yawned open like the maw of some gigantic, underground beast, its throat cloaked in darkness. Rusak moved to the side and peered into its shadowy depths.

"It's good to be back home," he said in a low voice. "The skeleton warlord will be pleased to know a host of villagers is following close behind. I'm sure he'll want to prepare a little reception for them."

The general removed the arrow from his bowstring, then dropped it on the ground. He smiled as he put his bow back into his inventory, then stared down into the dark hole once more. The light from the setting moon tried to pierce the darkness of the opening, but the magical enchantments wrapped around the entrance to the Hall of Pillars kept everything cloaked in an inky blackness. Only someone who knew the path and knew where to jump could avoid the fall to the ground, which would be fatal.

Rusak smiled. "Wizard, I wish I could be here to watch you try to do our little parkour course without any sunlight."

He could almost hear the screams of the villagers in his imagination as they plummeted to their deaths. It made his smile grow larger and larger. Then he leaped into the darkness and was swallowed by the shadows, his laughter echoing off the walls of the black abyss.

CHAPTER 30

Sunrise was a welcome relief; the painted eastern horizon, with its warm reds, oranges, and yellows, filled the villagers with hope.

"It's good to be able to breathe again," Blaster said. "My mouth felt as if I'd been licking the remains of an old campfire."

"Drink some water," Planter said. "It helps."

Blaster accepted a bottle of water and drained half of it, then poured the rest over his head, washing the soot from his hair and face. Removing the rest of his black leather armor, he replaced it with a set of white to match the birch trees in the forest.

"Where's our friend?" Cutter asked.

Watcher held Needle out before him and moved until the blade turned a bright purple, creating a small circle of iridescent light around the boy, driving back the colorful rays of the morning sun. "He's still heading to the southwest. Likely, that's where his Hall of Pillars is located."

Mapper opened his ender chest and rifled through the ancient books until he found the book of maps. "I see the Bad Lands on the map, and this birch forest, but to the southwest all there is on the map is something called *The Leap of Faith.*"

"That sounds familiar." Cutter glanced at Watcher. "Like the time you shoved us off that cliff . . . that was a leap of faith, wasn't it?"

"You shoved people off a cliff?" Cleric asked, a disapproving parental tone to his voice.

"Well . . . I was . . . umm . . ."

Cutter smiled at Planter, then both started to laugh, the big NPC slapping the boy on the back. He almost knocked Watcher to the ground.

"The Hall of Pillars must be near that spot on the map," Watcher said, changing the subject. "Everyone eat something, then we run."

The villagers gobbled up cooked meat, or bread, or pieces of fruit, then ran, following Watcher and his glowing sword. They moved quietly through the birch forest with archers scanning the surroundings for threats while the swordsmen stayed at the center of the formation, guarding the elderly and wounded, of whom there were many more now.

"What do you think this Hall of Pillars looks like?" Planter asked.

"When we were in the Capitol and I was wearing that magical chain mail armor we took from the zombie warlord, I saw the skeletons in their underground lair. There were huge pillars underground, each lit with redstone lanterns. The massive columns stretched up to a ceiling that was impossibly high." He moved closer to Planter and lowered his voice. "In that gigantic chamber, I saw the warlord and his army of monsters. There were hundreds of skeletons in there with him, every one of them armed and many wearing armor."

Watcher placed a hand on her arm and they slowed to a walk. Drawing her gaze to his, he lowered his voice to a whisper. "I don't know how we're gonna face that horde. If they're all at one end of the chamber, and we're at the other end, then we'll have to charge straight at them. With all those skeleton archers firing at us, they'll cut us to pieces as we run across that chamber.

Somehow we need to get close enough to make their bows useless."

"I'm sure you'll figure out how to do it. I have confidence in you," Planter said.

Watcher sighed. He didn't like all this responsibility.

"Archers, watch the treetops," Winger shouted. "There could be spiders up there."

His sister glanced at him for just an instant, then turned and continued walking through the forest.

I should have told them to do that, he thought. *I'm supposed to be in command, but I don't even know what I'm doing. Now I must figure out how to get past all the skeleton archers that'll likely be waiting for us. Sometimes I feel like I'm drowning in all this responsibility.*

He thought back to that obsidian tower in the ocean and the feeling of defeat when the chilling water started to flood the chamber. It was lucky they'd had the Frost Walker boots, or they would have all perished.

"We're almost out of the forest," a voice said to his left.

Turning, he found Blaster in gray armor smiling at him. "It's extreme hills next, with lots of stone-covered peaks. There's a trail that heads toward some big mountains. I bet that's where our friend went."

"I don't like the extreme hills biome," Winger said. "There are always lots of tunnels and caves all over the place."

"And caves mean monsters," Blaster said with a grin.

"Are we still heading for that skeleton general?" Cutter's voice boomed, far too loudly, if they were supposed to be sneaking up on the skeletons.

"Shhh . . ." Watcher replied in a quieter voice. He pointed Needle away from him, then slowly turned. The sword pointed still to the south west. "The skeleton went into the extreme hills biome for sure."

Watcher put away the weapon, then glanced at Blaster. His friend adjusted his gray leather armor, then cast him his ever-present grin, easing some of

Watcher's fears . . . but not all. "You said there was a trail that leads through the extreme hills?"

"Yep. It goes around the small mountains up ahead, then heads straight for the group of three really tall peaks." Blaster took out one of his long, curved knives and held it into the air. Light from the morning sun shone through the branches and leaves, hitting the blade. The keen edge reflected the light, making it glow as if heated from within. "There's a lava filled crevasse crossing the path, but I'm sure that's where the skeleton general went."

"We need to get that enchanted relic back." Watcher turned and found Mapper and his father, Cleric walking behind them. "If that skeleton warlord gets his hands on the Helm of Calling, he can bring thousands of skeletons to the Far Lands. Nothing will be able to stand against him."

"We aren't gonna let that happen, are we?" Cutter voice was filled with determination.

Watcher envied the NPC's courage, but when he saw Planter staring up at the big warrior, the envy was instantly replaced with a different sort of jealousy.

They followed Blaster through the edge of the forest and into the extreme hills biome. Patches of grass sat between blocks of stone. The grass was clearly crushed, as if this were a common path for the skeletons.

"Son . . . wait a minute." Cleric put a hand on Watcher's shoulder.

He stopped and faced his father, curious.

"I have something for you. I found it in one of the rooms in that building in the Bad Lands, and since it's a little cooler, I figured you could wear it now." Cleric reached into his inventory and pulled out a set of iron armor and tossed it to his son.

Watcher removed his chain mail and put on the chest plate and leggings. The metal glowed with a magical sheen, its surface shiny and reflective like Needle.

"It's so lightweight," the boy said, surprised.

"That's probably from the enchantment on it." Cleric tapped the chest with a knuckle. The metallic surface rang like a gong. "Hopefully this will keep you safe." A worried expression came across the old man's face.

"I know what you're gonna say . . . I'll be as careful as I can be." Watcher smiled.

Cleric nodded and rustled his son's reddish-brown hair with his hand. "Fearlessly believe in yourself without doubt or caution. The first step to success is believing you can do a thing . . . all the rest is just details."

Watcher smiled as the words sunk in, driving some of the lurking fear from the back of his mind. *Fearlessly believe in yourself,* he thought. *That's what I must do . . .* he glanced at Planter . . . *with everything and every*one.

They continued along the trail, with the archers watching the hills on either side and the swordsmen clustered at the center of the formation. They moved along the trail in complete silence. It curved around a small hill, then ended at the center of a trio of mountains, each capped with snow. A long, crashing flow of water fell down the face of the nearest peak. The liquid flowed across the stony ground and then fell into a wide ravine. Sizzles from water landing on molten stone filled the air, as did smoke and ash; it reminded Watcher of the Bad Lands, though not nearly as bad.

He found a narrow spot and placed cobblestone, forming an impromptu bridge for everyone. They crossed the deep gorge without incident and followed the skeleton's path until it ended at the edge of a huge pit, the interior cloaked in darkness.

"You can see the footprints lead straight to this massive hole," Planter whispered, confused. "But where did they go?"

Watcher knelt on the ground and extended his hand into the huge opening. It was instantly swallowed by the shadows, making it appear as if it were missing.

"There's some kind of enchantment on this hole,"

Watcher said. "Light from the sun can't seem to penetrate its interior."

"Then how do the skeletons go into it?" Planter asked.

"They take a leap of faith." Cleric put a hand on Mapper's shoulder. "Are there any clues in that book of yours that might help?"

The old man shook his head. "I checked when we stopped. There is no mention about this other than its name."

Watcher moved to the edge of the pit. He picked up an arrow he found on the ground, then tossed it into the darkness. Maybe ten seconds ticked by before they heard the shaft clatter to the bottom of the pit.

Blaster moved to the edge and stared down into the opening. "That took *way* too long to hit the ground. Nobody survives a fall like this. I'm thinking this is a bad idea."

"This is the way the skeletons get into their Hall of Pillars," Watcher said. "We have to do the same if we plan on taking back the Helm of Calling." He stepped to the edge of the pit. "I guess they call it the *Leap of Faith* for a reason." Watcher leaned forward and was preparing to jump when Winger reached out and pulled him back.

"Wait, I have an idea."

Winger pulled out the bow she found in the warlock's workshop. The magical weapon pulsed with power, the edges of it sparkling with purple light. When she notched an arrow to the string, the bow flashed red, as if something had just caught fire. The tip of the arrow gave off a crimson glow as thin tendrils of smoke snaked their way from the pointed shaft and into the air.

She fired the arrow into the dark abyss. The shaft caught fire when it left the bowstring, leaving a trail of sparkling embers as it streaked through the air. The arrow embedded itself into the far wall, the magical flames lighting the dark interior. Glancing at Watcher, she gave her brother a smile, then fired more shafts into the pit. In seconds, she had the dark hole fully lit with the flaming arrows. It revealed a series of tall columns of stone, each at a different level and spaced a few blocks apart.

"Apparently, the enchantment only blocks light from outside the pit." Mapper smiled and bowed to Winger. "Clever idea."

She smiled back proudly and returned the bow to her inventory with a flourish.

"It's a parkour course," Watcher said. "I can do this."

Jumping into the hole, Watcher landed on the first column, then moved to the second and the third, making his way to the bottom. The sound of boots thudding on stone filled the course as the other villagers followed him.

"I see a tunnel down there. It probably goes to the skeleton base." The boy glanced over his shoulder. The other villagers were following cautiously. "Come on, we can do this."

Watcher continued jumping from block to block, keeping his attention focused on the next column, the rest of the NPC army following. He didn't notice the pair of eyes, one pitch black, the other a hateful red, watching him from the darkness below.

CHAPTER 31

Watcher gazed nervously as the last of the villagers moved through the end of the parkour course and stood safely on the rocky floor. A few NPCs had fallen, but it had been near the end of the course and none had been seriously injured.

"Let's get moving," Cutter said, his voice booming off the cold stone walls. "I want to find these skeletons and crush them. The crops at the village could use some bone meal."

Some of the other villagers laughed, but most stayed silent, fear painted on their square faces. Before them now stood a wide passage that plunged deeper into the flesh of the Far Lands. The tunnel was perfectly circular and curved gracefully to the right as it descended into the darkness. Cutter moved forward, his iron boots clicking on the stone as he walked.

"How do you think they made this passage?" Winger asked, curious.

Watcher glanced at her. She had the enchanted bow in her hand and was anxiously playing with the feathers on an arrow.

"You can be certain skeletons didn't make this."

Blaster moved to her side. "If they used TNT or creepers, the tunnel wouldn't be so perfectly circular."

"They used magic," Mapper said. "There were implements of construction and mining that were made by the great wizards. This must be the result of one of those tools."

"It's spooky." Blaster took out one of his curved knives and tapped the stone wall. The sound traveled down the passage, echoing off the walls and returning back in seconds. The dark-haired boy cast Watcher a concerned look. "You can bet the skeletons will hear us coming."

Watcher nodded.

"Son, if you were going to protect this tunnel, what would you do?" Cleric laid a hand on the boy's shoulder.

"Well . . ." Watcher put a hand to his square chin and quickly was lost in thought. "I'd build some hidden rooms on either side of the tunnel, with an open block through which I could fire my arrows."

Cleric nodded. "We should prepare."

"Agreed." Watcher turned to his archers and gave a quick list of orders. With Blaster leading the archers on the right side of the tunnel and Watcher leading those on the left, the archers moved quietly along the walls. They stayed ahead of Cutter, who was placing torches in the center of the floor.

"What are you doing?" Cutter asked, his loud voice breaking the silence like a hammer shattering a vase.

Planter moved to the big warrior's side and explained what was happening. He smiled, adjusted his iron armor, then motioned the other villagers to stand back, away from him.

"I don't mind being the bait, but everyone else should stand back." Cutter tried to push Planter away, but she brushed off his attempt and pulled out her enchanted golden axe and shield.

"I'm with you on this." She glared at him, daring the big NPC to challenge her, but he wisely did not.

Watcher glanced at his two friends and admired their courage for acting as the bait. But the thought of Planter being out there terrified him. He wanted to say something, but knew Planter would be offended; she would want to share the same risk as Cutter.

But why Cutter? Watcher thought. *They seem to be whispering together a lot, and laughing . . . what's going on there?* Pangs of jealousy surged through his soul as he watched their arms gently brush against each other. With a sigh, he realized there was nothing he could do other than focus on the task at hand, and that was keeping everyone alive.

Watcher moved to the right side of the passage with his archers as Blaster and Winger led the other group to the left. Planter and Cutter walked down the center of the passage, their feet pounding the ground, making it clear they were there.

The tunnel made a turn to the right as it continued to descend. Watcher spotted a section of the wall that was unusually dark. Pointing to the opposite side with an arrow, he gestured to Blaster. The boy put on his black leather cap and nodded.

Watcher notched a fire arrow and aimed at the darkness on the opposite side, Winger doing the same but pointing her sparkling red arrow to the near side.

"Now." The brother and sister released.

Their arrows instantly caught fire when they left the bows, the fiery shafts streaking through the air and into the shadows. Instead of bouncing off a stone wall, the arrows slipped into the darkness and illuminated a hidden room filled with skeletons.

Before the skeletons could open fire, Watcher and Winger fired a pair of water arrows at the monsters. The blue shafts struck the back wall of the hidden chamber and created a water source. The liquid flowed across the skeletons' small chamber, pushing them against the wall, making it difficult for the monsters to fire. Taking advantage of their confusion, Watcher and his archers fired into one of the chambers while Winger and the others attacked the opposite side. The sound of flint arrow heads chipping through bone resonated from the hidden rooms as they quickly destroyed the skeletons.

Once the threat was eliminated, they continued, moving deeper into skeleton territory. Watcher spotted two more of the hidden traps, but this time, the hidden rooms were abandoned . . . and no skeletons in sight.

"It seems the skeleton warlord gave up trying to set traps for us," Cleric said.

"You can be sure he knows we're here now." Cutter placed a torch on the ground and scanned the surroundings.

"I'm going up ahead to look around." Before anyone could respond, Blaster had disappeared into the shadows.

They continued through the curving passage, heading deeper and deeper underground. A tense silence came over the army as their footsteps echoed off the walls. The silence allowed Watcher's famous imagination to start working. He imagined the skeleton general waiting in the shadows; at times, the image was coupled with that of the general's commander, the skeleton warlord. Watcher had no idea what that monster really looked like, and didn't want to know.

Fighting the monsters from a distance was one thing; he could launch arrows all day long at tiny little white spots. But when the monsters were up close, and he could see the unbridled hatred in their dark eyes, Watcher was petrified with fear. The ability to think seemed to leave him, as it did in that underwater structure and in the Swordsmith's Workshop.

What kind of leader am I if I can't stand up to my fears? he asked himself.

Glancing around, he saw expressions of determination and courage on the square faces of his companions. He put on the same mask, but Watcher knew it was a lie, his courage was a lie, his ability to command was a lie. He was just a scared kid.

"You okay?"

The voice startled him. "What?"

"I asked if you were okay," Planter asked. "You were turning the same color as the skeletons."

"It's just that . . ." He paused. *How do I tell Planter that deep down, I'm a coward?*

"You know, you can tell me anything and I'd understand." She put a hand on his arm . . . and it was fantastic. "We've been friends since . . . I guess, since we were toddlers, crawling around in the fields and getting yelled at by old Harvester. You remember?"

Watcher smiled and nodded. "Remember when you pulled up the carrots and blamed it on the chickens?"

"Yeah." She laughed. Her smile lit up her entire face. "Then we left some eggs in the fields and she was convinced it *was* the chickens."

"And that time in the winter when Harvester chased us."

"She couldn't keep up with us when we sprinted across the frozen lake, and she got stuck, waist deep in the snow," Planter said, grinning.

"My dad had to use some horses to help pull her out."

They both laughed as they moved through the huge passage. The memory pushed back his fear a little. But as the humorous images faded from his mind, Watcher grew serious.

"It's just that . . . I'm so afraid I'll mess this up and get everyone hurt, or worse." Watcher lowered his gaze to the tunnel floor. "I'm always so scared. I don't want to let everyone down." His voice became a whisper. "I don't want to let *you* down."

"Oh Watcher, you couldn't let me down. I have total faith in you that you'll know what to do or . . ."

"You see . . . that's just it. There's so much pressure for me to figure out what to do. And if I don't have a good idea then—"

"Would you just be quiet and let me finish!"

Watcher grew silent.

"What I was going to say is, I know you can come up with a great idea, but if you can't . . . you'll ask for help." She paused to let that sink in, then lowered her voice. "Think of Blaster. He's as brave as they come, but he'll never ask for help. That's true for a lot of people around us. But you're different. Your genius comes from knowing when to use the strength of the people around you, and not trying to do everything yourself." She stopped in the middle of the tunnel and grabbed his hand, pulling him to a halt. "It takes a brave person to admit they don't have all the answers, *and* are willing to ask for help. That is your strength, and that's what the skeletons will underestimate about you."

She continued walking, pushing him gently forward. Her touch was like fireworks to his soul.

"Just be you, and let the rest of us be there to help." Planter smiled. "I'm confident it will all turn out okay."

"What are you two whispering about?" a voice said from the darkness.

Cutter walked up to them and pushed his way into the middle. "Are you telling Planter your plan? Don't you think you should be telling me too?"

Watcher sighed. "There's no plan yet."

"Maybe you need to get on that instead of whispering in the dark like a school kid."

The big warrior looked down at Planter and gave her a smile, which she returned. Jealousy burned bright in Watcher's soul.

"I need to be alone and think," Watcher said, then veered away from the pair and walked by himself near the edge of the passage.

Suddenly, a dark presence appeared before him, startling Watcher. He reached for his bow and notched an arrow, but stopped when a wide grin spread across the mysterious face.

"Blaster . . . I wish you wouldn't do that!" Watcher scowled at the boy, but it only made his smile grow wider.

"Sorry," Blaster said, "but I do what I do."

"What did you see up ahead?" Watcher slowed his pace and moved back to the center of the tunnel with Blaster in tow. The rest of the villagers gathered around them.

"You wouldn't believe me if I told you," Blaster said.

"Then how 'bout you tell us?" Winger said, a scowl on her face.

"Is it the room with pillars?" Watcher asked. "All of them are white, with redstone lanterns near the base?"

Blaster nodded, a look of surprise on his face.

"The Hall of Pillars." Mapper whispered reverently. "This was the seat of power for the skeleton warlord, Ragnar the Tormentor. The ancient archives suggest he crafted countless terrible weapons in that chamber. At the end of the war, the wizards hid many of the weapons made by the monsters."

"Why didn't they just destroy them?" Planter asked.

"I don't know," Mapper said. "Maybe they hid them because they knew we'd need them in the future. Or maybe they couldn't destroy them."

"Well, whether it's destroyed or not, no one is using the Lightning Blade for a while," Cleric said. "Lava makes things very unattractive."

"My fear is the skeleton warlord found some of those relics," Mapper continued. "If he did, then we might be in serious trouble."

"Great pep talk." Blaster patted the old man on the back. "The entrance is just up ahead. I suggest everyone gear up and get ready. You can be sure the monsters know we're coming. But the strangest thing . . . I didn't see any skeletons."

"Did you go all the way into the Hall of Pillars?" Watcher asked.

"You think I'm crazy? I'll leave that for you and Cutter . . . you guys like that sort of thing, like the way you charged the entire skeleton army back there at that monster Workshop." Blaster smiled. "I'll leave all the courageous things to you."

The NPCs smiled and patted Watcher on the back. But the adulation just chipped away at his self-confidence.

"I didn't charge at those skeletons because I was being brave," Watcher said meekly. "I did it because I just lost control."

"Then maybe you should lose control a little more often." Blaster laughed a deep belly laugh that spread throughout the army, filling the passage with laughter, driving away their fears.

When it subsided, the villagers took out their weapons and notched arrows to bowstrings, each with a look of determination on their square faces, the humor driven away by the reality of the situation.

Watcher glanced around at his companions, and put on the same mask they wore, that of courage and confidence. But he knew his mask was a lie. He was terrified, but didn't want anyone to know . . . he had to be an example of bravery.

"Come on . . . everyone," Watcher said, his voice cracking a little. "Let's go take back the Helm of Calling, and teach that skeleton warlord a lesson about messing with villagers."

"Yeah!" they shouted and followed as Watcher ran through the passage toward the Hall of Pillars and whatever the skeleton had waiting for them.

CHAPTER 32

Watcher moved into the Hall of Pillars slowly, expecting a skeleton attack at any second. The chamber was eerily quiet, the only sounds being the soft scuffing sounds of their boots on the hard stone floor and the occasional squeak from bats fluttering about in the darkness. There was an ancient feel to the massive room, as if it had witnessed countless victories and defeats over the centuries, but the atrocities that had happened within this chamber seemed to leave a lingering echo of agony and despair. The Hall of Pillars had been part of the wizard and warlock war hundreds of years ago, and was now part of the struggle between the monsters and the NPCs of the Far Lands.

Moving further into the cavernous space, Watcher peered into its depths with his keen eyesight; he saw nothing. The chamber before him stretched out for what seemed like hundreds of blocks until the far end merged with the haze of Minecraft and disappeared. The gigantic pillars were placed at precise intervals, each spaced eight blocks from its neighbor. They created a uniform field of white columns stretching high into the air until they disappeared into the darkness. Redstone lanterns decorated each pillar, the glowing cubes all four blocks high off the ground.

"Where are all the skeletons?" Planter asked, her voice low, almost a whisper. The empty expanse allowed her words to travel to the far walls and reflect back, the echo barely audible, but there. "I thought they'd be waiting for us at the entrance."

"Me too." Watcher kept his voice quiet as he glanced at his companions. They all seemed nervous. "Maybe the ones in the tunnel were the only ones."

"No . . . they're here," Cutter said, his booming voice cutting through the stillness. "They know we're here and they're waiting for something."

The big NPC moved deeper into the chamber, the rest of the villagers following reluctantly. Suddenly, a high-pitched twang sounded in the distance. Watcher thought he recognized the sound, but before he could say anything, a shimmering something appeared out of the darkness. The boy stared at it as it approached, then was filled with fear when he recognized the threat.

"It's an arrow . . . EVERYONE TAKE COVER!"

Watcher crouched, keeping his eyes on the projectiles, but most of the villagers were confused and just stood there. The arrow arched downward and struck one of the NPCs, a young villager named Carver. It hit him in the chest and knocked him to the ground. He flashed red over and over as he writhed in pain, then disappeared . . . his HP depleted.

Twang.

"Another one's coming!" Watcher shouted. "Everyone scatter and get behind a pillar."

The villagers ran in all directions, terrified. Watcher could see the enchanted arrow approaching, its razor-sharp point glittering with magic. NPCs ran to the edges of the chamber, but the arrow seemed to track its target. It streaked down and struck a woman in the back. She fell face first onto the stone floor, then disappeared, only the items in her inventory showing she'd ever existed.

A dry, hacking laugh floated out of the darkness, a clicking sound added to each chuckle.

"I know that laugh." Watcher took out his enchanted bow and notched an arrow.

"Yeah . . . me too," Cutter said, anger filling his steely-gray eyes.

Just then, torches flared to life on the far side of the chamber. At least a hundred skeletons stood near the distant wall, many of them wearing different types of armor. And then a terrifying skeleton stepped out of the darkness and into the light, his eyes burning with hatred: it was the skeleton warlord. The other skeletons stepped back, making room for their leader. His size dwarfed the other skeletons, only his general, Rusak, being taller. Casting his gaze across his monster army, the monster stood a little taller, a look of satisfaction on his pale, bony face. He then faced the intruders and glared at Watcher and his friends.

The monster wore iron armor decorated with jagged strips of red and black, the metallic plates glowing with powerful enchantments. In the warlord's hand was a huge bow made of white bone, the weapon seeming to merge with his pale fingers. It shimmered with iridescent power, giving the weapon a lethal appearance. He drew the bow-string back. Instantly, a sparkling arrow appeared as he aimed up into the air. The warlord's eyes glowed with an iridescent, purple color, giving the monster a faintly magical appearance. The warlord then flashed red, as if taking damage, while he pulled back the arrow a little further and aimed at his next target. With a smile on his terrifying face, the monster released the string, causing the enchanted arrow to streak into the air.

"Everyone get behind a pillar." Watcher ran forward and put his back against the quartz column, the red-stone lantern glowing bright over his head.

Peeking around the edge of the pillar, Watcher tracked the glittering shaft as it arched high into the air then gradually descended, heading toward its target.

We should all be safe, he thought, though the words seemed hollow in his mind.

The arrow zipped past him, then struck a nearby pillar at incredible speed. It went straight through the quartz column and embedded itself into a villager. Cobbler fell backward with the glittering arrow sticking out of his leather armor, then disappeared with a pop.

"No," moaned the villager's wife. She ran to the pile of items and scooped them up, then collapsed to the floor in grief.

"You have come to the land of the skeletons," the warlord shouted. "This is my kingdom. I am the skeleton warlord, Rakir, and you will not be allowed to steal my relics. My Bow of Destruction will stop you."

"Oh no," Mapper moaned. "The Fossil Bow of Destruction."

"What are you talking about?" Cleric moved to the old man's side.

"It's one of the most powerful artifacts made by the warlocks." Mapper shook with fear. "That bow can fire an arrow incredible distances, and it never misses. You can dodge or hide behind a mountain . . . it doesn't matter. The magical arrow will go through anything to find its target."

"As we saw." Planter pointed to the shattered quartz column and Cobbler's wife, still weeping on the ground.

Watcher peered around the edge of the column and stared at the monster. Rakir took a step closer, then reached back to his general. Rusak took the Helm of Calling from his inventory and handed it to the warlord. With an evil grin on his face, he brought the shining helmet near his head.

"You don't frighten us!" Cutter shouted.

"Oh really?" Rakir tossed the Helm of Calling back to Rusak, then pulled back on the Fossil Bow's string. With another red flash and a grunt of pain, he released the arrow, then fell to one knee.

A skeleton moved to the warlord's side and gave him

food of some kind, allowing him to replenish his HP, but Rakir was terribly weak.

Glancing to the glowing shaft, Watcher could somehow tell the arrow was heading straight for Cutter.

We can't afford to lose him, Watcher thought. *Cutter's our rock . . . our courage. Without him, we've lost.*

The boy dashed to Cutter, then stood in front of him.

"Cutter, don't move." Watcher could sense the big warrior trying to move behind the nearby pillar. "I SAID, DON'T MOVE!"

The big warrior stopped moving. A silence, like that of a graveyard on a moonless night spread across the chamber. Watcher stared at the sparkling projectile as it descended toward his friend. He knew if he failed, then Cutter was dead . . . and he himself likely was as well. There was only one chance to save Cutter.

Dropping his bow, Watcher drew Needle and waited. He was terrified.

"Step aside, Watcher . . . it's okay," Cutter said in a calm voice.

"Be quiet!"

Gripping the handle of Needle firmly, the boy brought the enchanted blade up and pointed it at the deadly projectile. It was getting closer. He could hear it whistling as it descended closer and closer and . . . faster than he could think, Needle swiped through the air and knocked the arrow aside. The enchanted shaft flew to the side and embedded itself into the stone ground, then disappeared.

"That was close," Planter said as she rushed to Watcher's side . . . or did she go to Cutter?

A large hand settled on his shoulder.

"Thank you," Cutter said, voice sincere.

Watcher didn't speak, but gave him a nod. Turning, he faced the skeleton warlord and pointed with his magical blade.

"If we just stand here, we're dead," Blaster said. "We need to attack . . . now. No plan, no strategy, just attack."

"I agree," Watcher said.

Everyone looked shocked. Watcher was always the one that insisted on thinking through all the possibilities before coming up with a strategy. But now, he knew Blaster was right.

"No, I think we *have* to think this through," Cleric countered. "If we charge, it will take too long for us to get close. The warlord will just pick us off, one at a time."

"And when we get close enough, the other skeletons will open fire on us," Mapper said. "We'll have a hundred arrows raining down on us. We can't survive a storm like that."

The other nodded, agreeing with everything said.

"We attack," Blaster said, undeterred.

"I agree, we fight," Cutter said.

The villagers argued amongst themselves as Watcher considered the words. Something Mapper had said resonated in his mind.

"Rain . . ." Watcher muttered.

"What?" Planter asked, confused.

Watcher looked at his friend, then remember the story about Planter and him being chased across the ice by Harvester. Suddenly, the solution materialized in his mind.

"You're right . . . you're *all* right. We can't just run at them and attack, and we can't stay here." Watcher looked to the skeleton warlord. He was slowly getting to his feet, his health gradually returning. "I have a plan, but you'll all probably think I'm crazy when I tell you."

"We all thought that a long time ago," Blaster said with a smile. "Why don't you tell us anyway?"

Watcher grinned. "Okay, here's what I want you all to do."

And Watcher explained his plans to the other villagers. Some laughed, while others shook their heads, but they knew they had no choice. If they fled, then the skeletons would use their ancient enchanted weapons to take over the Far Lands. They had to make their stand here and now.

Watcher removed the Frost Walker boots from his inventory and placed them on the ground. Stepping back, he drew the wand he'd found in the desert temple with all the parrots. Waving it over his head, he flicked his wrist over and over. Balls of light shot from the wand and struck the boots. They gave off bright flashes, forcing many of the villagers to look away, but Watcher kept staring down. He shot another ball of light at more of the boots, flicking the wand over and over again. Suddenly, pain surged through his body as the wand reached out for energy and found the boy's HP. He flashed red, but kept replicating the boots.

A glass bottle shattered against his enchanted armor, the potion dripping through the gaps between the metallic plates, adding to his HP. It allowed him to continue without driving his health to zero. Flicking the wand faster and faster, he showered the frozen boots with magical energy. Finally, when there were enough, he stopped and put the wand back into his inventory.

"Well . . . that was quite the trick." Blaster patted him on the back. "How did you know that would work?"

"When I found this wand, I—"

"Explain later." Cutter tossed pairs of boots to each NPC.

The skeleton warlord was now back on his feet and getting ready to fire another arrow.

"Why don't you try to shoot me?!" Watcher yelled out, taunting the monster.

"Son, what are you doing?" Cleric moved to his son's side.

"It's okay, just stay back." Watcher put on a pair of the Frost Walker boots, then stepped away from the other villagers and held Needle at the ready.

An arrow from Rakir's bow streaked into the air, soaring high, then descending straight toward Watcher. When it was close enough, he brought Needle up. The enchanted blade flicked it aside again. Watcher shook with fear, hoping Needle would continue to protect him.

He gave out a pair of magical boots to every villager. Cutter refused them at first, the stubborn warrior saying he didn't need them. Planter gave him an angry glare, then smiled at the big NPC, successfully convincing him to wear the enchanted shoes. Once everyone had them on, Watcher gazed at his comrades. "Is everyone ready?"

They nodded.

"OK then, here we go." He glanced at his sister as he pulled out a blue-tipped arrow, Winger doing the same. They aimed high into the air and fired, the water-arrows soaring into the chamber and landing on the ground between them and their enemy.

Before the arrow hit the ground, Watcher and the others charged ahead.

"For Carver . . ."

"For Farmer . . ."

"For Baker . . ."

The villagers shouted the names of fallen comrades and family members as they followed Watcher, their leader, into battle, expecting a rain of arrows to fall down upon them at any second.

CHAPTER 33

Sprinting as fast as he could, Watcher charged straight at the warlord. Next to him, Cutter tried to keep up, his iron armor clanking with every step. For some reason, Watcher's own armor made no noise; the enchantment kept it quiet, somehow.

The skeleton warlord had a surprised expression on his pale face as the ragtag group of villagers ran forward, yelling the names of their fallen friends. The monster stared straight at Watcher, its dark beady eyes glued right to his.

Slowly, Rakir pulled back on the Fossil Bow's string and took aim.

"NOW!" Watcher skidded to a stop and quickly put on a set of the Frost Walker boots as the rest of the villagers did the same. He and Winger then fired water arrows at the ground ahead of them.

"RUN!" He took off, running atop the flowing water, the liquid freezing instantly.

Planter and Winger, on either side of him, fired more water arrows as Watcher put away his bow and drew Needle.

The warlord released his arrow. It streaked through the air, leaving a faint trail of sparks as it flew. Watcher tried to weave to the left, but the projectile turned, continuing to track its target. Increasing his speed, he dashed across the frozen water, heading straight for his adversary.

More water arrows fell onto the floor of the Hall of Pillars, coating the surface with flowing blue liquid. With the Frost Walker boots, the villagers were able to move two to three times faster than any skeleton expected.

The warlord's arrow sped toward him, the pointed tip glistening in the light from the redstone lanterns. Watcher relaxed his arm, holding the blade before him as he skated across the ice. It was almost to him, almost there, almost . . . Needle became a silvery blur as it brushed the arrow aside.

"You're pretty good at that," a deep voice said to his right. Watcher found Cutter at his side, diamond blade in his hand.

"Let's get this done," Watcher said. "More water!"

Archers, all wearing Frost Walker boots, fired water arrows ahead of them, but they also fired them at the skeletons who were now within range. They were moving so fast, the monsters' arrows were of no concern; the bony creatures always fired where they had been a moment earlier, and not where they were going to be by the time the arrow arrived.

The skeleton warlord pulled back on his Fossil Bow again, getting ready to fire, but a curved knife suddenly shot out of the darkness, spinning end over end until it hit the monster in the shoulder. Rakir dropped his bow and fell backward, already weakened from using the enchanted weapon.

Rusak, the skeleton general, quickly scooped up his wounded leader and carried him behind their troops, giving him bones to revive his HP. The skeletons formed a protective circle around their leader, but before they could ready another volley of arrows, Watcher and the others were upon them. The water arrows fell amongst the monsters, knocking them aside and making it difficult for many to stand. Some fell to the ground while others just tried to retreat.

Smashing into the skeletons at full speed, Watcher and Cutter knocked the monsters aside as if they were mere insects. They wanted the warlord and the general; the other villagers would take care of the skeletons.

By now, the other villagers were firing upon the skeleton army as they drew near. The monsters tried to respond, but swordsmen and swordswomen running across the frozen water were already within their ranks.

Screams of pain shouted out from both sides as the battle raged. Watcher heard the shouts of agony and fear, but knew he couldn't focus on them. His job was to stop the warlord and take any ancient relics that monster possessed before he could do any more harm.

Cutter's diamond blade slashed through the skeleton ranks, snapping bones and tearing at HP. Watcher fought at his side with Needle moving with lightning speed. Some of the skeletons came at them with swords, the bony creatures garbed in various types of armor, but it didn't matter. The speed and ferocity at which the two villagers fought was just too much for the skeletons.

Suddenly, a bright red shield appeared next to Watcher. Planter blocked an arrow, then turned with her golden axe and slashed at a nearby skeleton. Its bones shattered under the assault, the monster disappearing, a look of confused terror on its pale face. Blaster appeared at her side with only one knife; the other was still embedded in the skeleton warlord. He held a shield in his left hand, a handful of arrows already sticking out like feathered quills.

"Go get him," Blaster said. "We'll keep these monsters off your back."

Watcher nodded, then charged through a gap in the lines, heading for the warlord and general, who huddled near the far wall. Watcher and Cutter approached slowly, with Blaster and Planter following behind, knocking away arrows with their shields.

By now, the skeleton army was in complete disarray. Likely, the monsters expected to pick the intruders off from afar, but now they were standing face to face with the NPCs. Few of them had swords, which meant the skeletons were in serious trouble. The NPCs drew swords and axes and charged into the pale ranks. The skeletons tried to hold them back with arrows, but the projectiles were not very effective at close range.

At the same time, Watcher and Cutter closed in on the warlord and general. The two monsters stood on either side of a huge throne made of fossilized bone and redstone blocks. Redstone lanterns embedded in the floor around the ornate seat lit the scene with a warm yellow light, pushing back the gloom. A dark hole sat on either side of the throne, water flooding into each shadowy opening.

We must be careful not to fall into those holes, Watcher thought, noting their position in his mind.

"You think you can challenge Rakir, the skeleton warlord?" the monster shouted.

He reached into his inventory, clearly looking for the Fossilized Bow, but it lay on the ground when it had been dropped, a step in front of Watcher.

"Looking for this?" Watcher smiled, then bent down and grasped the bow with his left hand.

For some reason, the warlord only smiled as he watched the boy pick up the magical weapon.

Pain erupted in his Watcher's arm as the bow seemed to stab at him, but he did not release his grip. Quickly he put the bow into his inventory, then shook his tingling arm.

Rakir was shocked the boy was able to put the weapon aside. He glared at Watcher, then screamed. "You dare take the Fossil Bow of Destruction from me?!"

"You want it?" Watcher sneered at the monster. "Come and get it."

Rakir reached into his inventory and drew a long two-handed sword. It sparkled with magical enchantments but was also surrounded by a dark halo, as if the weapon were drinking in the light around it. The blade itself was black as midnight, its keen edge gleaming in the light from the redstone lanterns.

"You think that bow is my only weapon." Rakir glared at him. "You are a fool." The skeleton smiled. "Allow me to introduce to you the Widow-Maker, and it will soon destroy you and leave your widow sobbing in grief."

"Too bad I'm not married," Watcher returned with a grin, then glared at the monster.

Fear started to creep into the back of his mind; the skeleton was terrifying to behold, but he knew this monster would destroy every one of his friends if given the chance. He had to stop him, here and now . . . and that meant standing up to his fear, somehow.

"Skeleton warlord, I will not allow you to hurt my friends or any other villagers."

"What are you gonna do about it, boy-wizard?" Rakir sneered, then took a step closer, his massive broadsword held casually on his shoulder. "You don't have your powers, for if you did, you'd be using them. You're just a worthless kid, pretending to be brave, but I can see the fear deep within you. You don't stand a chance against me."

Watcher took a step back. The skeleton warlord was right; Watcher didn't stand a chance against this huge monster and his massive sword. He was just a kid, pretending to be a warrior, but he wasn't fooling anyone.

But then, a voice whispered something in the back of his mind. *A hero can be the smallest and weakest person, yet do great deeds if people believe in them.*

"Er-Lan believes in Watcher." The zombie was suddenly at his side, his razor-sharp claws extended and ready for battle. "Everyone believes in Watcher." The zombie laid a hand on the boy's shoulder. "Er-Lan have seen your victory already."

"You mean in your visions?"

The zombie hesitated for a moment, then nodded. "Become the hero Watcher was meant to be."

He'd seen my victory in the future—that must mean I can do this, Watcher thought.

Er-Lan's faith in him pushed aside any doubt or fear. He was here to protect his friends, and that's what he was going to do. Extending Needle, Watcher took a step forward, the enchanted blade glowing bright.

"Skeleton, I'm gonna punish you for your crimes," Watcher said, then stood a little taller, his courage pushing back his fears. He glared at his enemy, refusing to retreat. "Come on, Rakir. . . it's *go* time."

At that moment, Rakir swung Widow-Maker as Watcher swung Needle, starting the greatest PvP battle since the Great War.

CHAPTER 34

Their enchanted swords met in a shower of sparks, the blades crashing together with the sound of thunder. The force of the blow reverberated through Needle and into Watcher's arm, making it go numb for just an instant.

Rakir laughed a dry, scratchy laugh as he raised the massive blade for another strike. Moving fast, Watcher spun around, swiping at the skeleton warlord's ribs, his blade tearing into the monster's armor and finding a gap between the metallic plates. Rakir flashed red as Needle dug into the monster's HP.

At the same time, Cutter and Rusak circled each other like predatory cats. The glow from Cutter's enchanted armor cast a soft purple circle on the ground, but the sparkling light from the Frost Walker boots made the illumination pulse as if it were alive. The two warriors carefully assessed their opponent . . . and then they attacked, their swords clashing together, thunder filling the hall. Cutter grunted in pain as Rusak's sword slipped past his guard and dug into the NPC's shoulder, but Watcher had to ignore his friend, for now. He knew Cutter could take care of himself, and Watcher knew his own battle would take every bit of skill he had to defeat the skeleton warlord.

When he looked back to his opponent, Rakir was swinging Widow-Maker in a huge arc. Watcher brought Needle up just in time to deflect the blow, but the impact of the massive broadsword almost tore Needle from his grasp. Rolling to the side, he slashed at the skeleton's legs, but his enchanted longsword just missed its pale femurs. Pain erupted in Watcher's shoulder as the skeleton warlord's dark sword came down in a mighty blow. The razor-sharp edge of the enchanted blade cut through a section of his armor and dug deep into his flesh, making the young boy flash red with damage. At the same time, Watcher heard Cutter shout in pain as he too took damage; their battles were not going well.

Watcher stood, then charged at his opponent, his Frost Walker boots gripping the stone as if they had claws. He pretended to attack his right side, then twisted and attacked his left. Needle clanged off the warlord's armor, but had no effect.

Suddenly, the skeleton moved forward and wrapped his skinny arms around the boy. It felt as if a thousand spikes were stabbing into him as the monster held Watcher tighter and tighter.

His armor has the Thorns enchantment, he thought. *I must get away from him.*

Watcher twisted and squirmed, trying to get free, but the skeleton held on tight, his armor continuing to inflict damage. Reaching into his inventory, Watcher pulled out a water arrow and threw it onto the ground at his feet. Instantly, a pool of water spread out across the stone ground, making it slippery. The skeleton stumbled and fell, allowing Watcher to move away, the water instantly freezing under his feet and letting him step back quickly.

The skeleton warlord struggled against the flowing water, then pulled out a block of dirt and placed it on the water source. Gradually, the water flowed away, leaving the stone floor dry again.

"You can't get away from me, boy," the warlord said, his voice raspy. "Soon, the rest of my army will be here and it will be the end for you and all your friends."

Watcher glanced around the chamber, checking to see if more monsters were arriving. They weren't there . . . yet. And then the two warriors attacked again, their swords clashing together, making thunder fill the hall.

Ducking under Rakir's sword, he rolled to a side and stabbed at his legs. Watcher noticed many of the villagers had removed their enchanted boots. And then, out of the corner of his eye, he saw the boots just disappear from the feet of an NPC. The frozen water underfoot melted just as she attacked one of the skeletons. *That's curious . . . why would the copied boots disappear?*

Watcher pushed the thought aside and charged at his opponent, swinging Needle as fast as he could, allowing Rakir to block his attack, but then he spun around as he swiped at the huge skeleton's chest. His enchanted blade gouged into the monster's armor, but did little damage.

The skeleton brought the Widow-Maker down in a lethal, overhead strike, aimed at his head. Watcher got out of the way just in time, the vicious blade glancing off his shoulder and tearing into the metallic sleeve. Part of the armor fell to the ground, leaving his left arm unprotected.

Rakir laughed, pointing at the torn garment on the ground. Watcher took advantage of the distraction and rolled forward, then lunged at the monster's chest. The warlord brought the massive blade down just in time to deflect his attack, then hit Watcher hard in the head with the hilt of the sword. He staggered backward, his head spinning, the monster's laughter filling his ears.

"You don't stand a chance, boy-wizard. Soon, I will take the last of your HP and watch you disappear."

Watcher glanced around, looking for something to help. This monster was just too big, his armor and weapon too strong for him. *I can't do this . . . it's impossible.*

Just then, a sparkling red arrow streaked through the air and struck Rakir in the chest. The arrow bounced off his enchanted armor, but pushed him back a step. Another arrow followed the first, pinging off his chest plate, the *Punch* enchantment forcing the monster back again.

"Watcher, are you okay?"

He glanced up and found Winger standing over him. She fired another arrow, then helped him to his feet. Rakir's Fossil Bow of Destruction clattered to the ground as well as the cloning wand and other items that had been in his inventory. He thought about using the Bow on Rakir, but he doubted his HP could pay the price.

"I can't beat him, Winger . . . he's too strong."

"Er-Lan believes," a voice said in his ear.

Watcher glanced over his shoulder and found Er-Lan standing at his side.

"You said you saw me victorious in your vision?" Watcher accused in disbelief. "I can't beat him . . . he's four times stronger than me. It's impossible. Your vision must have been wrong!"

"Four times stronger?" Er-Lan asked.

"What?" Watcher was confused.

The zombie leaned down and picked up the wand of cloning and moved it in a circle over his head as Watcher had, then flicked it toward the boy.

A bright white light engulfed Watcher, every inch of his skin feeling burning hot and freezing cold at the same time. The faint outline of Rakir moving closer filled him with fear, but then the image of the skeleton seemed to split in two as if Watcher had double vision, then his sight cleared. He glanced at Er-Lan. The zombie was flashing red as he took damage, the wand demanding payment. With another flick, the zombie shot another ball of burning, freezing light at him. Again, Watcher was enveloped with magical power, his vision splitting again as needles of burning cold pierced his skin.

Er-Lan screamed in pain, then flicked the wand one more time, and collapsed.

Did that wand take too much HP from Er-Lan? Watcher thought, fear exploding throughout his body. *Is he dead?*

The twang of a bowstring brought him back to his senses.

Winger fired another burning arrow at the skeleton as Watcher's vision finally cleared. He looked around to find three other Watchers staring back at him, confused.

"What's going on?" he asked his sister.

"Talk later." She fired another arrow. "It's time to fight, and I'm talking to all of you!"

Watcher glanced at the other Watchers. Each wore the same shiny, enchanted armor with the left sleeve missing, each one with their own Needle glowing angrily in their hands. They all turned their gaze toward Rakir who stared at the quadruplets in disbelief, then sneered.

"One boy-wizard or four . . . it's no matter to me. I'll destroy you all."

"You think so?" one of the Watchers said.

Rakir laughed, then took a step forward, Widow-Maker held ready.

"Skeleton, it's time we taught you some respect," another Watcher said.

"Yeah," said the third, "and school is now in session."

The fourth Watcher banged Needle against his chest plate, then yelled his battle cry, his carbon copies all joining in. "ATTACK!"

CHAPTER 35

The Watchers charged at Rakir.

The skeleton, shocked at the multitude of opponents, took a step back, then gave his enemies a growl. "Four of you . . . Rakir can easily destroy four boy-wizards who don't have any power yet."

Leaping high into the air, the skeleton warlord landed between all of the Watchers. He swung his huge blade with two bony hands gripping the hilt, spinning in a circle. The tip of the enchanted blade cut a gash through the sparkling iron mail of his opponents. One of the Watchers charged at the monster, taking a savage hit to his ribs. The boy flashed red as he screamed in pain and took damage. Another Watcher attacked from behind, bringing Needle down upon the monster's enchanted armor. He hit the monster hard, causing a wide crack to form along the monster's back.

Rakir turned and lunged at the attacker, scoring a hit on the boy's shoulder. At the same time, two other Watchers charged, swinging their Needles with all their strength. Both blades came down upon the monster for a killing blow, but the skeleton warlord stepped away just in time, allowing the attack to miss. With the two Watchers off balance, Rakir stepped forward and slashed at them, tearing into their armor and chiseling away at their HP. The nearest boy screamed in pain, a look of fear on his square face. He glanced at his sister and started to say something, but Widow-Maker came down upon the boy's shoulder, taking the last of his HP. He screamed in pain and disappeared. One Watcher had perished.

"One down, three to go." Rakir laughed a hollow, hacking sort of laugh, then charged at the nearest adversary, his dark blade coming down like a bolt of shadowy lightning.

Watcher rolled to the side, the monster's blade narrowly missing. When he stood, the other duplicates charged at the skeleton, slashing at arms and shoulders and chest. Needles bounced off the monster's armor, causing wide cracks to form in Rakir's metallic skin. The warlord screamed in frustration, then slashed at his attackers, landing a hit on each.

Out of the corner of his eye, Watcher saw more of the Frost Walker boots disappearing right off the villager's feet. The villagers fell through the melting layer of ice, getting stuck in the water that flowed across the stone floor.

"Winger, help the others," the boy shouted as he brought up his blade to block an attack.

The skeleton kicked him hard in the chest, sending him to the ground. Before he could stand, Widow-Maker came down onto his leg, cutting through the iron leggings and digging in to his flesh. Pain shot through his body like fire as the sword tore into his HP; Watcher knew he was close to death.

The Watcher doppelgangers charged the skeleton warlord, trying to protect the wounded Watcher. They slashed at the monster, tearing chunks from his enchanted armor. Rakir turned and brought his shadowy blade onto the duplicates, causing them to cry out in pain.

He's destroying them, and when he's done with them, he'll turn on me. Watcher glanced across the chamber at Planter. She was locked in battle with two skeletons, her golden axe hewing into their bones, but she too looked terrified. *This must stop before all my health is gone. I need to get healed somehow.*

Just then, he remembered the arrows he still had in his inventory . . . but were there any left? Reaching into his inventory, he pulled out the last arrow of Healing. With the shaft gripped firmly in his hand, Watcher dropped Needle and allowed it to clatter to the ground. Rakir heard the sound and spun. Seeing the villager with no weapon and a single arrow in his hand, the warlord laughed.

Watcher glanced at the other Watchers, then held the arrow high over his head. They nodded and also dropped their swords, each pulling out a similar arrow.

"What are you gonna do with those, scratch your name into my chest plate?" Rakir laughed again.

"It's time for this to end." Watcher took a step forward. He glanced at his duplicate selves. They nodded, each understanding what must be done. "NOW!"

The three identical villagers charged at the warlord. Rakir swung his huge blade at one of the Watchers. The boy ducked under the attack and rolled across the ground. Then, as one, they all leapt into the air, holding their arrows like daggers. They fell upon the skeleton, the *Thorns* enchantment on the monster's armor stabbing at them, but the pain didn't matter, the agony didn't matter . . . all that mattered was the arrows of Healing. They each jabbed the arrows between the armored plates until the pointed shafts found bone, then pushed away from the monster.

The healing potion embedded in the arrows quickly spread across the monster. It coated his bones beneath the armor, the metallic layer doing nothing to protect him. Rakir screamed in pain. He dropped Widow-Maker as he flashed red, the healing potion acting like poison to the undead creature.

The monster fell to the ground, writhing as he flashed red again and again. The silvery Helm of Calling fell from his inventory and rolled across the ground. One of the Watchers stepped forward and stopped the ancient relic with a foot, then glared down at the skeleton warlord.

"I think the lesson is over, Rakir," Watcher said. "Class dismissed."

And with a terrified expression on his face, Rakir, the skeleton warlord, disappeared.

CHAPTER 36

"**T**he warlord is dead?!" one of the skeletons shouted. The fighting slowed as many of the monsters glanced at the pile of enchanted armor that had once been worn by their commander. A handful of the monsters turned and fled from the chamber, their will to fight now broken. Some of the skeletons continued fighting, but most chose to follow the examples of their comrades, and ran from the villagers.

Watcher glanced at Cutter and the general. They had separated, and Rusak was now staring at the pile of armor that had once been his skeleton warlord.

"No . . . it can't be true." General Rusak glanced at Cutter, then reached out suddenly and pushed the big NPC to the ground.

As the warrior struggled to his feet, the skeleton ran for the elaborate throne against the far wall. He stood next to the hole adjacent to the throne, water pouring into the opening. Rusak glared at the Watchers, then jumped into the watery flow and disappeared into the darkness.

Once he regained his feet, Cutter chased after the monster, ready to dive into the flowing liquid, following his enemy.

"No . . . you can't jump in there after him," one of the Watchers said. "He could have blocked off the water flow farther down and you could drown." He moved to his friend's side and placed a hand on his shoulder. "Let him go."

"But he might have more artifacts. Some of them could be dangerous weapons."

"It's okay; we stopped the skeleton warlord," Watcher said. "That's the important thing." Cutter nodded, then glanced past Watcher to see the other two Watchers. "There's three of you?"

The three Watchers nodded.

"But I don't think we're gonna be here for much longer," one of them said.

"Yeah, I saw the Frost Walker boots disappearing as well," another Watcher replied. "I think the items cloned with the magic wand only stay for a while."

"Er-Lan . . . he was hurt when he did the cloning. Is he okay?" The third Watcher scanned the room and found his friend lying on the ground. Winger was there at his side, offering the zombie a piece of melon. He ran to the zombie. "Are you alright?"

The zombie glanced up at Watcher, then cast his gaze on the other duplicates. "I think so." He took the melon slice and gobbled it down, then stood on shaky legs. Winger gave him an apple and a loaf of bread. "But Er-Lan has a confession to make. Watcher's victory was not seen in a vision."

"You mean you didn't see me defeat the skeleton warlord?"

The zombie shook his head.

"They why did you tell me that?" one of the Watcher asked.

"Belief was needed. Watcher doubted what he could do, and if that doubt lingered, Er-Lan knew victory could slip away." The zombie looked down at the ground as if he were ashamed. "Er-Lan lied to Watcher so success would seem possible. One can only do what they imagine is possible. If Watcher thought victory was impossible . . . then it would have been impossible." He took a step closer to his friend. "Er-Lan gave Watcher hope."

"I guess you did the right thing, but I'd rather hear the truth." Watcher glanced at his other doppelgangers. "How long do we have until we start to disappear?"

The others just shrugged.

"Er-Lan is confused. Watcher was cloned three times." The zombie bit into the loaf of bread and chewed as he thought. "There should be four, but only three are present. What if the original Watcher was killed?"

"Then all of us would disappear and there would be no—" That Watcher suddenly vanished in a puff of purple sparkles, the cloning enchantment having run its course.

"Oh no." Planter moved closer to one of them. "That means *all* of you might disappear."

The remaining Watchers both nodded their heads.

And then a second one disappeared, leaving only one remaining.

"I can't tell if I'm the real one or a clone." Watcher took a step toward Planter and held his breath, waiting for the moment when he would disappear.

The Hall of Pillars grew still, every villager staring at the boy, waiting to see what would happen. Watcher's heart pounded in his chest. *What will it feel like? Will it be like dying?* He felt a tingling sensation at his neck. *Was it beginning?* The tingling spread across his neck, then up to his cheek, and then suddenly . . . *SQUAWK!*

A parrot nuzzled his neck with his smooth beak, the bird's feathers tickling his ear.

"I'm still here . . . I'M STILL HERE!"

The villagers cheered, many of them struggling through the flowing water to reach Watcher's side. Those nearest gave the boy a hug as the celebration spread through the chamber.

Watcher felt as if he'd just narrowly escaped death. The skeleton warlord had been too much for him, and without the Wand of Cloning, he would have not survived. But if Rakir had killed him instead of one of the clones, the outcome would have been completely different.

If I had died, I wouldn't have had the chance to tell Planter how I really feel, he realized. *I need to take the risk and tell her while I still have the courage.*

He took a step toward her. "Planter, there's something I've been meaning to tell you."

Planter turned from a celebrating villager and faced her friend. "Yeah? What is it?"

"Well . . . you see . . . umm . . . I've been feeling—"

Suddenly, a shadowy presence appeared in the chamber. Instantly, the air grew frigid, a chill spreading throughout the chamber. It was as if the life had been sucked out of the air.

A wither appeared next to the warlord's throne, its three dark heads scanning the villagers with vile hatred in its eyes. The center head, larger than the other two, wore a golden crown with tiny black skulls embedded in the rim.

"So, wizard, I see you have destroyed my skeleton warlord," the monster said.

"Who are you?" Cleric asked.

"I am Krael, the King of the Withers, and I have come for what is rightfully mine." The monster glanced at the silvery Helm of Calling that lay on the ground a few blocks away. The monster floated toward it, no one close by.

"We have to stop him!" Watcher shouted.

Krael laughed as he drew nearer to the enchanted artifact. When the monster was just a block from the Helm, the ancient relic started to slide toward the wither. The other heads joined the center, laughing a maniacal laugh that made the villagers cringe. But before the enchanted helmet could slide into the monster's inventory, a flaming arrow streaked through the air and hit the Helm, pushing it across the ground, right to Cutter's feet. It moved quickly into the big warrior's inventory and disappeared.

Everyone followed the line of glowing embers still floating in the air along the path of the arrow. It led back to Winger and her enchanted bow.

"I think we'll be holding onto that artifact for a while." She glanced at her brother and gave him a wink.

"Archers, aim at the Wither King and get ready to fire," Watcher said. He drew his own enchanted bow from his inventory and notched a fire arrow to the string. "Ready . . ."

"Another time, wizard." Krael floated backward, away from the archers. "But our next meeting will not end so easily for you."

"Aim . . ."

And then then Krael, the King of the Withers, disappeared in a cloud of dark smoke.

"I hate those things." Blaster picked up his knife from amongst Rakir's belongings. "But I thought we already destroyed the king of the withers."

"Whichever one gets the Crown of Skulls becomes the Wither King," Er-Lan said. "There have been many who have worn the Crown and become ruler of the withers. That artifact seems to be able to find a new wither to control when the old one dies. Great magic flows through that golden crown."

"I'm just glad it's gone." Mapper reached down and collected the skeleton warlord's items and stuffed them into his already-bulging inventory. "And we should be gone as well. There must be a way out other than the way the general escaped. Everyone look around for a lever or button; there must be another way out."

The villagers spread out, moving along the walls looking for a secret exit.

"Watcher, you were saying something before the Wither King arrived." Planter put a gentle hand on his arm.

It felt like fireworks going off within his soul.

"What was it you wanted to tell me?"

"Well . . . umm . . . it's just that you and me have been friends for a long time. But now—"

"I found it!" a voice shouted from the darkness. A set of pistons could be heard moving, the sound of stone scraping across stone filling the hall. One of the villagers placed a torch on the ground, illuminating the secret passage. "Come on, everyone!"

The villagers all ran for the passage, anxious to get out of the Hall of Pillars.

Just as Watcher was about to continue, Cutter appeared at Planter's side.

"Come on, let's get out of this place." The big warrior grabbed her hand and headed for the exit.

She glanced over her shoulder and shrugged, then smiled and ran in lockstep with Cutter, her golden axe shining as brightly as her beautiful blond hair.

Watcher felt as if he'd been punched in the heart. "I just want to tell her how I feel." His voice as weak, barely a whisper.

"I know, brother," Winger said, her hushed voice in his ear. "Another time will come, Watcher. You'll have your chance."

"But what about Cutter? I mean . . . look at them running together. . . ."

"It probably doesn't mean anything."

"Or it means everything." Watcher stared at the ground, feeling defeated.

"Come on, son and daughter." Cleric put his arms around his two children. "Let's get out of here."

"Where are we heading?" Winger asked. "We need a plan."

"I was thinking about that," Watcher said as they walked toward the entrance. Most of the villagers had left the hall, leaving them alone in the Hall of Pillars with Blaster waiting near the exit. "There was the huge village in the savannah before we went into that desert temple. I think we should go there and rest up, and maybe build some defenses around that community in case Krael comes knocking on our door."

"That's a good idea." Cleric patted his son on the back.

"Will anyone listen to me now that all the fighting's over?" Watcher asked.

"Er-Lan will listen," a scratchy voice said from behind, his voice shaking as if afraid.

Watcher turned and found the zombie walking quietly behind them, an expression of guilt and fear on the monster's face. Reaching out, Watcher pulled the zombie into the group and put an arm around his green shoulders. Er-Lan smiled.

"You're still part of this family, no matter what you do or say," Watcher said. "You lied to me about your vision to help me defeat that terrible warlord, and in it, you taught me a valuable lesson. I must first believe in myself and see my success in my mind."

The zombie nodded. "Er-Lan's mother taught that to Er-Lan many years ago. That lesson reminds Er-Lan of her, and keeps the memory of mother alive in Er-Lan's mind . . . and heart."

Winger leaned over to the zombie and kissed him on the cheek. "We can learn a lot from you, I think."

"There is much that villagers can learn from zombies, and probably from skeletons as well," Cleric said. "Maybe one day, there will be peace in the Far Lands, and the different races will have the opportunity to learn from one another."

"That's not gonna happen while the Wither King is out there stirring up trouble," Watcher said. "We need to do something about that monster."

"Later," Cleric said. "For now, let's go to that village in the savannah and rest . . . we deserve it."

"Agreed." Watcher and Winger said in unison.

They looked at each other and smiled, then ran for the exit to the Hall of Pillars, putting their frightening adventure behind them . . . for now.

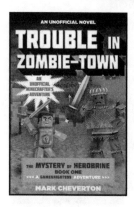  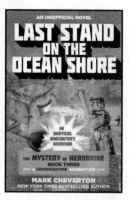

AVAILABLE NOW FROM MARK CHEVERTON AND SKY PONY PRESS

THE BIRTH OF HEROBRINE SERIES
Can Gameknight999 survive a journey one hundred years into Minecraft's past?

A freak thunderstorm strikes just as Gameknight999 is activating his father's Digitizer to reenter Minecraft. Sparks flash across his vision as he is sucked into the game . . . and when the smoke clears he's arrived safely. But it doesn't take long to realize that things in the Overworld are very different.

The User-that-is-not-a-user realizes he's been accidentally sent a hundred years into the past, back to the time of the historic Great Zombie Invasion. None of his friends have even been born yet. But that might be the least of Gameknight999's worries, because traveling back in time also means that the evil virus Herobrine, the scourge of Minecraft, is still alive . . .

The Great Zombie Invasion (Book One):
$9.99 paperback • 978-1-5107-0994-2

Attack of the Shadow-crafters (Book Two):
$9.99 paperback • 978-1-5107-0995-9

Herobrine's War (Book Three):
$9.99 paperback • 978-1-5107-0996-7

AVAILABLE NOW FROM MARK CHEVERTON AND SKY PONY PRESS

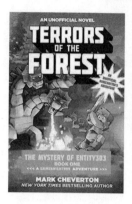  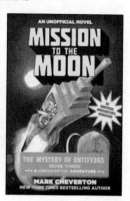

THE MYSTERY OF ENTITY303 SERIES
Minecraft mods are covering the tracks of a mysterious new villain!

Gameknight999 reenters Minecraft to find it completely changed, and his old friends acting differently. The changes are not for the better.

Outside of Crafter's village, a strange user named Entity303 is spotted with Weaver, a young NPC Gameknight knows from Minecraft's past. He realizes that Weaver has somehow been kidnapped, and returning him to the correct time is the only way to fix things.

What's worse: Entity303 has created a strange and bizarre modded version of Minecraft, full of unusual creatures and biomes. Racing through the Twilight Forest and MystCraft, and finally into the far reaches of outer space, Gameknight will face his toughest challenge yet in a Minecraft both alien and dangerous.

Terrors of the Forest (Book One):
$9.99 paperback • 978-1-5107-1886-9

Monsters in the Mist (Book Two):
$9.99 paperback • 978-1-5107-1887-6

Mission to the Moon (Book Three):
$9.99 paperback • 978-1-5107-1888-3

EXCERPT FROM
INTO THE SPIDERS' LAIR
A BRAND NEW FAR LANDS ADVENTURE

They slowed to a walk, everyone including Watcher tired from the chase. Moving next to Planter, he looked down at the black-and-white bunny she held in her hands.

"Have you been carrying that all this time?" Watcher asked.

She looked at him with her bright green eyes. Planter said something, but Watcher wasn't paying attention; he was lost in those emerald pools.

"What?" He shook his head to clear it.

"I said no, I just found this one and picked her up." She smiled as she scratched the fluffy animal's ears. "Aren't they fantastic?"

"It's just a rabbit." Cutter's voice boomed through the forest, always louder than necessary.

Planter scowled at the big warrior, but he didn't notice; he was adjusting his armor. Watcher smiled.

"I didn't know rabbits were part of the mega taiga biome," she said.

"Yep, there are lots of animals in this forest." Mapper paused to catch his breath, then continued. "Let's see, there are chickens and sheep and wolves and—"

"Wolves?" A concerned expression came across Planter's face. "Don't wolves eat rabbits?"

"Wolves eat just about whatever they want to eat," Cutter added. The big warrior moved between Planter and Watcher, feigning interest in the tiny animal in her arms. His armor clanked as he walked, scaring the little rabbit. It squirmed in Planters arms, then jumped to the ground and scurried away. "I love wolves. They're a ferocious animal that know how to fight and won't just run away when attacked. Wolves are a creature to be respected."

"Sometimes standing your ground isn't always the right thing to do," Watcher said.

Cutter remained silent.

"Mapper, do you have any idea where these spiders are heading?" Planter asked as she stopped walking, pulled out a loaf of bread, and took a huge bite.

"I'm not quite sure," the old man replied. "I saw some ancient structures made by the wizards on the map, but the spiders don't seem to be heading toward them. It's almost as if they just want us to follow them . . . strange."

Just then, a sound, like distant thunder, floated through the forest. The noise was almost imperceptible, but was still detected by Watcher's sensitive ears.

"Did any of you hear that?" The boy scanned the forest, looking for threats.

"Hear what?" Cutter moved to his side, his diamond sword drawn and ready.

"I thought I heard something like thunder, but look up . . . there are no clouds overhead." Watcher glanced up and could easily see the sparkling stars overhead, the occasional cloud drifting by.

"I didn't hear anything." The big warrior surveyed their surroundings one more time, then put away his sword. "I think it was nothing, maybe something from that famous imagination I've heard so much about."

Watcher blushed when Planter giggled, then put away his bow.

"It's okay, Watcher, sometimes I hear things too," Mapper said in a soothing voice.

"But I felt something in the ground rumble as well, like a very faint tremor." Watcher lowered his voice and whispered to the old man. "Something's coming toward us . . . I can feel it."

"Just keep it to yourself until you know what it is for sure," the old man said. "We don't want to panic everyone for no reason."

"Right." Watcher nodded, but he knew his face showed what he was feeling: fear.

Er-Lan moved next to Watcher and grabbed his arm. "This is the forest."

"What?"

"From the vision," the zombie said. "The black rain . . . it draws near."

Glancing to the sky, Watcher checked for storm clouds. "I can see the stars, Er-Lan. There aren't any clouds up there. I think you are mistaken about the black rain."

"Visions are never mistaken." Er-Lan glanced around, fear covering his scarred face. "All must be careful . . . the black rain comes."

Watcher nodded and patted his friend on the back, then focused his attention on the surroundings. They continued through the spruce forest, the massive trees looming high overhead, the treetops barely visible in the darkness. The path before them was difficult to see; the few rays of moonlight piercing the leafy canopy were not very bright. Only Watcher's keen eyes could still discern the trail of the spiders.

Suddenly, a clicking sound seemed to filter down through the branches and leaves ahead. Watcher skidded to a stop and peered into the forest. The moon lit the forest with its silvery light, struggling to push back the night. It allowed Watcher to see the forest around him, but sections further away were completely masked in darkness; anything could be out there, including that rumbling something.

Just then, a huge cluster of clouds floated across the moon's pockmarked face, masking the lunar glow. Darkness enveloped the forest like a black velvety curtain. More things clicked in the treetops.

"Everyone look around." Watcher's voice was barely a whisper.

"I don't see anything," Cutter boomed.

"Shhhh." Planter took out her enchanted shield and golden axe. An iridescent glow surrounded the girl, the purple radiance pushing back on the gloom.

With his bow in his hand and a sparkling fire arrow notched to the string, Watcher closed his eyes and allowed his ears to direct his attention. He listened to the strange clicking, then finally recognized it.

"Spiders . . ." his voice was barely a whisper, "in the trees."

He aimed at the tapping sound, he drew back the bowstring, focusing his shot on the noise, and then he raised his bow the slightest amount. Stilling his body and his mind, he loosed. The arrow burst into life as it streaked through the air. A magical halo of light surrounded the shaft as it zipped through the air, shining a radiant glow on the treetops.

Planter gasped. "Spiders . . . in the trees."

Watcher's arrow sliced through the air and embedded itself onto the thick trunk of a towering spruce. The flicking glow of the burning shaft revealed countless spiders, all descending from the forest roof on the end of thin strands of spider's silk.

"Fire at the spiders!" Watcher launched his fire arrows at the treetops, lighting the green canopy so the others could see.

The others pulled out bows and launched arrows at the monsters descending from the treetops like a deadly, dark rain. Pointed shafts streaked through the air, striking the dark, fuzzy bodies. The spiders screeched in pain, clicking their mandibles together rapidly. One of them disappeared, its glowing balls of XP falling to the ground like a rainbow hail.

"Work in pairs." Watcher sliced through another web with his flaming arrow. "Fire at the same spider!"

Moving next to Planter, he pointed at a spider then fired. Their arrows flew in parallel, both hitting the creature in the side. After another volley, the monster disappeared, adding more XP to the ground. They fired as fast as they could, but there were so many spiders. The monsters slowly moved down their thin strands of web, their eyes glowing like hot, angry embers.

"They're all around us." Planter fired at a nearby monster, cutting through its web. The monster fell to the ground screaming, then became silent.

Watcher turned, taking in everything around him. There were just too many of them; their arrows weren't slowing the mob at all. Some were close by and easier to hit, but others were far away, the gossamer threads from which they hung invisible in the distance.

"I don't like this." Mapper fired his bow as fast as he could, but everyone knew he was a terrible shot. "When they reach the ground, they'll charge and overwhelm us."

"Just keep shooting." Blaster shot at the monsters nearest to the ground, his shafts hitting with deadly accuracy. When the first of the spiders touched down, he took out his dual curved knives and charged at them.

"Blaster . . . wait!" Watcher yelled, but the boy ignored him.

The spiders clicked their mandibles together excitedly. Blaster streaked toward the monsters, his dark armor making him nearly invisible. He slashed at the creatures as he darted by, tearing into their HP. Some, who had been wounded by his arrows, disappeared under the first knife thrust, while others lingered a bit before the boy destroyed them.

"Blaster, get back here!" Cutter boomed. "More spiders are landing on the ground. We need to stick together."

The monsters settled noiselessly on the ground, forming a thick, angry ring around the villagers. Blaster dashed back to his friends and stood between Cutter and Mapper. The companions held their weapons at the ready as hundreds of angry red eyes glared at them from the darkness.

"We're surrounded," Watcher moaned, the taste of defeat heavy on his soul. "Everyone get back to back, form a circle."

The villagers pressed their backs together with Mapper at the center. The old man fumbled with potions, but he had nothing that would harm the monsters. They launched their pointed shafts at the monsters, but there were so many of them, their scant few arrows had negligible effect. The spiders moved forward, slowly closing their trap.

Watcher slowly lowered his bow. *We're trapped . . . it's over.* He glanced at Planter and a sadness such as he'd never experienced washed over him.

"Keep firing," Cutter yelled in desperation, but Watcher was numb to everything, the feeling of despair overwhelming his mind.

The ground shook again, as it did before, but this time, the thunder boomed from the darkness, as if the storm was about to descend upon them. But it didn't matter; he'd failed, and now all of his friends would be destroyed as well.

Planter, I failed you the most, he thought. *You relied on me to keep you safe, and I foolishly thought I could do it, but my courage was just a lie.* Drawing another arrow, he shot at one of the closest spiders, but knew the situation was hopeless.

Maybe that storm will just wash us all away and end this nightmare. He fired as fast as he could, hitting spider after spider as their circle of claws drew tighter around the defenders, getting ready for the final charge.

This was the end.

COMING SOON:
**INTO THE SPIDERS' LAIR:
THE RISE OF THE WARLORDS BOOK THREE**